I'M NOT YOUR

MANIC

PIXIE

DREAM

GIRL

· GRETCHEN McNEIL ·

BALZER + BRAY

An Imprint of HarperCollinsPublishers

Balzer + Bray is an imprint of HarperCollins Publishers.

ISBN 978-0-06-240911-9

Typography by Ellice M. Lee
16 17 18 19 20   PC/RRDH   10 9 8 7 6 5 4 3 2 1
❖
First Edition

For my Beatrices:

TARA CAMPOMENOSI MURPHY,
RACHANEE SRISAVASDI,
AND JEN WOLDMAN

"Sadness is easier because it's surrender.
I say, make time to dance alone
with one hand waving free."

—Claire from *Elizabethtown*

ONE

"YOU'RE NOT LATE, Beatrice," my mom said as she rolled the Prius to a stop in front of Spencer's house at exactly two minutes to eight.

I glanced at her out of the corner of my eye. "Only because you hit three out of seven green lights, blew through a questionable yellow, and cut off that old lady trying to make a left into her driveway."

It had been a miracle of modern commuting that we were on time, and I wanted to make sure she understood that our punctuality was a fluke. My mom was late for pretty much everything except Mass and the hair salon, a trait that had driven my dad crazy since before he'd married her, when she was his legal secretary. She'd even shown up a half hour late to their final divorce mediation, though I was relatively sure she'd done that on purpose.

My mom let out an audible sigh. "You don't even have class until nine."

She was right. The first day was a delayed start, and I was only meeting my friends for bagels and coffee, so it wasn't like I was going to be marked tardy (which would have counted on my permanent record). But that wasn't the point.

"If I'm not five minutes early," I said, matter-of-factly, "I'm late."

"Beatrice . . ." Her lilting Tagalog accent always made my name sound regal. "You need to loosen up. You're a senior now. Have some fun."

I grabbed my wheelie bag, mentally ticking off the seconds. This conversation was eating up precious time. "I have *plenty* of fun, Mom."

She sighed dramatically. "Don't call me that, *Anak*."

Whenever my mom renewed her hunt for Husband Number Two, I was no longer allowed to call her "mom." Why? Because she thought she could pass as my older sister.

"Sorry, *Flordeliza*," I said, opening the car door. "Who's the new prospect?"

My mom sighed again, deeper this time. "Benjamin Feldberger, Esquire."

So that explained her outfit. I eyed it with a mix of horror (65 percent) and awe (35 percent). She had chosen a red dress, sleeveless with a draped neckline and a thigh slit that effectively negated the knee-length hem. Don't get me wrong; she looked fabulous. My mom had this sexy *pinay* charm about her that had been completely lost in the genetic translation when it came to me. Probably because, as my mom loved to remind me, I was only half-Filipino.

"Is that work appropriate?" I asked.

She clucked her tongue. "Maybe if you dressed with a little more pizzazz, you might make a few friends at school." She paused. "Girlfriends."

I smoothed down my navy blazer piped in white. "I have friends."

"Mmhm."

Spencer and Gabe might have been nerds and outcasts, but they were *my* nerds and outcasts, and contrary to my mom's belief, dressing like an extra in a Katy Perry video wasn't going to increase my popularity at school or win me any female friends. I'd tried that freshman year after my parents' divorce had pulled me from the safety of St. Anne's Academy and tossed me into the shark-filled waters of Fullerton Hills High School, and it hadn't worked.

"Quality over quantity," I said, quoting one of my dad's favorite sayings (which had a 95 percent chance of making my mom cringe), then I slammed the door and dragged my wheelie bag up to Spencer's garage.

"I'm here!" I announced as I pushed open the side door. "Forty-five seconds early." Okay, it was more like fifteen, but since Spencer was standing at his easel, brush flying across the canvas, I doubted he was paying close attention.

Spencer Preuss-Katt and I had met in Honors English freshman year. He was the epitome of a brooding, absent-minded artist, which, unfortunately, went unappreciated by the jocktocracy of Fullerton Hills, where he was picked on ruthlessly for being short and skinny and quiet. Thankfully, his moms not only appreciated his artistic abilities but encouraged them. Two years ago, they'd remodeled their garage into a weatherproofed, sound-insulated, air-conditioned art studio for their son, which had become our de facto hangout space.

I left my bag by the sofa and tiptoed over to the easel. "Do I get to see this one?"

"Do you ever?" he replied without looking at me.

I frowned. Three years of friendship and, other than some doodles and sketches, he'd never let me see any of his work. I knew he was protective of it, but if he couldn't show his art to Gabe and me, how was he ever going to share it with the world?

"No," I said simply. "You don't. But maybe you should start? First day of senior year. Perfect time for—"

He held up his free hand, demanding silence while he added a few finishing strokes to the canvas. I clenched my jaw. Nothing pissed me off more than being interrupted, which Spencer knew damn well. Finally, he whisked a tarp off the floor and flung it over the easel. "Now you can talk."

"That's a horrible way to greet a friend you haven't seen in two months."

Spencer dropped his brush into a jug of murky water, then wiped his hands on a rag of questionable cleanliness. "I missed you too."

I rolled my eyes as he stood smiling down at me. He was taller than he'd been last time I saw him, and his body was broader, less boyish, a mix of angles and sharp lines. Spencer and his moms had spent most of the summer on an art tour of Western Europe, and it was as if an entirely different person had returned in his place.

"You look weird," I blurted.

Not offended in the least, Spencer laughed. "Now who's being horrible?"

"I mean different, not weird." I could feel the heat mounting in my cheeks. Why was I embarrassed? I didn't want him to see me blush, so I threw my arms around his waist instead. "I *did* miss you."

Spencer stiffened. "Yeah?" he said softly.

Well, duh. I'd missed both my friends. While Spencer had been in Europe, Gabe had spent most of his free time at the comic book store. I was the only one stuck at home with nothing to do.

Except hang out with Jesse.

A nervous fluttering spread upward from my stomach. I'd told Jesse to meet me at Spencer's, which meant he'd be here any minute. How was I going to explain him to my friends?

I felt Spencer's arms tighten around me and caught the unmistakable scent of cologne, something rich and spicy and, in my limited imagination on the subject, utterly European. I took a deep breath, attempting to place the fruit and floral notes, and the fluttering in my stomach stopped, replaced by a sharp pain as if my intestines were being twisted in a vise. Nerves. But why should I be nervous with Spencer? It was utterly illogical. Perhaps I was having an allergic reaction to the cologne? A synaptic response to an action potential?

Before I could further examine my current physical and emotional state, the side door flew open and Gabe barged in.

"The bus broke down!" he cried. "I got stuck exiting behind a hipster with a penny-farthing bicycle that barely fit down the stairs and then there was a nun in line ahead of me at the bagel shop who I swear to God"—he made the sign of the cross—"was buying bagels for the entire convent, which seemed strange to me, but whatever. *And then* I had to walk ten blocks in this heat." He paused, panting heavily. "So it's not my fault. I would've been on time, I swear."

Gabe always knew how to make an entrance.

Spencer broke away from me. "That's okay. Bea was late too."

I shoved him. "Was not."

"I don't believe it," Gabe said with an arched brow as he dropped a brown paper bag on the coffee table. He certainly hadn't dressed up for the first day of school: baggy cargo shorts and a T-shirt sporting a geektastic "<sarcasm>" HTML code under a well-worn flannel shirt.

"I was exactly forty-five seconds early," I said, and shot Spencer a withering look.

He met my gaze coolly. "Fifteen."

"Which is exactly four minutes and forty-five seconds late, according to Beatrice Standard Time," Gabe added.

"I know. But I'm at the mercy of Flordeliza, who spent an hour in the bathroom getting tarted up for work." I opened the bag and began removing a spread of precut bagels and cream cheese, laying them out on napkins in a neat, orderly row. Plain bagels in the middle with the fruity ones on the left and the savory varieties on the right so they wouldn't contaminate each other.

Gabe grabbed half a blueberry bagel and slathered it with whipped cream cheese. "You didn't tell me your mom was on the prowl again."

I shrugged. "You weren't around."

"I was here all summer!"

"Yeah," I said. "But you spent almost all of it gaming down at Hidey Hole."

He narrowed his eyes. "Actually, I was researching a new article for the school paper on the cultural impact of miniature tabletop warfare games on a generation of future politicians and military strategists."

"That sounds significantly less incendiary than your last article," Spencer said.

Gabe winced. "Tell me about it." His exposé on the dangerous workouts Coach Summers was forcing on the football team last year had gotten the coach fired, and hadn't exactly endeared Gabe to the jocktocracy in the process. Not that they'd loved him before: his penchant for smart-ass one-liners and class clownery had earned him plenty of ass kickings even before he'd turned his caustic journalist's pen on Fullerton Hills' protected class.

But as much as Gabe would love to claim that all his hours at Hidey Hole were spent pursuing a new lead, I knew better. "I'd hardly call playing Warhammer all day 'research.'"

Gabe held up two fingers. "A of all, yes, it is. And B of all, I wasn't playing the whole time. Kurt got me a job there."

"Who's Kurt?" Spencer asked.

I grabbed an onion bagel. "That doughy junior with the big head and the tiny face."

"I like his tiny face," Gabe muttered. "Oh, Spence. Have you seen the new video on YouTube with the kitten riding around on the back of a llama?"

"Of course," Spencer said. He had a weird affection for home videos of pets. "Totally staged, but I appreciated the tweeness nonetheless."

My phone buzzed in my pocket. Balancing my bagel in one hand, I fished it out.

What's Spencer's address? I think I'm lost.

"Is that your mom?" Gabe asked.

"No." I typed a quick response to Jesse so I didn't have to look them in the eyes.

"Maybe it's Cassilyn Cairns," Gabe said. "And Bea's her new bestie."

Spencer snorted. "Zero percent chance of that."

"More like five percent." The idea that the most popular girl in school would befriend me, Queen of the Outcasts, was ludicrous but not technically out of the realm of possibility.

Spencer smiled wickedly. "Then maybe it's a hot new boyfriend."

"Thad Everett?" Gabe suggested, naming one of the most loathsome members of the football team.

Spencer laughed. "No way, dude. Milo Morris. The way

he calls her 'Math Girl' is so romantic."

I really didn't care that most of the Fullerton Hills student body knew me only as "Math Girl." Our school was filled with jerks and asshats, and their dismissive nickname for me just made it easier to ignore them all.

"Hold up." Gabe dropped his bagel onto a napkin. "Other than Spence and me, you don't talk to other people at school. Ever. So, if that's not your mom, who's texting you?"

"Um . . ." I was working up the courage to explain when there was a soft knock at the door and we all turned to the window where Jesse stood with a dorky little smile on his lips.

Gabe turned to me, his eyes wide. "Is that Jesse Sullivan?"

TWO

"HEY!" JESSE SLIPPED into the garage, his beat-up back-pack slung over one shoulder. "Am I late?"

I jumped to my feet, hands trembling with a mix of nervousness and excitement. My boyfriend. My first boyfriend. My first *anything*.

He'd transferred to Fullerton Hills last winter, halfway through the school year, and though he wasn't in any of my honors classes, we'd sat next to each other in my Comparative World Governments elective. Jesse had never volunteered to answer questions in class, until one day when we were discussing Israel and his hand shot up in reaction to the question "What can you tell me about Benjamin Netanyahu?"

"He has an architecture degree from MIT," Jesse had said, naming my absolute dream college. After class I'd tracked him down in the halls to ask how he'd known, breaking my cardinal rule about talking to my classmates.

Turned out that Jesse's dad used to be a professor of architecture at MIT.

And just like that, my neurochemical processes were excited by his external stimuli.

Not that I fell in love with Jesse just because he'd grown up on the campus of my dream school. But it definitely made me pay attention. As the semester wound down, I noticed the charm in Jesse's half smiles, and the way his brown eyes were so dark you couldn't even discern the pupils most of the time. So when we'd bumped into each other at the bookstore the first week of summer and he'd asked me if I wanted to get coffee (with him, on a date, *a real date*), I'd surprised myself by saying yes. It had been weird and uncomfortable and glorious all at the same time. Coffee turned into "hanging out," which basically meant watching TV, playing video games (which I was horrible at, but willing to learn), and making out. Before I knew it, we were a couple.

I enjoyed Jesse's quietness and patience. He had a calming effect on me, unlike, say, Spencer, who was always pushing my buttons, as if his day wasn't complete without getting a rise out of me. Jesse would let me prattle on about my plans for MIT next year, answering all of my questions about the campus to the best of his ability. He didn't protest when I explained how he could probably get into Boston College and be near me if he just added Advanced Econ as his elective, and he indulged my excitement for my favorite topics: information theory and applied mathematics. He had no idea what either of those things were, but he'd smile and listen and not make me feel like a total and complete freak. We didn't fight, didn't rile each other up, and didn't make each other crazy.

Basically, the opposite of every other relationship I'd witnessed in my seventeen years—aka my parents, my mom's string of potential second husbands, my dad's first ex-wife, and my dad's current wife—which all seemed to be enveloped in a stifling cloud of anger, resentment, and unfulfilled expectations.

It had been a great summer with Jesse. Really great. So why hadn't I told my friends we were dating? We'd decided not to change our relationship statuses on Facebook, which seemed kind of sweet, like our time together was our own little secret, but we hadn't explicitly kept our relationship confidential. And now, with Spencer and Gabe staring at me like I'd just spoken in tongues, I kind of wished I'd mentioned Jesse to them earlier.

"You're not late at all," I lied, then dashed over and grabbed his hand, dragging him to the sofa. I was on edge, unsure how I was supposed to act in public as a girlfriend, a role I'd never played before in my life. "Right on time."

"Right on time?" Spencer muttered.

Jesse smiled, and reached around to unzip his backpack. "I was halfway here when I remembered something. Had to go back and grab this for you." He pulled out a copy of *MIT News Magazine*. "There's an article about a scholarship for incoming freshman. Something about information math? My dad said you should look into it."

I sucked in a quick breath. "Information theory?"

"Yeah," Jesse said. "That."

I quickly flipped to a dog-eared page where a small blurb had been circled in black marker. A brand-new scholarship sponsored by the applied mathematics department for research on information theory and its applications in everyday life.

This scholarship was tailor-made for me.

My mind raced, trying to think of ways to apply my geeky hobby to daily life, when behind me Gabe cleared his throat.

Oh crap, that was right. I still hadn't explained my boyfriend.

I tucked the magazine under my arm and turned to face my friends. "Guys, you know Jesse."

"No," Spencer said. "I don't."

He wasn't going to make this easy on me, was he? "Jesse, these are my friends, Gabe and Spencer."

"What's up?" Jesse said, no hint of nervousness in his voice. His clothes were just as relaxed as he was: Vans and baggy jeans, an extra-large grandpa sweater over a plain blue shirt, and his favorite navy beanie perched on his head.

"Nice to meet you," Gabe said, then practically shoved a bagel half into Jesse's hand. "Bagel, cream cheese. Good? Good. Now . . ." He arched an eyebrow. "So you and Bea are a thing? Boyfriend-girlfriend? Hot dates and making out and—"

I cut him off. "Seriously?"

Gabe shrugged. "If you're not going to fill us in on the details, I thought Jesse might."

Jesse turned to me, head cocked to the side. He still held the dry bagel half in his upturned palm. "You didn't tell your friends about us?"

Dammit. The answer was that there were too many emotional wild cards with making our relationship public. Would my friends accept him? Would he accept them? And how would he fit in with our lowly social position at school? I'd managed to avoid these questions all summer, and even though it was only the first day of school, I was already feeling nostalgic for those days when Jesse and I could just hang out in my living room without any pressure.

So instead of telling him the truth, I changed the subject. "We should probably get going. Don't want to be late on the first day, right?"

"Don't we?" Gabe slouched back against the sofa, all thoughts of Jesse and me forgotten. "I mean, I'm not exactly in a hurry to get my ass kicked."

Spencer snorted. "If you could just remember to not mouth off in front of the football team or get their beloved coach fired, you'd be golden. Now me, on the other hand . . ." He drew his thumb across his throat and lolled his head to the side, tongue hanging out of his mouth. "I'm a dead man."

"Maybe it'll be different this year," Jesse said. "I mean, you're seniors now. Won't those guys have freshmen to pick on?"

Jesse had only been at Fullerton Hills a semester, but that

had been long enough to know exactly where Gabe, Spencer, and I fell in the social hierarchy at school—i.e., the bottom—so I really had to appreciate his optimism.

Gabe propped his feet up on the coffee table. "Dude, even the freshmen pick on us."

"Maybe if you toned it down a little bit?" Jesse suggested. "Blended in?"

I winced. As much as I would love for us to fit in, the last thing I'd want would be for my friends to change who they were.

"How exactly should I blend in?" Spencer asked, his eyes cold. "Do you think if I pretended I were actually gay they'd stop calling me a fag in the halls?" He nodded at Gabe. "No offense."

"None taken," Gabe said. "But, you know, if you were really a flaming queer, they'd probably leave you alone. They wouldn't want to be anywhere near that stereotypical homo-sexual bullshit for fear it might rub off on them." He pursed his lips and drew his hand up to his chin, posing like a cover model. "Thad, your cheekbones are *fabulous*. Has anyone ever told you that? I just want to run my tongue up and down them." Then he roared like a tiger.

Spencer laughed. "I'd pay to see the look on Thad's face."

"Right before his fist connected with your nose," Gabe said, then turned to me. "And I don't know what Bea could do to shake her nickname."

"If she'd just agree to do their algebra homework," Spencer said, naming the one thing I absolutely refused to do, "she'd probably be able to hang out with Cassilyn and her crew whenever she wanted."

Jesse grabbed my hand. "Maybe that could be your thing? You could be a math tutor."

I jutted out my chin. "I'd rather cut off my arm than help those half-wits figure out the value of x. It's insulting to the memories of Diophantus and Brahmagupta."

Jesse blinked. "Huh?"

Gabe waved him off. "Math stuff. Don't ask or you'll get a lecture."

I took a deep breath. "Jesse's right." Sort of. Though I disagreed with his suggestion that we tone down our personalities, my boyfriend did have a point. "We're seniors now. Definitely not the freaks and weirdos we were freshman year. This is our school, and our last year at it, and we're not going to let a bunch of 'roided-up assholes take that away from us. We have to act like we're not afraid of them."

"Exactly," Jesse said. "Just act like you're cool and everything will be fine."

I smiled at him. I wasn't sure it would work, but I was willing to give it a try.

THREE

SPENCER PULLED HIS 1970s diesel Mercedes (a hand-me-down from his grandmother) into the spot next to Jesse's Scion, and we all silently stepped onto the black pavement. No one spoke as we trudged up the steep concrete stairs that led from the student parking lot to the main campus, but I could feel the tension bubbling beneath the surface.

Above us, the glass-and-chrome facade of Fullerton Hills gleamed in the bright Southern California sunshine, its sleek, modern construction and green manicured lawns seemingly out of place on the parched hillside. The city had spent a small fortune on the newest high school in the district, and to me, it was a perfect analogy to the student body: all flashy, expensive exteriors with very little substance once you got inside.

But there had to be a way to combat the bullshit we faced every day at school. I took Jesse's hand. Maybe he was right. Strength and confidence, those were the keys to success.

Maybe if we just acted like we weren't intimidated, people would leave us alone? It was worth a shot. I pulled open the double doors and strode purposefully into the foyer, head high, unafraid. Spencer and Gabe hesitated.

"Come on, guys," I said, trying to rally the troops. "According to Dr. Mannheim's treatise 'On Mathematics and Human Behavior,' as long as we don't act like prey, we have a sixty-two percent chance of being left alone by the predators."

Gabe pursed his lips. "Right, because that's totally how it works in the Serengeti."

I elbowed him. "Stay positive."

"I agree with Bea," Jesse said.

"You would," Spencer mumbled.

Gabe cleared his throat, then started to sing, "'Where can I find a woman like that?'"

Spencer's jaw clenched as he glared at Gabe.

"What song is that?" I asked.

"Never you mind." Then Gabe backed down the hallway toward his homeroom, blowing us a kiss as he went. "Hello, Fullerton Hills!" he cried out, arms flung wide. "I'm here to give you a big hug." A gaggle of girls scurried by and he pointed right at them. "You heard me. Hugs for all!" Then he half tackled them, their shrieks of laughter pinging off the highly polished tile floors.

Well, at least he was taking my advice to heart.

Spencer, Jesse, and I were in the same homeroom, so after quick stops at our lockers, we hurried upstairs to the freshman English classroom—the same one in which I'd met Spencer years ago. We were halfway down the hall when a group of short, scrawny guys barreled toward us. One of them shouldered Spencer's forearm so hard his book bag went flying onto the ground.

"Watch where you're going, loser," the jerk said, smiling at his buddies for approval.

Instead of getting angry (Spencer never got angry), he ignored them and calmly retrieved his bag. But whether it was because Jesse was with us or because I was relatively sure the perpetrator was a sophomore with absolutely no social standing of his own (or a 78 percent chance that it was both), something inside me snapped.

"You know," I said, standing my wheelie bag on its legs and approaching the group with arms folded across my chest, "I feel sorry for you."

"Aww, Math Girl feels sorry for me?"

I nodded. "Absolutely. Because based on the remedial level of the textbooks you're carrying and your obvious lack of adequate adult role models as exhibited by your behavior, I estimate you have an eighty-five percent chance of living with your parents until you're forty. So have fun with that."

And before he could answer, I spun around, caught the handle of my bag, and strode resolutely into homeroom.

Jesse slipped his arm around my waist. "That was pretty cool."

"Thanks." I blushed as we snagged desks on the far side

by the windows, exactly ninety-three seconds before the final bell.

"Welcome, seniors!" Mrs. Murphy, our freshman English teacher, breezed into the room. She was a prim, well-dressed woman in her midfifties, with an ever-present string of pearls and a short, tidy hairdo that looked as if she got it set once a week and slept with a cap on each night to keep its shape. "I hope your last year at Fullerton Hills is one you'll remember as you move forward to college and beyond."

A low beep signaled the beginning of morning announcements, which should have been read jointly by our student body president and vice president, Gus Hendrickson and his younger brother Gary, who'd been elected in a landslide last spring, but instead, Principal Ramos took the microphone. A general welcome, a mission statement, a call to action to make Fullerton Hills the best high school in Orange County. The usual BS.

My mind wandered to the copy of *MIT News Magazine* in my bag. I estimated my current chances of getting into MIT at approximately 87 percent, but winning that scholarship would guarantee me not only admission but early decision. MIT had been my dream school since I was ten, when I realized there were colleges that actually specialized in math and sciences. My goal was to study applied mathematics, and winning that scholarship would make me a rock star in the department. People would know who I was, know my actual name instead of just calling me Math Girl. Because everyone there would be Math Girl or Math Boy, and I would be the

Cassilyn Cairns of the MIT math department.

I had to come up with an amazing project, backed by the most original, most out-of-the-box research anyone had ever seen.

I sighed. No pressure.

The announcements ended, and Mrs. Murphy picked up her iPad. "Let's do a quick roll." She went through the list, alphabetically calling out the names of the thirty seniors in the room, all present, until she got to the bottom of the list. "And I see we have a late addition. Toile Jeffries?"

"*C'est moi!*"

I turned toward the affected French accent, which appeared to come from the hallway. Instead of a person standing in the door, there was just a head peeking around the door, her face obscured by an enormous black-and-white striped sun hat and a tangled mass of blond hair.

"Toile Jeffries?" Mrs. Murphy repeated.

Without a word, the new girl stepped into the room. She was pretty—porcelain skin with high cheekbones, unnaturally violet eyes, and a delicate, ballerina-like figure—but her looks were overshadowed by the most outlandish outfit I'd ever seen. She wore bright yellow tights, thick and opaque, disappearing into shiny black patent Mary Janes, and a vintage floral dress, empire-waisted, with tiny puff sleeves trimmed in lace. Over that, she'd thrown a gray crocheted vest with green and pink flower appliqués, and on her shoulder, she clutched an oversize white canvas hobo bag, scribbled all over in multicolored Sharpie ink with words like "beauty" and "magic" alongside longer phrases in what appeared to be French and Italian. The effect was disorienting, like staring into a kaleidoscope.

She paused for a moment, a smile twitching at her lips, then dropped into an awkward curtsy. "I'm Toile."

Mrs. Murphy beckoned her to the front of the room. "Welcome to Fullerton Hills. Why don't you tell us a little something about yourself?"

Toile approached the whiteboard, blinked several times, her tiny smile deepening, then she bit her lower lip. "I like birds." She was very matter-of-fact. Like a child proclaiming a newly discovered truth.

Mrs. Murphy arched an eyebrow.

"I know it's weird and totally not cool, but I like the way they look when they soar across a blue sky, wings out-stretched, glimmering in the sunshine."

"Okay . . ." Mrs. Murphy looked confused. "Are you a bird-watcher or—"

But Toile barreled on, ignoring the interruption. "And Tennyson. I love Tennyson."

"Wonderful!" Mrs. Murphy exclaimed. "I believe English 12 does a module on British poetry, and you might enjoy—"

The bell rang, signaling the end of homeroom and of Toile Jeffries's official introduction. Which was good because I wasn't sure how much more of her scatterbrained babbling I could take. Why couldn't she just state the facts? Name, grade, city of origin. Short and to the point.

"A moment, please!" Mrs. Murphy cooed above the

excited throng of newly minted seniors bustling out of the room. "I need a volunteer to help our new student get to her first-period class." She rested her hand on Toile's arm. "Where are you going, dear?"

Toile's glassy eyes lit up. "Show choir," she said reverentially.

Of course she was in the show choir.

"Is anyone going near the theater?" Mrs. Murphy asked.

"Uh, I guess I am," Jesse said, staring at the schedule printout in his hand.

"Wonderful, Jesse," Mrs. Murphy said, beaming. "Since you were new here last year, I'm sure you'll be able to offer Toile some advice."

Jesse glanced at me, an apology in his eyes. "I guess I can't walk you to class."

"That's okay," I said. "See you at lunch, okay?"

He smiled, then shuffled to the front of the room to claim his ward as Spencer and I hurried off to AP English.

FOuR

LUNCH AT FULLERTON Hills was a big deal. I suppose that's true for every high school, but the imposing magnitude of Fullerton Hills' cafeteria made the location of your table monumentally important. And the first day of school, when you staked your cafeteria claim, could literally make or break your year.

There were three interconnected eating areas, each with its own predetermined label of social importance. The main room—a long, rectangular space with a high arched ceiling and massive windows at each end that resembled a small airplane hangar—offered maximum exposure to a select mix of upper- and lowerclassmen, a plus if you wanted to show off your social supremacy but a minus if you wanted to remain in the shadows. On either side, the cafeteria opened up into two smaller eating areas, like the north and south transepts on a medieval cathedral, with diner-like booths tucked against the walls.

Spencer, Gabe, and I preferred the north room, the dominion of the unseen. It was safer to be out of sight, a strategy that had served us well through six semesters' worth of lunch periods, and I wanted to make sure we were discreetly ensconced in a quiet, secluded booth—with room for four, of course—before the tables filled up. As soon as the bell rang at the end of third period, I headed to the cafeteria, where a quick scan of the north room showed it to be 95 percent unoccupied.

Excellent.

I maneuvered my wheelie bag through the smattering of round tables, eyes fixed on my first choice in seating location (in the corner, near the exit in case we ever needed to make a quick getaway), when a figured stepped in front of me, blocking my view.

"Beatrice Giovannini." Michael Torres stood with his hands on his hips, legs spread shoulder width apart like a drill sergeant addressing the new recruits.

"Michael Torres." I wasn't entirely sure my upper lip didn't curl as I said his name. On paper, my archenemy, Michael Torres, and I should have been friends. We had been the only two freshmen in Trigonometry and AP Physics I, but instead of us forming a bond, it had been hate at first sight.

"Where are you going?" he demanded.

I strained on my tiptoes to see over him. Tables were beginning to fill up, but no one had claimed any of the booths in the north room. Yet. "It's lunchtime. So I'm going to eat lunch."

He squinted at me. "And your 'friends,'" he said, using air quotes as if Spencer and Gabe weren't real people but figments of my imagination, "will be joining you?"

Michael Torres and I rarely interacted unless forced to, so I had no idea what his game of Twenty Questions was about. There was a shiftiness in his brown eyes, as if he was hiding something, and I couldn't help but wonder if he'd seen the MIT scholarship announcement. Did he want to ask me about it? Would he be going for it too?

"So you and Spencer and Gabriel Muñoz will be sitting back there for the entire lunch period . . . ," he said slowly, as if trying to grapple with the information.

I had no idea what was going on in that devious mind of his, but I was officially done with the conversation. "If you're fishing for an invitation, the answer is no. We have a strict no-douche-bag rule at our table." I strong-armed him out of my way. "Later."

The booth near the emergency exit was still empty and I immediately nabbed it, breathing a sigh of relief as I parked my wheelie back next to the cushioned bench. Safety had been attained for one more year.

"Hey," Spencer said, sliding in next to me. "You want to go to LACMA this weekend? There's a Fauvism exhibit I want to see."

I nudged him. "Sit on the other side."

"Why?"

"Hey, Bea." Jesse shuffled up, bag lunch in hand. "Is there room?"

Without another word, Spencer slid out of the booth and took a seat across from me. "Of course."

"Sweet." I felt my heart rate accelerate as Jesse sat beside me. I was in the cafeteria with my boyfriend. For a split second, I almost wished we were sitting in the main room so the entire school could see us.

"This is great," I babbled, feeling the need to speak but not quite sure what I should say. "You're here and I'm here and we're all eating lunch together."

"Which is what you do in a cafeteria," Spencer said, staring at his lunch.

His snark only intensified my nervousness, as if I needed to make up for it somehow. "How were morning classes, Jesse?" I asked, talking so fast the words practically blended into one another. "Did you make it to first period okay? And did you like Advanced Econ? I know I made you take it, but if you really hate it—"

Jesse laid his hand on my arm, and instantly the nerves in my stomach vanished. "It was great. So was English 12. Toile's in my class."

I snorted. "That space cadet from homeroom?" I was suddenly grateful I was on the AP track.

"Yeah," Jesse said. "She's pretty cool. She lived in Hawaii before she came here. Honolulu, I think. She's really into singing and she knows how to surf."

"Wow," Spencer said, "did you read her autobiography?"

Jesse laughed. "No, we just talked a lot."

He meant that *she* had talked a lot. I pictured Jesse smiling and nodding and hardly following along with her mindless chatter.

"Oh," he continued, as if he'd just remembered another factoid, "and she collects hats. It's kind of her signature thing."

"Signature crazy is more like it," I said.

Jesse shrugged.

"Guess what?" Gabe dropped his lunch tray on the table. "Mr. Poston wants me to be the editor of the *Herald*."

"That's amazing!" I squealed. "You'll make a kick-ass editor."

"Thanks. He told me there's another applicant and he's thinking about making us coeditors, which blows, but it's someone who hasn't been in journalism before and he wants my experienced eye on the editorial side. So basically I'll still be in charge."

I laughed. "Can't share the spotlight, can you?"

"Shouldn't have to." Gabe flipped imaginary hair out from his face. "But it gets better. Poston wants me to submit an article to the *Orange County Register* for their high school internship program. He's going to personally recommend me! That could totally be my ticket to—"

The giant black-and-white brim of a sun hat appeared out of nowhere. "Hi, Jesse!"

"Hey!" Jesse shot to his feet.

Toile placed a dainty hand on his arm, and I felt my body tense up. "Thank you so much for showing me around this morning. I really appreciate it."

"No problem," he said.

Was that a blush creeping up Jesse's neck?

"It's *so* amazing here," Toile continued. "How can you guys stand to go to school in such a beautiful place? There's this secret patch of wildflowers on the hillside next to the track. Have you seen it? It's like a little oasis! And we're doing a whole two weeks on Tennyson in English 12. I just *adore* Tennyson."

"So I've heard," I muttered.

"And did you know," she barreled on, "that Fullerton Hills has one of the best show choirs in Orange County? I don't even mind that it's first period. Kinda warms me up for the day. I don't have much of a voice, but I *love* to sing, and we do all these cool dance moves. Sometimes, I just need to get up and move, you know?"

Yeah, it's called walking.

She stretched her arms out to either side of her body and started waving them back and forth like an octopus, then she broke into some outlandish choreography, culminating in an off-balance pirouette. She stumbled, bracing herself against Jesse's chest. Everyone was staring at her, including Michael Torres, who I noticed lingering near the entrance to the north room, but instead of being self-conscious or embarrassed by the attention, Toile threw her head back and laughed. Not a cute, twittering kind of laugh, but a hearty guffaw that seemed more appropriate coming from your great-uncle after he made an off-color joke.

Our daily lunchtime goal was to attract as little attention

as was humanly possible, but Toile had 40 percent of the cafeteria focused on us. To make matters worse, Cassilyn Cairns was making a beeline for our table.

Blond and blue-eyed, Cassilyn could have been the poster child for Orange County. Her skin was perfectly tanned at all times, her makeup perfectly applied. Her hair was perfectly curled in loose ringlets that framed her face, and her outfits were perfectly stylish without being gaudy, flirtatious without being lewd. I was pretty sure she'd never voluntarily said a word to either me or my friends in our three years at school together, but Toile had attracted her attention, and she was coming over. This wasn't going to end well.

"Sit down," I hissed. Maybe Cassilyn would get distracted and go back to her own table.

"You're sweet," Toile said with a delicate smile, misinterpreting my comment for an invitation. "But I promised some new friends I'd eat with them."

"Toile!" Cassilyn grabbed Toile's hands and kissed her on both cheeks as if she were greeting an old friend. "Our table's over here." She tugged her toward the main room.

"You know each other?" I blurted out. Cassilyn wouldn't have invited a complete stranger to eat at her table. Maybe they went way back? Childhood friends?

Toile laughed again, loud and carefree. "We have algebra together. Totally bonded over our mutual dislike of numbers."

"Dislike of numbers," I repeated slowly. Who the hell were these people?

Cassilyn scanned our table; her eyes lingered on Spencer.

"Have you guys met?" Toile asked.

I wanted to scream. Fifty percent of me was irritated by her disparagement of algebra, and 50 percent of me was insulted that the new girl was trying to introduce us to the most popular person in school. "Yes," I said through clenched teeth.

Which wasn't a lie. I'd introduced myself to Cassilyn freshman year, back before I learned that talking to my fellow students was a bad idea. But clearly, Cassilyn had no memory of this meeting. She cocked her head to the side and stared at me with vacant blue eyes.

"Math Girl," she said at last.

Fibonacci's balls.

"I'm Jesse," my boyfriend volunteered.

"Hey," Cassilyn said, smiling weakly. "Nice meeting you guys." Then she quickly dragged Toile away.

Jesse's eyes trailed after them as he sank back into the booth.

"That went well." Spencer smirked at me. "She even knew your name."

"No," Jesse said, still glancing over his shoulder. "She didn't."

"Which one of you is Gabriel Muñoz?"

I'd been so pissed off about Toile and Cassilyn, I hadn't seen Milo Morris, Thad Everett, or a half dozen other members of the Fullerton Hills football team approach our secluded table until it was too late. They surrounded us, cutting off our escape, and judging by their combative stances, they were out for blood. Gabe's blood.

"Who?" I said, trying to display a mix of nonthreatening confidence and upbeat naïveté. Despite multiple confrontations over our high school career, Thad and Milo didn't actually know Gabe's name. Maybe I could stall them until a teacher walked by?

Milo nodded behind him. "Some geek over there said that Gabriel Muñoz was sitting at this table. That bitch got Coach fired."

I saw Michael Torres waving at me from the main room of the cafeteria. He'd led Milo and Thad right to Gabe. I knew he hated me, but what did he have against my friends?

No time to puzzle it out. I had to soothe the angry beast.

"May I inquire as to the nature of your question?" I began.

Thad pointed his forefinger at me. "Is it you?"

"You think Gabriel's a girl?" Gabe snorted. "Dumber than I thought," he said to Spencer out of the side of his mouth. Only too loud. Loud enough for everyone to hear.

Shit.

Milo's dark skin flushed red as he grabbed the collar of Gabe's flannel shirt. "What did you say?"

"Leave him alone!" I cried.

Thad glared at me. "Shut the fuck up, Math Girl."

"She has a name, you know." Spencer stared hard at Thad, refusing to look away. I saw the lines of his jaw ripple as he clenched.

"Yeah?" Milo said, loosening his grip on Gabe's shirt.

"And do you have a name? Wouldn't happen to be Pussy, would it?"

Here we go again. Same church, different pew. We were starting senior year as victims, the one role we were trying to avoid. But I'd promised my friends that things could be different this year. Just like in the hallway this morning, I had to do something.

"Look, gentlemen," I said, kneeling on the bench to make myself look taller. "I understand that feelings were hurt by Gabe's article last year, but those are the risks we take to live in a society where we enjoy freedom of speech and freedom of the press. Gabe is entitled to his opinion—"

"Based on facts," Gabe added.

"Bea," Jesse whispered. "Don't."

Seriously? He'd gushed when I'd stood up for Spencer this morning but now he wanted me to back down? "And you are entitled to yours."

Gabe spread his hands wide. "Based on bullshit."

There was a split second where Gabe's quip seemed to hang suspended in space and time, an elongated moment where I almost thought he might not have said it and I'd just imagined that my friend had waved a red flag in front of an angry bull. Then the world shifted back to regular speed, and as Thad, Milo, and their goons lunged at Gabe, I was sure the next red thing I saw would be blood.

Instead, I heard a high-pitched voice piercing the angry shouts.

"Here he is, Mr. Poston," someone said. Then I saw Kurt

Heinzmueller's round baby face pushing through the crowd with the journalism teacher in tow. "Gabe's right over here."

The instant a faculty member arrived, it was as if a bomb had been defused. Football players scattered, the pitch of tension lessened, and all around us, the student body turned back to their lunches as if no one wanted to get caught rubbernecking.

"Thanks, Kurt," Gabe said with a huge sigh the second Milo and Thad backed away.

Kurt's face relaxed. "No problem."

"Is everything okay here?" Mr. Poston asked.

Gabe nodded. "Don't worry. I can handle them."

But not to be completely emasculated in front of the student body, just before Milo disappeared into the hallway, he turned and shouted one final threat across the cafeteria. "Watch your backs, losers. I'm coming for you."

FiVE

"SO DO YOU think Milo meant it?" Jesse asked as he drove us to Spencer's after school.

I cringed at the name. All my hopes that somehow my friends and I would fly under the radar this year and emerge at graduation physically and emotionally unscathed from the bullying of the jocktocracy had gone up in flames the moment Thad and Milo appeared at our lunch table. They were never going to leave us alone, and if Milo was true to his word, senior year would be our worst yet.

"I'm sure he'll forget about us in a day or two," I lied. Jesse didn't respond right away and I felt the need to fill the uncomfortable silence. "By Monday, I bet. Totally back to normal." Normal isn't actually a good thing, Bea. "I mean, not normal like *we'll get picked on in the halls all the time* kind of normal. More like we'll go back to being invisible. Which sounds really awful, but actually isn't so bad at all."

I was talking fast, the words tumbling one upon another.

Was I afraid Jesse wouldn't like me anymore if he thought I was going to be even less popular this year than I had been before? And if so, what did that say about our relationship?

"Normal," he mused. Then he cleared his throat. "I was thinking, maybe at lunch you and me could find our own table. You know, in the main cafeteria maybe?"

My eyes grew wide. "With all the popular kids?"

He shrugged. "Yeah, why not?"

I could think of twenty-seven reasons right off the top of my head, including but not limited to the almost 100 percent chance of daily humiliation at the hands of Milo and Thad.

But instead of admitting that, I made a more practical argument against Jesse's plan. "There wouldn't be room for all four of us," I said. "And I can't abandon my friends."

"Oh." He paused. "And why are we hanging out with them after school?"

"Because I always do," I blurted out. That was the norm. Homework for me, while Spencer painted and Gabe worked on his newest article.

Jesse eased the car to a stop at the next light and turned to me for the first time since we left school. "I was thinking maybe we could go to D'Caffeinated," he said, naming the coffee shop where Cassilyn and her friends sometimes hung out.

I'd never set foot in D'Caffeinated: not on the way to school, when businessmen and -women were lined up out the door for their daily fix, not on the weekends, when it was mostly college students working on research papers or screenplays that were going to take Hollywood by storm, and certainly not after school, when Fullerton Hills wannabes camped out around the lacquered wood tables hoping to be seen in the same vicinity as the most popular girls in school. "I guess we could go sometime."

"Today?" he asked eagerly.

Why was he suddenly so interested in artisanal coffee beverages? "Spencer and Gabe are waiting for us."

"Oh." Jesse sat up, eyes back on the road. "Right."

Gabe was slumped in the corner of the sofa, head resting against the torn fabric of the arm with his knees drawn up to his chest when Jesse and I arrived at Spencer's studio.

He heaved a sigh. "I'm sorry I ever wrote that stupid article."

"No, you're not," I said quickly.

"You shouldn't be seen with me in public," he continued, wallowing in the drama. "You should cut ties with me to save yourselves."

Spencer leaned back against the sink, preparing for one of Gabe's monologues. "Here we go again."

"I mean it," Gabe continued. "I'm an albatross around your necks. Without me, you have a chance. I'll just start eating lunch in the journalism classroom. Or . . ." He placed his hand on his chest. "Under the football bleachers like a true outcast."

I sat down beside him. "You're being ridiculous."

"Am I?" He cocked his head to the side. "And what, exactly, do you suggest we do?"

"Move to Siberia," Spencer said, "and pray they don't find us."

I smirked. "Funny."

Jesse checked his phone. "You could transfer," he suggested, typing as he talked. "Or maybe try homeschooling?"

He was attempting to be helpful, but those were cowardly options, bordering on insensitive. "We can't run away from this," I said. "There's got to be a solution we're missing."

"Like what?" Gabe uncurled his legs and planted his feet on the ground. "Talk to them? My mom suggested that freshman year. 'Just have a conversation with them, *mijito*. They'll understand.'" He snorted. "I came home with a wedgie so deep I had to send in spelunkers to get it out."

"Go to the principal?" Jesse said.

"We've already tried to get Ramos involved," I explained. "We're not important enough for her to discipline her championship football team."

"See?" Spencer said. "Siberia doesn't sound so bad."

Jesse shoved his phone into his pocket. "I have to go," he said.

I turned to him, confused. "What? Why?"

"I forgot I have an appointment," he said. "Do you want me to take you to your mom's?"

"She's at her dad's tonight," Spencer said before I could answer. Three and a half days split evenly between the two households, and Spencer always remembered when I was where. "I'll take her home."

"I'll call you later, okay?" Jesse took my chin in his hand, angling it up toward him. "Meanwhile, you can use that math brain of yours to figure out this problem. Bye!"

I stood rigid beside the sofa, Jesse's words echoing in my ears. *Figure out this problem.*

"You okay, Bea?" Gabe asked.

I nodded. Problems had solutions. Solutions were equations. And who was better at solving equations than I was? No one. Without thinking, I moved toward my wheelie bag and pulled out a notebook and pen, then sat down on the sofa next to Gabe.

"What is it?" Spencer squeezed in beside me.

Something was percolating inside me, that familiar flutter of excitement I got whenever I was on the brink of a mathematical breakthrough. There was always a moment when I shifted my perspective, and in an instant, all the elements would come together with a beautiful simplicity that made me feel like a moron for not having seen it before.

This was one of those moments.

Our current sociological predicament could be boiled down to a simple linear equation. We knew the result, i.e., a tolerable school environment where we weren't living in fear of an ass kicking every five minutes. I just had to work backward from there.

"We've been looking at this all wrong," I said, noting the tremor in my own voice.

"How?" Spencer asked. "Milo and Thad are misunderstood? They just need a hug and everything will be fine?"

"No one has to hug anyone," I said. My pen began to fly over the page, an automatic flow of symbols and letters. "Unless you're both hugging me in gratitude."

Spencer leaned over my shoulder and glanced at my preliminary scribbles. "For what?"

I held my notebook out in front of me. "The Formula for Happiness in High School."

The Formula™:

$$\int_{f}^{s} F(x)R^{v} = \emptyset$$

If F is a continuous real-valued function defined on a closed interval [f, s] between freshman and senior years of high school, R is the social role played based on v, the relative void in which R does or does not exist, then the exponential product R^v is equal to the empty set, i.e., "eternal happiness."[1]

Or, in layman's terms:

(1) Find the niche.
(2) Play the role.
(3) Fill the void.

1. Taken from Smullyan's ham sandwich argument to present eternal happiness as an empty set.

SiX

SPENCER AND GABE stared up at me from the sofa with looks of abject confusion on their faces while I math-splained my new baby in what I hoped were easily understandable terms.

Gabe's eyes slowly crossed. "I literally have no idea what you just said. Was that even English?"

Spencer raised his hand as if he were in class. *"¿Dónde está la biblioteca?"*

"You guys are such arithmophobes." If only more people could see the beauty of mathematics, the endless possibilities of its application to our everyday lives, I swear calculus would be the most popular class in high school. "It's simple."

Spencer slouched on the arm of the sofa. "Liar."

I sketched axis lines on the page and then drew a curve through them, roughly coloring in the space below. "This is happiness, defined by the points f and s, i.e., the four years we spend in high school. In order to maximize the amount of happiness—um, that's this shaded space below the curve—we need to raise the line, increasing its area."

Gabe leaned forward, elbows on his knees. "How?"

I bit my lip. This was the hard part. "We need to establish new roles at school."

Spencer shook his head. "Impossible. Those dickheads aren't going to wake up tomorrow and think of us as totally different people."

"Why not? I mean, people change who they are all the time." I pointed at Gabe. "Remember that guy in your US history class sophomore year? The one with the weird growth on his face?"

"Lyle Kontos," he said. "He had that thing lanced off and suddenly he was God's gift to chicks."

"Exactly. He'd been shy, kinda quiet before, and then he came back from summer vacation a completely different person."

"Bea, the guy had corrective surgery." Spencer walked over to the minifridge beside the sink and grabbed a bottle of Perrier. "It's not like he just woke up one day and decided he was going to be a different person."

"Didn't he, though? I mean, simply removing a giant boil didn't transform him from a wallflower to a playboy. He had to make a conscious decision to change."

"You're right." Gabe scooted forward to the edge of the sofa, and I could see by the lightness in his eyes that he was excited by this idea. "So what do we do? What roles could possibly make the three of us socially acceptable?"

"This morning when you were joking about how Spencer should play up the gay thing. Could you do that again?"

Gabe stared at me blankly. "Do what?"

"You know, the voice, the hand gesture . . ." How was I supposed to explain?

"She wants you to flame on, Johnny Storm," Spencer prompted.

I cringed. It sounded gross when Spencer put it like that. "Er, yeah."

"Okay." Gabe straightened up, cracked his neck, and shook out his hands like a boxer preparing for the first round, then lowered his chin and smiled wickedly. "Sweetie," he said, "that color is absolutely divine on you. Makes you look ten years younger, like a Botox-Kybella cocktail." He pursed his lips for an air kiss, held the pose for a moment, then dropped the act. "Like that?"

Spencer leaned back against the sink, sipping his Perrier. "A piece of me just died inside."

"You and me both," Gabe said. "I think I just lost my gay card for that."

While I shared their aversion to a derogatory portrayal of flamboyant homosexuality, it could be Gabe's ticket to safety at Fullerton Hills. "Do you still have the bow tie and suspenders from when you went as the Eleventh Doctor for Halloween last year?"

Gabe jutted out his chin, as if the mere suggestion that he would have discarded his beloved *Doctor Who* cosplay garb was an insult to his nerd cred. "Of course."

"Excellent." Now I just needed to deal with Spencer. I stood up, eyeing him closely as he continued to lean back against the sink. He'd always had a disheveled, unkempt air to his style, but now his hair was bleached from the hot European sun, and it had the shape of an actual haircut—close cropped in the back but longish in the front, sweeping over his eyes. Even his clothes looked more sophisticated than they had a few months ago. He was still in his usual uniform of black jeans and a button-down shirt, but the jeans were crisp and tailored, the shirt slim-fitted with a scroll of embroidery across the chest.

He looked cool and edgy, like the artist he was.

And how do you make an artist socially acceptable in a typical American high school?

You make him paint something people want to see.

"Spencer, haven't you always wanted to do portraiture?"

He arched an eyebrow. "Maybe."

"What if you offered to paint some of your fellow Fullerton Hills Honchos?"

"Slow down, Machiavelli." Spencer held his hands up before him. "I don't want any part of this little makeover."

"I'm not trying to make you over," I said, which was almost entirely true. "But do you remember last year when Milo and Thad cornered you in the locker room after you'd stood up for Gabe?"

Spencer couldn't meet my eyes. "I remember the choke hold."

"I know I've told you this a thousand times," Gabe said,

"but I really am sorry I called Thad a 'nad knocker.'"

"If Coach Summers hadn't walked in," I continued, "who knows what would have happened."

Spencer's bright blue eyes (how had I never noticed they were that blue before?) turned to me. His face was pinched, practically pained, his eyebrows drawn together in silent pleading.

"I don't want to change who I am," he said, "because of them. Then they win."

I joined him at the sink. "I don't want to change who you are either. I like you. I like *us*. But we need to think of this like the ultimate *Fuck you* to Milo, Thad, and the rest of those assholes who have made high school a living hell."

Gabe shifted on the sofa and the ancient coils groaned in protest. "You mean like going undercover?"

I spun around. "Yes! You could write an article about your experience—infiltrate the popular crowd, change them from within. This is the perfect opportunity to make Fullerton Hills a more tolerant place." I smiled wickedly. "And don't you think the *Orange County Register* would go nuts over an article like that?"

Gabe's eyes grew glassy. "I can see the headline now: 'Nerdy Queer to Fashionably Fey—My Journey from Outcast to A-list.'"

"Brilliant." I turned back to Spencer. "My formula gives you a chance to add portraiture to your portfolio *and* keeps Milo and Thad off your back. Wouldn't that be worth it?"

Spencer looked skeptical. "This wouldn't have anything

to do with a certain MIT scholarship, would it?"

I caught my breath. "I hadn't even thought of that." He was right, though. This formula I'd come up with . . . It was exactly the kind of everyday application of mathematics MIT was looking for. If it worked, if we actually pulled this off, it could mean more than just our security at high school. It could literally mean my future.

"Sounds like a no-brainer to me," Gabe said.

"Just hear me out," I said to Spencer. "If you hate my plan, you're free to continue on your path toward an ass kicking."

He took one last chug of his Perrier, then banged the empty bottle loudly against the counter. "Fine. I'm listening."

I hugged him, pressing my face against his chest.

"But only because you asked me to," he said.

I pulled away as my stomach tightened, once again feeling vaguely uncomfortable for reasons I couldn't quite define.

"Okay, yay!" Gabe said with over-the-top enthusiasm, shooting his hands into the air like a cheerleader. "Go, team!" Then he folded his arms across his chest. "Now what?"

"Gather 'round, kids," I said, pulling a chair up to the coffee table. "We've got work to do."

SEVEN

WE MET IN Spencer's studio bright and early the next morning for one last strategy session before we unleashed our new personae on Fullerton Hills. It was a bold move we were about to make, and everything had to be just right. I'd outlined our new roles, including the most minute details of wardrobe, attitude, vocabulary, even the way we carried ourselves. The more I thought about the Formula, the more I was convinced it was going to work.

(1) Find the niche.
(2) Play the role.
(3) Fill the void.

GABE

(1) Find the niche: The article on Coach Summers aside, Gabe's issues with the jocktocracy at Fullerton Hills had nothing to do with his homosexuality (I doubt Milo and Thad even

knew he was gay) and everything to do with the fact that he was an attention-seeking smart-ass who didn't know how to keep his mouth shut. Of course, I liked that attention-seeking smart-ass, but we needed to find a way to make his one-liners and subtle cutdowns more socially appropriate. Embraced, even. How? Keep the snark, and add a dose of gay stereotype.

(2) Play the role: Instead of baggy cargo shorts and flannel shirts, Gabe's new wardrobe was colorfully nerd chic with a hint of retro flamboyant. He wore a slim-fitting blue plaid shirt with the sleeves rolled up crisply so they hit just above his elbows. The collar was buttoned to the neck and affixed with a burgundy clip-on bow tie. His blue jeans were also tightly fitted, cuffed at the ankle to reveal a pair of white loafers he'd borrowed from his mom, and instead of a belt he wore a pair of dark blue suspenders. He had also slicked his usually messy hair up into a tightly coiffed pompadour with a pair of white heart-shaped sunglasses perched gingerly on top.

(3) Fill the void: Fullerton Hills lacked an outspoken gay best friend. Gabe would be the cool, hip new thing, a fabulous accessory to Cassilyn's clique, and she and her fashion-conscious friends should fall all over themselves to befriend him. Popularity was all about trendsetting, and Gabe would be the hottest trend of all.

And he'd get something out of it too. This would be the ultimate test of his journalistic prowess—a full-immersion undercover assignment, the opportunity to view high school social hierarchy from the top down and dissect how something as simple as changing one's appearance and attitude could affect their role within it. That's the kind of article that the *Orange County Register* would pounce on.

SPENCER

(1) Find the niche: Fullerton Hills High School lacked a resident *artiste*. So we'd give them one.

(2) Play the role: Instead of trying to hide Spencer's predilection for painting and drawing, we'd highlight it. He already had the clothes, and his newly acquired Euro-cool attitude. We just had to put them to good use.

(3) Fill the void: How does an artist gain cachet in the typical American high school? From the top down. In the case of our sport-crazed campus, Spencer was going to offer up his painting skills in the name of school spirit, creating portraits of Fullerton Hills' fastest, strongest, and most skilled athletes—the very douche bags who wanted to kick his ass. The jocktocracy would love seeing themselves immortalized on canvas, and though, as Spencer whined last night via text, painting sportsball portraits was going to destroy his soul, he would be honing his portraiture skills in the process.

Spencer may have been loath to admit it, but he needed this push. Despite some amazing feedback from a few gallery owners downtown, Spencer had very little confidence in his art. Which was why he hated letting his friends see any of it. Doing portraits for the A-list would force him to be more public about his art and boost his confidence while simultaneously bulking up his portfolio. If he was going to apply to art schools for next year, he was going to need both.

BEATRICE

(1) Find the niche: Gabe had told me a million times that if I just agreed to nurse the mean girls through algebra, I wouldn't be such an outcast. Even Jesse had realized that if I embraced this as my "thing," I'd have a surefire way to fit in. I'd been fighting against the label of Math Girl since freshman year, but maybe it was time to own it.

(2) Play the role: I had the easiest transformation. I was already a know-it-all math genius. Didn't really need to change anything there. The hardest part for me would be actually talking to my new client base without disdain radiating from every pore. Maybe not so easy after all.

(3) Fill the void: All I had to do was swallow my pride and offer my services as a math tutor. Free of charge. They might not like or accept me, but they definitely needed me. And as with Gabe and Spencer, it wasn't like I'd get nothing out of the experience. Spencer's comment about the MIT scholarship had lit a fuse. The Formula was the perfect research: mathematics and information theory applied to everyday life. I could chronicle how the Formula worked for us, and present a surefire proof of my equation. "Math Girl" may have made me cringe, but it was going to be my ticket to MIT.

I smiled at my friends, standing before me in their new skins. Even the combative glint in Spencer's eyes was somehow perfectly in character. This was totally going to work.

"This isn't going to work," Spencer said.

"Of course it will," I snapped.

"I look like an eighties gay stereotype on glitter rainbow crack," Gabe said.

"You look fabulous," I said. "Now, did you come up with a catchphrase like we discussed?" Based on my research, a catchphrase was of vital importance to any over-the-top character.

"Yeah, how's this?" Gabe fanned his hands on either side of his face like Judy Garland in *A Star Is Born*. "Zoopa!" He dropped his hands to explain. "It's like 'super' with a highly affected German accent."

I gave him a thumbs-up. "And what are you going to say when you see Cassilyn in the halls today?"

Gabe took a deep breath. "Oh em gee, Cassilyn! I'm *so* glad you went with the Michael Kors over the Tory Burch! That bitch is so last spring."

It was disturbingly perfect.

Spencer was also impeccably in character. He'd followed my instructions and put together the most emotastic outfit possible. Black boot-cut jeans over a pair of heavily buckled motorcycle boots. On top, a black V-neck T-shirt and a distressed pin-striped jacket, and even though he stood before me with his hands shoved into his pockets, trying with all his might to throw me some shade, he still looked like the epitome of a brooding, mysterious artist.

As for me, I hadn't changed much. I'd pulled my long wavy hair into a high ponytail, and instead of my contacts, I'd fished an old pair of cat-eye glasses out of a drawer. I certainly looked like a nerdy Math Girl, which, let's face it, wasn't that much of a stretch.

"I don't like this," Spencer said for like the fortieth time that day.

"I don't like it either," I said. Which was partially true. I wasn't much of a fashionista, but I cringed at the idea of Jesse seeing me in all my nerd glory. "But we have to focus on the positives. Gabe gets his article. You get a portfolio. I get a scholarship. And we all get a break from the daily bullying."

"Dahlings." Gabe sailed forward and whisked his shoulder bag off the floor with a ballerina's grace. "Let's go show Fullerton Hills what we're made of."

EiGHT

GABE PUSHED OPEN the double doors at the front entrance of Fullerton Hills High School and strode into the two-story foyer. "I just *love* the smell of freshman boys in the morning." His voice, higher-pitched than usual, pinged off the tile floor and vaulted ceiling.

Gabe might not have had any formal theater training, but his flair for the dramatic meant he was perfectly suited for this new persona, and he'd thrown himself into the role like it was the ultimate LARPing experience.

"Freshman boys are hardly your type."

He grazed his chin with his forefinger, supporting his elbow with the opposite hand. "Touché."

I glanced around the foyer, looking for Jesse. I'd texted him last night and asked him to meet us there before class so the sight of me all dorked out wouldn't be a horrifying sur-prise at lunch, but he hadn't responded, and was nowhere in sight. Which sucked. I was dying to explain the Formula and how it would change everything for us at school.

But though Jesse wasn't there to see it, our entrance had definitely turned some heads. I could feel the subtle shift in the energy of the foyer. People were whispering, pointing fingers, staring. It was working. We were making a splash.

Then a doughy face emerged from the thickening crowd.

"What's this?" Kurt Heinzmueller asked, examining Gabe up and down. "Dress-up day? Did I miss the memo?"

Gabe didn't drop his pose, just his voice. "Trying something new," he said softly.

Kurt laughed. "I'll say. Where the hell did you find these clothes?"

"Not now, Kurt," Gabe said out of the corner of his mouth.

"What do you mean, 'not now'? You don't want to talk to me in front of your friends?"

He was going to ruin everything. "Kurt," I said, drawing him aside. "Gabe's just conducting an experiment on social acceptance. For a new article he's working on." Technically, it wasn't a lie. "And you're going to blow his cover."

Kurt tilted his head to the side. "His cover in the gay mafia?"

With that, Gabe broke character. "I'll talk to you later," he said, his affected attitude gone. "Okay?"

Kurt stared at him for a moment. "Whatever." Then he bounded across the foyer and disappeared down the hall.

The whispering and finger pointing doubled, only instead of excited curiosity, I sensed derision and ridicule in the attention. Had I miscalculated somehow?

"This isn't working," Spencer whispered in my ear. "What do we do?"

"Maybe we should just head to class," I suggested, "and try this again later."

"Screw that," Gabe said, then he swung around and started blowing kisses toward the balcony above us. "Dahlings!"

I froze as the four most popular girls in school descended the stairs to the foyer.

Esmeralda Juarez led the way. The daughter of Fullerton's deputy mayor, she looked like a twenty-five-year-old Playboy centerfold. Flawless brown skin—darker than my own but with a radiance that meant she either was a master of bronzer or had a megawatt bulb lighting her from within—doe-like eyes, and enormous boobs that seemed to hang suspended from her chest without any sign of adequate support.

Behind her trailed stepsisters Dakota Mills and Noel Tattinger. They came from more money than God, which a dizzying array of stepparents seemed to throw around with reckless abandon. I wasn't even sure if they were technically related—their parents changed partners faster than square dancers—but I assumed they still resided in the same house at least part of the time, considering their wardrobes, as well as their personalities, were interchangeable.

"Who's tha . . . ," Dakota said. Her voice trailed into lazy silence. Consonants and punctuation were just too much effort.

"I dunno," Noel echoed. I could barely discern the last

syllable as the vocal fry drowned out her diction.

And then came Cassilyn. Beautiful and poised as ever, as if she were an actress in a high school sitcom with wardrobe, hair, and makeup crews at the ready for instant touch-ups.

"Oh em gee," Gabe said, taking Cassilyn's hand as he examined the designer bag on her arm. "I am *so* glad you went with the Michael Kors over the Tory Burch! That bitch is so last spring."

Cassilyn blinked, taking in Gabe's ridiculous getup. I could see her register the bow tie, the hairdo, the suspenders, and heart-shaped sunglasses. And then, just like that, she accepted him.

"I know, right?" She laughed, tossing her hair. "I was just telling Esme the same thing last week. Tory is done."

Esmeralda turned to the side, flashing her own Michael Kors handbag. It was the same shade as Cassilyn's—an off-white snakeskin—but it was twice as large and twice as expensive.

"As if I didn't own one already," she said. Her eyes flew to the bag dangling from Cassilyn's shoulder, as if desperately trying to prove that she wasn't copying her friend's style. Which meant, of course, that she was.

"We love Michael Kor . . . ," Dakota and Noel said in perfect unison, even leaving out the final *s* together.

But Cassilyn had already moved on. "What's your name?" she asked Gabe, smiling sweetly.

"Gabriel Muñoz. And these are my friends, Spencer and Bea."

Four sets of eyes turned to us blankly. They'd bought Gabe and his gay-best-friend routine, but the two of us? Not so much. Hopefully, I could fix that.

"Math Girl," I said, pointing to myself. Self-deprecation might ingratiate me. "That's how you guys know me. Highest GPA in school and I aced every exam in Algebra II, so if any of you—"

"Who are you?" Cassilyn asked, her wide blue eyes fixed on Spencer.

"Spencer," he replied, then looked away, refusing to elaborate.

"He's an artist," I said, doubling down. "Maybe you've seen some of his portraits at the Heinzmueller Gallery downtown?"

Gabe choked as I used Kurt's last name for my fictitious gallery. "Sorry," he said, recovering quickly. "I'm okay. *Zoopa*, really."

"Portraits?" Cassilyn asked. "Like with paint and stuff."

Oh boy. "Yeah," I said, forcing myself not to roll my eyes. "Spencer just came back from a tour of Western Europe, and he's planning an entire show based around portraits of the Fullerton Hills football team."

Cassilyn took a step toward him. "Really?"

For a split second, I wasn't sure if Spencer was going to play along or tell me to piss off and storm out of the foyer. I held my breath.

"Yeah," he said. His whole body seemed to go limp with the word. "Portraits. Football team."

Cassilyn sucked in a breath. "That is so awesome."

I wanted to dance around the foyer. The Formula had worked. We were in public having an actual conversation with the most popular girls at school, and no one was making fun of us. If only Jesse had been there to see it.

The electronic buzzer ripped through the foyer. Five minutes until class. Spencer jumped at the opportunity to extricate himself from the situation.

"Gotta go," he said, hurrying off, not even pausing to wait for me even though we had first period together.

"See you later," Cassilyn cried after him, then turned to Gabe. "You too. You're my new favorite."

Cassilyn trailed down the hall, followed by her friends. The instant they were out of earshot, Gabe draped himself over my shoulder. "That was truly *zoopa*."

NINE

"SO HOW DID it go this morning?" I asked the second Gabe joined me at our lunch table. I noticed that he'd greeted a dozen people as he promenaded across the cafeteria.

"*Zoopa!*" I held up my hand for a high five, which he playfully smacked. Then, making sure that no one was paying close attention, he leaned forward and dropped the act. "I talked to Poston in his office after second period," he said. "Told him about my idea for the article. He thinks it's brilliant. Perfect for the *Register*."

"Awesome."

He pulled a small notebook out of his breast pocket and flipped it open, revealing a page and a half of scribbles. "I've already documented instances of people treating me differently. And the more outlandish I behave, the more attention I get."

I smirked. "Sounds like you're enjoying it."

"A little." Then he sighed. "Now if I can just stomach

this stereotype for a few weeks."

"At least twenty-five percent of the student body already knows your name," I said, mentally calculating it based on the response I'd just witnessed. "Gabriel is already significantly more popular than Gabe."

"I know," he said. "That's what bothers me."

"Eyes on the prize, Muñoz," I said, patting his hand. "If you nail that article, the internship is yours."

"Which might make all this crap worth it." Spencer slid into the booth next to Gabe and slouched down, propping his legs up on the seat next to me.

"Speaking of crap," Gabe said, smiling sweetly, "any takers on your portraits?"

He wrinkled his nose. "Ha-ha."

I pushed his shoes off the cushioned bench. "Seriously. Have you mentioned it to anyone besides Cassilyn?"

"Oh yeah," Spencer said, head tilted to the side. "I marched right up to Thad and Milo and said, *Dudes, how about I paint you?* I thought the idea was to avoid getting my ass kicked. Not invite it."

"You have to make an effort at some point or this won't work."

Spencer nodded across the cafeteria. "I don't see you over there chatting them up about the Pythagorean theorem."

"Nice reference," Gabe said.

"Thanks."

I knew Spencer was just trying to annoy me, so I ignored the jab and turned to check out the cluster of lunch tables in the middle of the main dining room. Cassilyn, Esmeralda, and the stepsisters were there, as well as Milo, Thad, and a coterie of football players and wannabe fashionistas, one of whom was telling a very animated story that seemed to have everyone's rapt attention. Her arms gesticulated wildly, and blond hair fluttered around the side of her sparkly hot-pink snood.

Toile.

Okay, fine. She'd been accepted by the cool kids after only twenty-four hours. So what? Who cared if she was already popular while I'd been at that stupid school for three years and no one even knew my name?

I did.

As I continued to watch her hold court, a figure approached Toile's table, tall and lean and wearing a navy beanie.

I shot to my feet. "Jesse!" I cried way too loudly, and waved my arms over my head like I was trying to guide a 747 to the runway. He hesitated, casting a glance at Toile's table, then turned and walked toward me.

"Amazing," Spencer said while Jesse was still out of earshot, "that he managed to forget where we sit after only one day."

"It's a big cafeteria," I said.

"Mmhm."

Jesse stared at me as he lowered himself onto the bench. "You look different."

That's right. I hadn't gotten a chance to tell him about

the Formula yet. "Long story," I said, laughing. "I'll explain after school when you drive me home."

"Oh."

Gabe arched an eyebrow. "I think she's got kind of a sexy-librarian thing going on. What do you think, Jesse?"

"I guess," he said. "I've never seen you in glasses."

Did that mean he liked them? Or didn't like them? Jesse's dark brown eyes were unreadable, and suddenly, I felt incredibly self-conscious. "I never wear them," I said quickly, snatching them off my nose. The cafeteria went fuzzy. "Just today, really."

"Oh," he repeated.

Spencer glanced up at me. "I like the glasses."

"'Where can I find a woman like that?'" Gabe sang.

"I'm going to kill you," Spencer said through gritted teeth.

Jesse cocked his head. "I thought you didn't like girls."

Gabe grinned. "I don't."

A bleating laugh carried across the cafeteria, above the fevered pitch of the assembled student body, and we turned to see Toile giggling hysterically with the popular people.

"I wonder what they're talking about," Jesse said.

I wasn't sure if it was the wistfulness in his tone or Spencer's goading that made me do it, but I hooked my glasses over my ears and nudged Jesse out of the booth. "There's only one way to find out." Then I turned and marched toward Cassilyn's table.

In my three years at Fullerton Hills I'd never once

approached a table in the center of the main cafeteria. Even clueless freshman Beatrice had known better than to swim with the big fish in open water, and the closer I got, the harder my heart pounded in my chest.

You'll be fine, I told myself. *Don't panic.* Right. I remembered how easily Gabe and Spencer had been accepted this morning, simply by following the Formula. That's all I had to do. I was a math nerd coming to offer my services as a tutor. I had something they needed. They would respect that.

Then why are your palms sweating?

I felt as if every pair of eyes in the cafeteria was on me, watching the bespectacled nerd Math Girl approach the forbidden zone. Realistically, I estimated a mere 5 percent of students had even noted my migration from the north room, but in my mind, it was as if a giant spotlight were following me, drawing focus. I wanted to turn around and flee, but I couldn't. I'd gone too far, past the event horizon to the point of social suicide. Close enough to hear their conversation.

"What is that?" Cassilyn said, eyeing the hot-pink monstrosity hooked to the back of Toile's head.

Toile smiled. "It's called a snood."

"That sounds dirt . . ." Dakota's voice trailed off.

"Total . . . ," Noel echoed.

"It's my new favorite," Cassilyn said. A queen laying down the law.

Esmeralda tossed her long black hair. "I have one at home. Had it for ages."

Cassilyn smirked at Toile. "Sure she does."

Thad spun around from the adjacent table. "Yo, Cass," he said. "How about we go to the back-to-school dance together?"

Was that how popular guys asked girls out? It seemed so impersonal.

Cassilyn was equally unimpressed. "How about you ask me nicely?"

"He did ask you nicely," Esmeralda said, her eyes narrowing on Cassilyn. For best friends, there was a lot of Haterade being consumed.

Thad was about to respond when his eyes landed on me. "Who are you?"

Crap. Not the entrance I wanted to make. "I'm Beatrice," I blurted out, momentarily forgetting the reason I was there. "I mean, Math Girl. That's how you know me."

Thad blinked. "What do you want?"

I took a quick breath. Play the role. "I just wanted to let you guys know that I'm offering free tutoring for anyone who might need help passing Algebra II or Trig and—"

"Algebra is so hard," Toile said with a pitiful little sigh.

"I know," Cassilyn said. "I hate math."

"Math sucks," Thad chimed in, right on her heels.

Esmeralda wasn't to be outdone. "Math is the worst. I hate it more than anyone."

I gritted my teeth. "Algebra isn't the worst." How could they hate math? What was wrong with them? Couldn't they see the beautiful order of a perfectly constructed equation? No, of course not. They could barely add.

Thad rolled his eyes. "Whatever, Math Girl."

Ugh, I was losing them. "Well, if you need help passing exams, I'd be happy to—"

"Are you friends with Jesse Sullivan?" Toile asked. "He is *such* a sweetie."

I was so confused by the speed at which she'd changed the conversation, I was momentarily struck dumb.

"Who?" Cassilyn asked.

Toile pointed Jesse out to her. "He's over there in the navy beanie. He totally showed me around school on my first day."

"Actually," I said, my brain finally catching up with the conversation. I didn't like the way Toile was talking about my boyfriend. "Jesse and I are—"

Cassilyn stood up, her gaze still locked on our lunch table in the north room. "You're friends with that painter guy, right?"

"Spencer?"

She nodded and glanced toward the north room. "Is he really painting portraits now? Like of real people?"

No, he's painting portraits of fake people, Cassilyn. "Yes."

She bit her lower lip. "I'd love to have my portrait done."

"I don't know." I glanced at Milo and Thad. "He wanted to focus on the athletics program."

"Oh my God!" Toile grasped Cassilyn's arm. "You would look absolutely ethereal in pastels."

Cassilyn tilted her head to the side. "I'm more of a spring. Bright colors with warm undertones."

Toile laughed. "No, silly. They're paints! And they'd totally bring out your coloring."

Cassilyn's eyes grew wide. "Do you think?"

"Of course!" Toile squealed. "Can you imagine? A portrait of you gracing a museum wall? Immortalized for all eternity."

"For all eternity," Cassilyn repeated.

"You'd be perfect as a model." Toile turned to me. "Don't you think?"

I wanted to kill her. "Sure."

"Awesome." Cassilyn took my hand, squeezing it gently. "Can you tell Spencer I'm interested and I can start right away? Thanks. Bye!"

TEN

I HURRIED TO my locker after the final bell, ready to get the hell off campus for the day. It wasn't as if I hadn't been humiliated at school before, but somehow it felt so much more pathetic when it came at the hands of Toile, the new girl, who had been there for two days and was already approximately 91 percent more popular than I was.

To make matters worse, Jesse had witnessed my failure firsthand. As soon as I'd returned to our table, he'd asked what Cassilyn and I had been talking about, and if we'd been invited to eat lunch with them or join them at D'Caffeinated after school for tutoring. I told him that we'd talked about Spencer, and no, I didn't actually have a tutoring date with anyone from Cassilyn's circle. I could see the brightness fade from Jesse's face, and by the time the bell rang, he'd practically raced from the cafeteria.

I just needed to explain to him what we were doing. On the drive home I'd lay out the whole Formula and tell him how he'd practically inspired this new role for me when he suggested it yesterday. I'd point out that the Formula had an 89 percent chance of success, which meant I'd probably be at least marginally popular by midterms. Not only that, but with the Formula, I had the perfect research to submit for the MIT scholarship. Which meant our plans to go to college together in Boston were still on track.

I slammed my locker door, still picturing Jesse and I traipsing through Boston Common together next year, when I caught sight of my boyfriend's navy beanie at the end of the hallway heading out to the parking lot. At his side, a sparkly, hot-pink snood.

Jesse was leaving with Toile?

They were halfway down the steps to the parking lot when I burst through the door. "Jesse!" I picked up my wheelie bag by the handle and hustled after them. The over-stuffed bag slapped against my thigh, and I had to lean to one side like a listing ship to keep the wheels from smacking onto the ground. I managed to overtake them just as they reached his car. "Jesse."

He stopped, and turned toward me. "Oh, hey, Bea. What's up?"

What's up? "You're driving me home."

He blinked. "Sure, yeah. I'm taking Toile home too."

"That's fine," I said, even though it was not. For the second time that day, Toile was messing up my plans. I wrenched open the front passenger door and slipped into the seat. It was sweltering in the car, which had been sitting in the blazing

Southern California sun all day, but I didn't care. No way was Toile riding shotgun.

"Sorry." Jesse's voice was muffled through the tinted glass window. I wasn't sure if he was talking to me or to her.

I clutched my bag to my chest as we backed out of his spot. The silence was almost as thick as the stifling air in the car.

"Are you going to your mom's?" Jesse asked when we were a few blocks away.

He never could remember whose house I was at on any given day. "I'm at my dad's Wednesday night through Sunday morning," I explained for the dozenth time.

"I love your school," Toile offered, unsolicited.

I turned to look at her. "Yay. I'm so glad." I couldn't even manufacture the fake enthusiasm required to make that comment sound less bitchy.

Toile reached forward and patted me on the head, like a mom commending a small child. "You're sweet, Bea." Then she caught her breath and pointed over Jesse's shoulder, through the front windshield. "Look!"

I spun around and braced my arms against the glove compartment expecting to see an eighteen-wheeler barreling toward us for a head-on collision. Instead, there was an ice cream truck parked across the street.

Toile gripped Jesse's arm. "Can we stop? Please, please, pretty please, with sprinkles and a cherry on top?"

A traveling food dispensary? Gross. "You know, even with modern regulations in the wake of the food-truck craze, unlicensed vendors like this are notorious for substandard hygienic condi—"

"Sure!" Jesse cranked the wheel to the left, performing a tight, less-than-legal U-turn that sent me flying into the window.

"Be careful!" I cried, wincing on the inside as I realized how much I sounded like my mother.

From the backseat, Toile squealed with delight, then laughed hysterically. Jesse joined in as he screeched to a halt in a red zone behind the ice cream truck. "Come on!" He hopped out and opened Toile's door. Then they hurried to get in line behind a group of ten-year-olds, leaving me alone in the car.

What the actual fuck?

I leaned over and engaged the hazard lights (perhaps a passing Fullerton PD cruiser would attribute our illegal park job to a mechanical issue), then fished my wallet out of my bag and pushed the door open with my foot. This day was rapidly unraveling.

Five minutes later, we resumed our drive. Jesse's chocolate malt was in the cup holder, Toile happily licked at a rainbow Popsicle, and I held a disturbingly accurate facsimile of Tweety Bird's head on a stick, made out of some kind of ice cream–like substance the color of yellow snow. I hadn't wanted to get nothing, so just pointed to the closest thing on the menu, which I thought was going to be a fairly safe and respectable ice cream sandwich and ended up being this toxic substance molded to look like a beloved cartoon character.

Was I supposed to relish biting into Tweety's bulbous skull? And why were these things being marketed to kids? What was wrong with everyone?

The car slowed while I was mid–mental rant. I glanced out the window, expecting to see an unfamiliar house that Toile's family had just moved into, and instead saw the cactus garden in front of my dad's place.

"You're supposed to drop off Toile first," I blurted out, unable to hide my disappointment.

He avoided my eyes. "She lives closer to me."

Of course she did. Because, apparently, the universe hated me.

Fine, whatever. I'd give him twenty to twenty-five minutes to get her home and then call him. Maybe suggest that he drive back over? I wrangled my bag and my sweating Tweety Bird out of the car with more awkwardness than I would have preferred. "I'll call you in a bit, okay?"

I fought the urge to lean across the seat and kiss him, asserting my claim in front of Toile. But that would prove that I felt threatened, and I wasn't going to give her the satisfaction. So instead, I just smiled and closed the door.

As I reached the porch, I heard a car door close. Was Jesse coming to say something? Kiss me? Anything? I turned just in time to see Toile slip into the front seat before Jesse peeled away from the curb.

Tweety Bird hit the ground, a sticky, melting lump on the stoop.

ELEVEN

I TEXTED JESSE. Twice. Once about thirty minutes after he'd dropped me off and once at ten o'clock before I went to bed. He didn't respond to either.

I'd broken down at some point and Googled "Toile Jeffries." Not out of jealousy, I'd told myself, just curiosity. But the internet was oddly devoid of any information on the new girl. Just a Facebook page that hadn't been updated yet. It was as if she didn't exist at all.

I was still antsy the next morning at breakfast, lost in my own thoughts as I narrowed Jesse's behavior down to two likely scenarios: family emergency or lost phone. I was so preoccupied even my dad noticed, which was a rarity.

"BeaBea, is everything okay?" he asked as he pored over emails on his phone. There was a pinched look around his dark eyes, deep crow's-feet extending toward his graying temples like shadowy chasms in his tanned skin. Even when he was trying to look kindly sympathetic, there was something hard in his features—a trait that made Andrew Giovannini an imposing opponent in the courtroom, and a difficult parent to relate to.

"Boy stuff," I blurted without thinking.

At the word "boy," Sheri, my stepmom, rushed over to the kitchen table and pulled out the chair next to me. "Boy stuff? I can totally help with that! Tell me everything!"

Sheri was sweet. I could have done way worse in a stepmom considering that the prerequisite for the job was, essentially, being my dad's secretary while he was married to someone else. What she lacked in brains she made up for in enthusiasm, and every sentence out of her mouth, whether it was delivering news of a death in the family or announcing what she'd made for dinner, sounded as if it ended in an exclamation point.

She'd probably been really popular in high school, a Cassilyn type who had boys fighting with one another for the chance to ask her out. That wasn't my reality. And though I appreciated her willingness to help, I wasn't in the mood for a pep talk.

"It's nothing."

"Are you sure you don't want to talk about it?" my dad asked, more out of courtesy than from a burning desire to hear my boy problems.

"Yes."

He pushed his chair out from the table and reached for his briefcase. "Good. I mean, okay. Whatever you want, BeaBea." He kissed Sheri on the cheek. "I'll be home late. Client dinner."

I cringed, noticing that he didn't look Sheri in the eye as he said it.

Her face fell. "Another one?"

"I'm sorry."

Sheri sighed. "I have an appointment with Dr. Aaronstein today. About . . ." She dropped her voice as if she was about to mention an adult topic a child shouldn't overhear. "About the fertility stuff."

"Excellent," he said, grabbing his car keys. "I want to hear all about it, okay? Come on, BeaBea. We're going to be late."

With roughly six and a half minutes until first period, I hurried through the halls toward Jesse's Advanced Econ elective class. I'd have just enough time to see if he was there or if, as would confirm my worst fears, he was absent and I needed to start calling the four major hospitals in the greater Fullerton area, searching for a member of the Sullivan family. By the time I reached his classroom, I had fleshed out an entire vision of Jesse huddled by his father's bedside, his face drawn with worry, unable to leave his ailing parent to check in with his anxious girlfriend.

I waited until the last possible second before the late bell, but Jesse never arrived for class.

That sealed it. Something awful had happened.

I was sweaty and panting by the time I dashed through the door of AP English just nanoseconds before the bell, and dropped into my desk behind Spencer as Mr. Schulty began the day's lecture on John Donne.

"You okay?" Spencer asked.

"I think something horrible happened to Jesse."

He arched a brow. "Why?"

Mr. Schulty loosened his tie and took up his battered volume and began to read aloud. "'Fond woman,'" he droned, slipping into a faux British accent, "'which wouldst have thy husband die, And yet complain'st of his great jealousy.'"

"He's not here today," I mouthed, my voice barely a whisper.

Spencer half turned in his chair, leaning his elbow on my desk and propping his head up with his hand, as if concentrating intently on Mr. Schulty's recitation. "Yes, he is."

"What?" I blurted out.

Mr. Schulty cleared his throat. "Beatrice Giovannini? Is there something you'd like to share with the class?"

"No, Mr. Schulty."

"Are you not interested in the poetry of John Donne?" he continued, clearly miffed that I hadn't been paying attention.

I should have just placated him, but of course, I had to say exactly what I was thinking. "Based on my choice of major and university, I have only an eight percent chance of referencing John Donne once I graduate."

"That's not really the point of poetry, Beatrice."

"Poetry," I said, "is a necessary evil of high school education."

He blinked, perhaps not quite sure if he'd heard me

correctly, then slowly shook his head. "I'll remember that on your final exam."

As if.

I waited until Mr. Schulty had resumed his performance, then leaned my face close to Spencer's.

"Are you sure?"

He nodded. "Saw him in the parking lot."

Why hadn't Jesse been in first period? Why hadn't he returned my texts? What the hell was going on?

"He'll be in the cafeteria," Gabe said as we crossed campus after third period. He looped his arm through mine and laid his head on my shoulder. "Don't stress."

Spencer fell into step beside me. "I'm sure he's not dead."

I was glad they were so confident.

We were crossing the foyer when someone called Gabe's name. Cassilyn, alone, without her entourage.

"Dahling." Gabe kissed her on both cheeks, European-style. "How are you?"

Instead of answering, Cassilyn just smiled, her eyes fixed on Spencer. "Where do you guys usually eat lunch?" she asked, even though Toile had pointed out our table to her just yesterday.

"Oh, you know," Gabe answered noncommittally. "Here, there."

"Want to join us today?" she asked Spencer. "You *and* your friends, of course."

I blinked, not trusting my own ears. Had the most

popular girl in school just offered us a spot at her lunch table?

"*Zoopa!*" Gabe said, using that ridiculous German accent. He blew her a kiss as he followed her into the cafeteria. "So sweet of you."

Before yesterday I'd never gotten within five feet of the popular kids' tables in the cafeteria, and now here I was among them for the second day in a row. Proof that the Formula worked? Absolutely. At least something was going according to plan.

"Can you believe this?" Gabe whispered, reading my mind. "Your formula totally works."

"I know!"

"This is going to be the opening line of the article: 'It took twenty-eight hours for me to permeate the A-list.' I mean, won't that be an amazing hook?" Then he squeezed my arm and pranced over to Cassilyn's side.

"You look pleased with yourself," Spencer said. He didn't mean it as a compliment.

"Yes," I said. "I am."

I glanced at the north room as we passed, hoping to see Jesse at our table so I could beckon for him to join us, but the booth was empty. I did, however, catch sight of Michael Torres watching me with a gaping jaw, his skin a sickly shade of yellow.

And Michael Torres wasn't the only one watching; Milo and Thad glared at us as we approached, their faces anything but inviting. But Gabe either didn't notice them or didn't care. He spun onto one of the curved benches, like he was in a choreographed dance number, then grabbed Cassilyn's hand as he came full circle. She lowered herself onto the bench beside him, crossed her hands daintily over her knee, and gestured for Spencer to sit on her other side. It was every inch the queen granting permission for an audience. "Will you paint my portrait?"

Spencer stiffened. "I don't know . . ."

"My father will pay you, of course. A commission, just like Van Gogh."

I was impressed she knew his name. "I think that sounds amazing, Spence."

Cassilyn turned her cool blue eyes to me, as if appraising a piece of jewelry, then smiled. "See? Math Girl thinks it's a good idea."

I flinched. *Math Girl.*

"You'd make the perfect muse," Gabe cooed.

Cassilyn's big blue eyes lit up. "Like the band?"

Um, no. "More like Ancient Greece," I muttered.

She placed her hand on Spencer's arm. "I'd be honored."

He laughed weakly. "Okay. I'll do it."

I should have been elated that the Formula was working. The pieces were falling into place, which meant my research for the MIT scholarship was going to be stellar, but for some reason, the way Cassilyn looked at Spencer irritated the hell out of me.

But wasn't this what we wanted? Milo and Thad were just feet from us, sitting at the same group of tables, and yet no one had threatened to kick anyone else's ass. That was the goal.

"I see we have guests." Esmeralda rounded our table slowly, a lioness circling her prey.

"Spencer's going to paint my portrait," Cassilyn said, tossing her hair like a shampoo model. "Isn't that exciting?"

"So . . . ," Dakota drawled, following close on Esmeralda's heels.

Noel finished the thought. "Excitin . . ." She sounded anything but.

Esmeralda didn't join Cassilyn at our table, but instead sat with Milo and Thad. I noticed that she purposefully squeezed in between them, snuggling up to Thad, who looked jittery and uncomfortable. He repeatedly craned his neck to get a clear look at Cassilyn's hand (which resided in close proximity to Spencer's), his lips pressed together into a thin line. Meanwhile, Dakota and Noel flanked Gabe, doting on his plaid bow tie and his striped yacht shoes as if they were playing with a dress-up doll. He beamed and laughed and tossed *zoopa*s around with abandon. Like Spencer, it was as if he belonged there.

Suddenly, I needed to get out of the cafeteria. I felt tears welling up, and I shook my head, frustrated at the illogical display of emotion. Why was I upset? This was exactly what I'd planned.

"Bea?" Gabe asked, his queen routine forgotten. "Are you okay?"

I didn't trust my voice, afraid I would burst into tears the instant I opened my mouth, so I just nodded quickly, grabbed my bag, and fled.

I paused around the corner from the cafeteria and pulled my phone from the pocket of my blazer. Still no response from Jesse.

I opened a text bubble and typed quickly. **Where are you? I really need to talk.** It felt so pathetic, like I was pleading with my boyfriend to answer me. That was awful. I knew that was awful. I shouldn't feel as if I was begging him to acknowledge my existence, yet at that moment, I would have given up all of my dignity just to feel as if I was more important at this school than the nameless Math Girl.

I just needed to find Jesse. Of course that's what was upsetting me. I was worried about my boyfriend. I power walked through the halls, the wheels on my bag squealing in protest every time I took a hard corner. He had to be somewhere. I searched all the obvious places and was moving on to the nonobvious ones when the door to the music room opened and my boyfriend stepped into the hall.

"Jesse!" I cried, relieved at finding him alive and well.

Alive and well and not responding to my messages.

He jolted, clearly startled. "Oh, hey."

Oh, hey? He'd left me hanging for sixteen and a half hours and that's all he had to say? "Did you lose your phone?" I asked, trying to give him the benefit of the doubt.

He patted the front pocket of his jeans. "No."

"Then why didn't you text me back?"

The door opened again and Toile bounded out. She was wearing a green dirndl, those yellow tights, and a bright turquoise beret perched on the side of her head. "Thanks for the help," she cried, waving back into the music room. "I'll let you know how it goes." Then she saw me. "Hey, Bea! What's up? Did you hear any of the rehearsal?"

"Rehearsal?" I asked, staring right at Jesse, willing him to answer me.

He didn't.

"Yeah!" Toile chimed in. "Mr. Terranova helped us pick out a song for Jesse's audition, and we—"

I felt my pulse accelerate. "Audition?"

"Jesse's auditioning for show choir." Toile hung on him, head against his arm. It was a complete and utter display of ownership.

I should have confronted them right then and there. Called Toile out for trying to steal my boyfriend, called Jesse out for allowing her to. But I couldn't. No coherent words were able to travel the distance between my brain and my mouth, and all I could do was stand there lamely, staring.

"I need to go," I mumbled, peeling my eyes from Jesse's face. And as Toile uttered a painfully perky good-bye, I barreled blindly down the hall.

TWELVE

SPENCER DROPPED ME off at my dad's after school;
thankfully no one was home. I'd planned to go straight
to my room and have a good, therapeutic cry, but no tears
would flow. Not unusual. I hadn't cried since the day my
dad told me he was moving out. But I thought it would help,
somehow, to eradicate whatever it was I was feeling. Instead,
I just lay on my back and stared at my ceiling fan as I pored
through scenarios in my mind.

FACT: Jesse was my boyfriend. I wasn't making that up.
We'd had several date-like excursions over the summer, had
held hands in public, and though we hadn't gone all the way,
we had engaged in eleven make-out sessions. These were all
solid, universally acknowledged boyfriend-girlfriend activities.

FACT: Despite official boyfriend-girlfriend status, Jesse
had been acting differently since the episode in the cafeteria
on the first day of school. This was . . . not good.

FACT: Toile was a negative influence on Jesse. While I couldn't rationalize away his fascination with her, I could construct a plausible scenario in which he was somewhat of an innocent victim to her romantic machinations. She'd twisted Jesse's naïveté toward her own goal: stealing my boyfriend.

FACT: Almost all of my interactions with Jesse since the first day of school had been in Toile's presence.

I sat upright. Of course! I hadn't been alone with him. Maybe if Jesse saw me without Toile around, I'd be able to break her spell?

I grabbed my purse and sprinted down the hall before I could change my mind. I had to talk to my boyfriend. Alone.

By the time I turned onto Jesse's street, my heart was pounding. Less from the physical exertion of walking uphill from the bus stop and more from pure excitement. I had convinced myself that Jesse had no idea what Toile's intentions were in regard to their relationship. Thankfully, he had me. I just needed to point out to him that this whole show choir thing was just Toile's excuse to spend more time with him and, more important, isolate him from his girlfriend.

I took a deep breath and tried to calm myself as I rang the doorbell. This wasn't a conversation I was looking forward to, but it had to be done.

Jesse had a hint of a smile on his face when he opened the door, as if he'd just woken up from a delicious dream. "Oh, hey, Bea."

"Hi!" I slipped my arms around his waist and hugged

him, resting my head momentarily against his chest. "Can we talk?"

I felt him shrug. "Sure." He stepped aside and let me into the family room separated from the kitchen by an enormous island. As usual, the house was immaculately clean, all gleaming tile and shiny chrome. I waited as Jesse closed and locked the door, then followed him through the kitchen and up the back stairs.

Just inside his bedroom door, I froze. Strung diagonally between two corners was a large canvas hammock.

"What is that?"

"It's a hammock."

"Well, yeah," I said lamely. "But what is it doing in your room?"

"I sleep in it."

I snorted. "Since when?"

Jesse strode defiantly over to the hammock and swung his body onto it. The hammock swayed to and fro, creaking at the fulcrum of each arc, and I couldn't help but wonder how long it would be before the studs ripped out of the wall. "It's relaxing," he said. "Calms me down so I can think. Dream."

Jesse wasn't exactly a ball of tension. "Dream?"

He pulled a curled-up paperback from the front pocket of his sweatshirt, and flipped it open to a random page. I recognized the volume immediately: it was Tennyson's *Idylls of the King.* "Sometimes I just need to let the rhythm of the poetry fill my being and allow my mind to drift far away."

I stiffened. He sounded like Toile. "So you're a hammock guy now, is that it?"

Jesse spun around and planted his feet on the carpet, stopping his momentum. "Is that a thing? Can that be my thing? Can I be the hammock guy?"

Jesse's obsession with having a "thing" was starting to grate on me. "Jesse, what the hell is going on?"

"What do you mean?"

"Since when do you read Tennyson?"

"Toile gave it to me."

Of course she did. "You don't even like poetry."

"Yes, I do." He sounded unsure.

"Since when?"

"Since . . ." He dropped the book onto the canvas. "Whatever. I do now. I read poetry and I sleep in a hammock."

This was my worst nightmare. "Jesse, look, this isn't you talking. This is Toile. She's planting all these crazy ideas in your mind."

"Toile?"

"Yeah." He needed to hear the truth. "She's trying to steal you."

He tilted his head to the side. "Really?"

He was so cute when he was naïve. "She wants you to be *her* boyfriend."

Jesse rocketed to his feet, pushing the hammock away with a violence that made me jump. "She does? Do you think? I mean, did she say that to you?" He pulled off his beanie and ran his fingers through his disheveled hair.

Now, if I'd been reading his words via text message, I could have interpreted them spoken with horrified shock tinged with pity that his innocent actions had unwittingly caused such a reaction in Toile. But because I was standing three feet away, I could see that Jesse was neither concerned that he'd led Toile on nor worried that he'd offended me in the process. Instead, as he paced the room, hands grasping his hair, he looked ignited, like a switch had been thrown inside of him.

I squared my shoulders and jutted out my chin as a knot formed in my stomach. I was having difficulty suppressing my anger. "I don't think you should hang out with Toile anymore."

Jesse paused. "What?"

"I mean it. I can't be your girlfriend if she's going to be around." He stared at me blankly, clearly not grasping the meaning of my words, and for the first time in our short relationship, his slowness got on my last nerve. "You need to choose. Toile or me."

He didn't even hesitate. "Sorry, Bea. I choose Toile."

THIRTEEN

THE ONLY REASON I knew it was morning was because one sliver of light managed to penetrate the darkened confines of my bedroom. It was a tenacious little bastard, finding the minuscule gap where my thick, double-lined curtains came together without overlapping, and invading my place of mourning with its cheerful yellow beam.

Normally on a Saturday morning, I'd have slid out of bed and thrown the curtains wide, inviting the sunlight to wash over me as I faced the day with unwavering confidence. But not today. I rolled over, turning my back to the repellent sunlight, and hitched my comforter over my head.

I was never getting out of bed again. Ever.

It had been roughly sixteen hours since Jesse had dumped me, most of which I'd spent in bed. My mom had been surprised to see me, since I was supposed to be at my dad's until Sunday morning, but I just couldn't take Sheri's good-intentioned questions or my dad's endless descriptions of his workday. So after I'd left Jesse's, I texted Sheri to say I wasn't feeling well, and headed back to the town house.

Friday night meant my mom probably had a date, and when I showed up unannounced, the bright red lipstick, dusting of glitter, and lined cat eyes proved that I was right. Mom had freaked out a little, but I had assured her that I didn't want dinner (my stomach felt like the inside of a tumble dryer) and she should go on her date. Her reaction had been less relieved than I'd expected, and as I'd climbed the double flight of stairs to my room, I realized that she'd been hoping to bring her date home.

Which meant my mom was getting more action than I was.

Which was officially the most depressing thought I'd ever had.

I'd gone to bed fully clothed and hadn't even bothered to text Gabe or Spencer to tell them what had happened. I just couldn't. They'd either try to cheer me up (which I didn't want) or try to convince me that I was better off without Jesse (which I didn't believe).

I didn't even cry, which was disturbing in and of itself. Getting dumped by your first boyfriend had an almost 100 percent probability of making you cry, and yet there I lay, unable to muster even a single tear.

In my defense, tears never improved your situation or helped you figure out a problem. So in that way, my response or lack thereof made perfect sense. Tears hadn't helped Sheri get pregnant or found my mom a second husband. And they sure the hell hadn't helped my parents get along better while they were married, and in that particular case, the tears had come from all three of us.

So I'd taken my lack of mourning as a sign that there was a solution to my problem, and I'd spent the night trying to puzzle it out. But so far, a solution hadn't presented itself. Which was disturbing on a variety of levels. I could *always* find a solution. Hell, I'd designed a mathematical formula to protect my friends from school bullies—shouldn't I have been able to fix anything?

"Anak!" My mom's singsong voice drifted up the stairs and beneath my door. "Are you awake?"

No.

I braced myself for the inevitable onslaught. My mom wasn't the type of parent who took her teenage daughter's silence as a signal that she wanted to be left alone.

My door flew open. "Beatrice, you're still in bed?" She floated across the room and whisked aside my purple damask curtains, flooding the room with light. "It's almost eight thirty."

"I'm not feeling well," I said without turning over. "Remember?"

"You'll feel better after some breakfast."

Doubtful.

"Come downstairs," she continued. "You can tell me all about what's bothering you, and I can tell you all about my second date with Benjamin Feldberger."

Don't ask. She wants you to ask.

She took a deep breath, then exhaled a particularly dramatic, melodic sigh that seemed to go on for a full minute. "He's like no one I've ever met."

Be strong.

"So kind. So smart."

Just play dead.

She leaned closer and dropped her voice. "So tender."

Gross. I sat up and faced her. "Stop! For the love of all that's holy, stop talking."

She smirked. "At least I got you to sit up."

I narrowed my eyes. "I hate it when you do that."

"I know." She stood up, and I noticed that she was smiling. "You really like this new guy?"

"Mmhm."

She seemed so happy. She always did at this point in the game. I tried not to think about the almost inevitable post-breakup meltdown that lingered three to six months down the road, complete with weeklong crying jags, an elaborate *I'm never leaving the house again* routine, and my personal favorite, the *I'm going to die alone* monologue.

"Then I'm happy for you, Mom." *For now.* I truly wanted her to be happy, and since I knew that her happiness, however pathetic that might sound to me, was tied up in finding Husband Number Two, I was all for it.

I just didn't want to hear the blow-by-blow of their date.

"Thank you." She cupped my cheek in her hand. "Now come downstairs and I'll tell you all about the thirty minutes we spent kissing in his car."

"Mom!"

"What? It's normal, Beatrice. And if Benjamin and I get married, you'll have to get used to—"

I was saved from more details by the doorbell.

"I'll be right back," my mom said, patting my leg, then she sailed through the door and down the stairs, humming softly to herself.

I flopped back against my pillow. So that was love, huh? These were romantic relationships? Jesse, who got distracted the second someone new waltzed into his life. My mom, who was so laser focused on finding a second husband, she was already talking about marriage after two dates. My dad, whose feelings of love and commitment were short-term and relegated to the women who sat at a desk outside his office.

Maybe I was better off without a boyfriend. Maybe Jesse had been holding me back, distracting me. I needed to focus on the Formula, and organizing my research to submit for the scholarship. That had to be the most important thing in my life right now, not . . .

Heavy footsteps on the stairs, definitely not my mom's light tread. Jesse? He'd realized he'd made a stupid, thoughtless mistake and he'd come to beg my forgiveness, to proclaim his undying love and devotion, to plead with me to take him back. I had a vision of tears and embraces and passionate make-up kisses . . .

And then Gabe walked in. Followed by Spencer.

I was instantly on alert. "What are you guys doing here?"

Gabe plopped down on the edge of my bed. "Oh, you

know. We were in the neighborhood."

I wasn't that stupid. "I'm supposed to be at my dad's house."

"We were in that neighborhood too," Spencer said.

Gabe nodded. "Sheri redirected us."

I glanced pointedly at the clock. "It's eight thirty. The only time either of you is voluntarily awake this early on a weekend is if you've stayed up all night."

Spencer dragged my desk chair over to the bed, spun it around, and straddled it. "Jesse changed his relationship status on Facebook this morning. Everyone knows."

I pushed the comforter down to my waist. "He did what?"

"Good Lord," Gabe said, eyeing my jeans and rumpled gingham blouse. "Did you sleep in that?"

I turned to Spencer. "What does Jesse's Facebook say?"

He took a deep breath. "'In a Relationship with Toile Jeffries.'"

"When?" I asked, my voice steadier than I thought it would be.

"Kurt saw it this morning," Gabe said. "But apparently Jesse posted it last night."

If ever I was going to break my ban on crying, this should have been it. Choosing Toile over me was one thing. Hooking up with her mere hours after breaking up with me was rubbing salt in my wound. But tagging her in a relationship post on Facebook? That was the ultimate blow. He'd never tagged me in a relationship post, but apparently, he'd had no trouble telling the world about Toile. Had he been embarrassed by me? Had he not wanted people to know?

This news should have left me huddled in a ball on the floor, rocking back and forth, muttering Jesse's name, but instead of hot tears and a hysterical episode, I just wanted to throat-punch someone.

I leaped out of bed, fists clenched at my sides, and marched to the corkboard where I kept a little collection of mementos. I searched the contents of my shrine, past ticket stubs from concerts Spencer and I had gone to last year, a picture of Gabe from his last Warhammer tournament, a photobooth triptych of the three of us from the homecoming dance sophomore year, a Paris postcard from Spencer, a fan of museum tickets from our many visits to the Getty, LACMA, and the Norton Simon. Finally, my eyes rested on a cluster of keepsakes from my short relationship with Jesse: a doodle he'd made on one of my notebook pages and a napkin he'd twisted into a rose for me at the coffeehouse on our first date. I ripped the offending pieces of tainted memorabilia from the corkboard, crumpled them into a tiny, mashed-up ball of woman scorned, and launched it across the room.

"What the actual fuck?" I said to nobody in particular. "What the hell does Toile have over me? And what kind of name is 'Toile' anyway? Who names their kid after fabric?"

"Celebrities," Gabe said.

"Musicians," Spencer added.

I ignored them as my brain chewed on this problem. What did Toile have that I didn't? "I mean, I know she's prettier than I am."

"What are you talking about?" Gabe spun me around to face the mirror. "Look at you. You're gorgeous."

I patted him on his cheek. "You're sweet, but I wasn't fishing for compliments. Just stating the facts. Toile is pretty in the traditional sense." I pictured her fair skin and large violet eyes, her tiny waist and her elegant, long arms. "Like maybe even gorgeous. Which I can admit, despite the fact that I hate her guts." I examined myself in the mirror. Short, curvy in a weird way, and lacking either of my parents' best attributes, namely my mom's petiteness and my dad's sharp Romanesque features. I was more mutt than purebred, the cute puppy at the shelter with an indefinable lineage and intelligent eyes.

"I don't think Toile's that pretty," Spencer said.

Gabe laughed. "Yeah, that's because she's not Cassilyn Cairns."

"Who's also gorgeous. I'm cute at best." I sighed, turning away from the mirror. "But I thought cute was good enough for Jesse. I guess I was wrong."

"For fuck's sake." Spencer grabbed me by the shoulders. "You are way too good for Jesse, okay? Completely out of his league."

I hated it when he was illogical. "Then why did he dump me?"

"Toile's type is heroin for a guy like Jesse."

"And what type is that?" I asked.

Spencer laughed. "Duh. She's a manic pixie dream girl."

FOURTEEN

"MANIC PIXIE DREAM girl!" Gabe practically shouted. "Of course."

It was like they were speaking a language I didn't understand. "A manic pixie what what?"

"Have you ever read *Paper Towns*?" Gabe asked.

I shook my head.

"Do you know who Audrey Hepburn is?" Spencer asked.

"Or Zooey Deschanel?" Gabe suggested. "She's an actress on a sitcom. Do you know what *that* is?"

Spencer laughed. "You know she hasn't watched a scripted TV show in ten years."

"I just prefer nonfiction television, thank you very much," I said with pursed lips. "Besides, you watch too much TV."

He lowered himself to the edge of my bed and leaned back on his elbows. "Don't get bent out of shape, Spock. A manic pixie dream girl is a character trope: a quirky, effervescent female who walks to the beat of her own drum and makes the male lead feel like she's changed his world."

Quirky and effervescent. Those adjectives definitely applied to Toile. "What else does she do?"

"Not much," Gabe said.

"What do you mean?"

Spencer shrugged. "That's just it. Her entire existence in the framework of a fictional plot is to improve the male character. She makes him better so he can make the world better."

I sat down next to Spencer. "Let me get this straight: She exists solely for the guy in her life?"

"Yep," Spencer said.

"That sounds horrible."

Gabe shrugged. "But it works. Toile's clearly charmed Jesse, and pretty much everyone else at school too."

He was right. I remembered how Cassilyn and her friends had fawned over Toile in the cafeteria from day one, and how Jesse knew more about her after an hour of English class than he knew about me in two months of dating. She might have been a flighty space cadet, but there was something about Toile that made people like her.

"Guys dig it when a girl thinks they're interesting." Gabe jabbed his thumb at Spencer. "Just look at Picasso here. Cassilyn bats her eyelashes and asks about his painting and suddenly they're inseparable."

I turned to Spencer. "Inseparable?"

He cleared his throat. "Gabe's being dramatic."

"That's not what I heard." He pursed his lips and made a

kissing sound as he pulled his phone out of his bag. "Check this out. A few days ago Thad was trying to kick my ass in the cafeteria, and yesterday I got this."

He turned the phone so Spencer and I could see it, and I read a text from Thad to Gabe out loud. "'Dude. Can I call u dude? K. Dude. Has Cass said anything about going to the dance with me? Do me a solid and bring it up.'" I glanced up at Gabe. "Thad is asking for your help?"

"Yes! Isn't that amazing? And then . . ." Gabe scrolled through his text conversations and I saw that he had them from Cassilyn, Esmeralda, and a group text from Noel and Dakota. "Apparently, one of the benefits of being the newest girlfriend in the A-list is that they tell me all their secrets." Gabe pumped his eyebrows. "Seriously, Bea, this formula of yours is brilliant. I'm putting a whole subsection in the article about how quickly they've taken me into their confidences, as if the gay guy can be trusted with secrets they wouldn't share with the other girls, and the jocks forget they hate me because they're so desperate to get in some girl's pants. It's totally fascinating."

"So Cassilyn talks about Spencer?" I asked. It was the only piece of Gabe's monologue that stuck in my brain.

"All the time." Gabe smirked at Spencer. "She thinks she's your inspiration. Hey! It's like you have your own manic pixie dream model."

"She is *not* my inspiration," Spencer said through gritted teeth.

This topic was growing increasingly irritating. I shot to

my feet, suddenly desperate to move around the room again. "Women are not on this planet exclusively to inspire men and make them happy. We have our own dreams and needs, our own shit to get done. We run companies, countries, international organizations. We're not props, and we're certainly not here to cater to men's egos."

"Fight the power!" Gabe said.

"Okay, calm down." Spencer tugged on my hand, pulling me back onto the bed. "You're preaching to the choir here."

I sat stiffly at his side, breathing heavily. "Manic pixie dream girl." I spit out each word with a considerable amount of disdain. I needed to learn more about her, about Toile. "Gabe, can you hand me my laptop?"

He lifted the thin metal clamshell off my desk, eyebrows raised. "Are you about to go down a research rabbit hole?"

"Yep," Spencer said, answering for me.

Gabe sighed. "Then that's my cue to exit." He pulled the strap of his messenger bag over his head. "I've got a shift at Hidey Hole till six."

I waved at him with one hand while I typed "manic pixie dream girl" into the Google search box with the other. "Sure, sure."

"I bet it'll be nice to drop *zoopa* Gabe for a few hours," Spencer said.

"You have no idea."

Spencer laughed. "I have some."

Gabe paused at the door. "Spence, you coming?"

Spencer didn't move. "I'll hang for a bit. Make sure she doesn't go full stalker mode."

I paused and glanced at him sidelong. "Thanks, Mom."

"Bye, you two," Gabe cooed. "Don't do anything I wouldn't do."

Spencer lounged on my bed flipping through a book while I combed the internet. I couldn't believe how many results came up in my search. Films dating back to the thirties, foreign and domestic. Television shows. Even books. This manic pixie dream girl phenomenon had legs, deeply entrenched roots in our society, and yet somehow I'd never heard of it. I grabbed pen and paper and started jotting down a list of films.

"How did I not know about this?"

"You don't go to movies, read books with plots, or have the TV on after eight o'clock," he said without looking up.

"I see movies."

He closed the book. "Oh yeah? Name one."

I looked at him pointedly. "We saw that new Will Ferrell comedy together before you left for Europe, remember?"

"I remember." He paused while I returned to my list. "So you didn't see any movies with Jesse?"

I winced at his name.

"Sorry," Spencer said. The bed rocked as he shifted position. "I brought you something."

"Yeah?"

"Yeah." He dropped a red plastic thumb drive onto my laptop.

"What's this?" I pushed it aside and began to cross-reference my film list against accessible online streaming sources.

He cleared his throat. "Plug it in. You'll see."

Probably more YouTube videos to cheer me up. But I didn't have time for cats dressed as sharks riding around on Roombas. I had work to do. "Thanks, Spence. I'll watch it later, okay?"

"Oh." He sounded disappointed.

"I need your help with this," I began, glancing up at him. "If I were to watch a movie with one of these manic pixie dream girl characters, where should I start?"

Spencer blinked several times, his eyes shifting to the thumb drive I'd placed next to me on the bed, then he sighed. "What's on your list?"

"How did you know I had a list?"

Spencer snorted. "You make a list for everything. Pros and cons, pluses and minuses, ranking probable outcomes from their least to most likely occurrence."

I hated the fact that he could read me so easily. "Fine. I've got *Betty Blue, Garden State, (500) Days of Summer, Sweet November, Ruby Sparks, Almost Famous, Elizabethtown, Bringing Up Baby, Breakfast at Tiffany's,* and *Annie Hall.*"

Spencer whistled. "Well, *Elizabethtown* is the movie that inspired the term. Maybe we should start there."

"We?"

He leaned his long body back on his elbows. "Your boyfriend just dumped you and now you're on a crusade to figure out why. Do you really think I'm going to let you endure that death spiral alone?"

I wanted to be pissy at the implication that I needed to be protected from myself, but deep down, I knew he was right, and I really appreciated his company. "Fine," I said, suppressing a smile while I tossed him the Roku remote. "But be prepared to take notes. There'll be a quiz at the end."

FiFTEEN

SOMEWHERE BETWEEN THE lobster scene from *Annie Hall* and when the goob from *Garden State* told Natalie Portman that she'd literally changed his life in four days (seriously?), I had a revelation.

The wacky outfits.

The unexpected actions.

The positive feedback loop.

The relentlessly sunny dispositions.

Manic pixie dream girl was a formula.

"Spence."

"Mmhm." He was curled up on his side next to me in bed, head cradled in the crook of his arm, half-asleep. Apparently, the manic pixie marathon hadn't circumvented his need for a weekend nap.

"Wake up, princess," I said, patting his cheek.

"Did you open my thumb drive?" he muttered.

"Not yet. I've got some science to lay down on you."

He yawned. "Already laying down."

I pushed myself off the bed and planted both hands on the mattress, then shook it violently. "It's the big one! Duck and cover!"

Spencer jolted awake, flailing his arms as he rolled off the edge of the mattress, collapsing in a heap on the floor.

"Oh shit!" I leaped across the bed and peered down on him, a tangle of limbs. "Are you okay?"

Spencer sat up and ran his fingers through his hair. "Not funny."

"I don't know. It was, kinda."

He pushed his palm against my forehead and rolled me back onto the bed. "Oh yeah? How do you like it?" Then he pounced on top of the mattress and jumped up and down in his bare feet. The headboard banged against the wall and the metal legs groaned in protest.

"Stop!" I shrieked through my laughter. "You'll bust through the floor."

"It's the big one!" he cried, mimicking me. "Duck and cover!"

"Cut it out!" I grabbed Spencer's leg while he was midjump and yanked it toward me. He lost his balance and came crashing down on top of me; his elbow barely missed knocking out a couple of my teeth.

"You wanna play rough?" Spencer asked, trying to sound mean but coming off more like a Disney villain. Then he went for my weak spot: my feet. He grabbed my legs together, flipping me onto my stomach, then wiggled his fingers lightly on the soles of my feet. "Vee have vays uf making you talk," he said, using a fake German accent.

"Stop!" I was laughing so hard tears were welling up in my eyes.

"Oh!" Spencer said, feigning surprise. "You want me to stop?" He tickled my feet again, and I let out a howl. "Are you sure?" Then he leaned back so he could see my face.

I took advantage of his lapse in concentration and twisted my torso, ripping my legs from his grip, then I went for his ticklish weak spot: the side of his stomach. "Payback's a bitch."

I heard a creak on the stairs. "*Anak?*" my mom called up. "Is everything okay?"

We froze, limbs tangled. "Fine, Mom!"

"Don't call me that," she snapped from the other side of my bedroom door.

I looked up at Spencer, who pressed his lips together to silence his snickering, then composed myself. "I'm fine, Flordeliza."

"Good." Then the stairs creaked again as she retreated.

I lay there panting, Spencer hovering over me. His goofy, toothy grin reminded me of the younger, smaller version of the guy I'd known for so many years. As I stared up at him, the smile faded. His breaths slowed and deepened, and the muscles around his eyes softened. I thought maybe he'd roll to the other side of the mattress, but he stayed put, balancing over me with stiff, outstretched arms, his blue eyes locked onto mine.

I felt my face grow hot, and for the second time that

week, I felt embarrassed with my best friend.

"Bea . . ."

I didn't even give him a chance to finish. Something in my stomach gurgled and tightened, like I'd eaten raw eggs. Whatever I thought Spencer was about to say, it instilled an instantaneous panicked reaction, and I needed to do something—anything—to cut him off.

"I have a plan to get Jesse back," I blurted out.

Every muscle in Spencer's neck tensed up at once, giving him the wide, veiny look of a pro wrestler posing for the camera. His eyes darted away from my face as he pushed himself off me. "Oh yeah?"

I swallowed, my mouth suddenly dry, a sensation that happened only when I was overwhelmed by nerves. "Yeah." The playful mood was completely shattered and the air in my bedroom hung heavy between us. "This manic-pixie-dream-girl thing is a formula."

Spencer swung his legs over the side of the bed and bent down to put on his shoes. "Uh-oh."

I grabbed my notebook, happy to have a prop. "I made a list of all the attributes these characters have in common. Unique fashion sense, unorthodox approach to social boundaries, absence of a filtering mechanism between the brain and the mouth, lack of self-awareness, and a rejection of class structure. I mean, I can do that. I can make myself into one of these girls and win Jesse back."

Spencer turned around and folded his hands in his lap, looking very much like my mother when she was attempting to lay down some parental knowledge. "Answer me one question, Bea. Why do you want him?"

I pulled my chin back, confused. "He's my boyfriend."

"He *was* your boyfriend."

"Still *would* be," I said, mocking his tone, "if it weren't for Toile."

"That's my point." Spencer shook his head. "Do you really want to be with a guy who would dump you the moment someone else is interested him?"

I bit the inside of my lower lip, rolling the dimply bit of skin back and forth between my teeth. Spencer was right. How important had our relationship been to Jesse that he'd dump me within days of meeting Toile? I could make excuses until the end of time: Jesse was susceptible to outside influences, Toile had taken advantage of his kindness, I'd been dealing with my friends and hadn't been there for him, he'd been seduced by her popularity. They were weak rationales, and I knew it.

And yet I remembered the good times. The way Jesse made me feel when he asked me out on that first date. Like I was special. He saw me in a way no one else at school ever had, like I was funny and interesting and desirable. Spencer certainly didn't think of me that way. I was just good old Beatrice to him. But to Jesse, I was a girlfriend, and I didn't want to lose that feeling.

"Is it about winning?" Spencer said before I could explain what I was feeling. "About beating Toile? I know how competitive you get."

The cheeky little smile on Spencer's face made me bristle.

"I love Jesse," I snapped, annoyed both at Spencer and by my own irrational anger. "That's why I want him back." See? A logical rationale.

He blinked twice in rapid succession. Then stood up. "I've gotta go."

"Are you meeting Cassilyn?" I said. I hadn't meant them to, but the words sounded bitter. For some reason, this whole conversation had gotten me riled up—defensive and raw.

Instead of answering, Spencer just opened the bedroom door. "I'll talk to you later, Bea."

And then he was gone.

SIXTEEN

I STOOD IN my room long after Spencer left, breathing heavily. I was upset, that much I could self-diagnose, but I wasn't sure exactly why. Upset by the realization that Jesse had dumped me for a manic pixie dream girl? Upset that Spencer had suggested I only wanted Jesse back so that I could "win"? Upset that he was possibly going to meet Cassilyn?

Cassilyn? No, definitely not that. I wanted Spencer to infiltrate the A-list. That was all part of the Formula.

I recalled the way she touched his arm in the cafeteria. Well, maybe I didn't want him to infiltrate *that* deeply.

But before I could ponder my mood any further, my mom poked her head into my room. "Was that Spencer?"

"Yeah."

"Has he been in your room all day?"

"Um . . ." Why did I pause? Spencer was just a friend, and it shouldn't have been any more scandalous to be alone in my room with him than with Gabe. "Yeah."

Now, a normal mother would have either freaked out or taken the opportunity to engage in a calm discussion of male-female relations, safe sex, or *No means no*. Flordeliza? Not exactly normal. She pumped her eyebrows and smiled knowingly. "Were you having fun?"

"I have a boyfriend." I couldn't look at her as I said it, so I turned to my bed and started straightening up the bedsheets.

"Mmhm."

Had she been listening? Did she know Jesse had broken up with me or did she just suspect it?

I leaned across the bed to fluff the pillows when I felt the weight on the mattress shift. "*Anak*," my mom said, her voice softer than before. "Is there anything you want to talk about?"

I'd stopped sharing the details of my personal life with Flordeliza when I was thirteen. With good reason. Every time I mentioned a boy I thought was cute (there were a few) or one that I thought might think *I* was cute (there were far fewer), my mom inevitably turned the conversation from my puppy love to cheating spouses, custody battles, second marriages, and general relationship bitterness. As if my short-lived crush on Carlos Velasco freshman year would have ended a decade later in a messy divorce.

Then every time she had a new boyfriend who was absolutely, positively "the one," she'd start pressuring me about finding one of my own because being in a relationship was the single greatest thing in the world. Until she'd get dumped and the cycle would begin again.

Mother-daughter heart-to-hearts about boys weren't really part of our repertoire, so I think she was as surprised as I was by the words that came flying out of my mouth.

"Jesse dumped me."

"And Spencer was consoling you?"

That was the last question I'd expected. "Yeah."

"That's a good friend," she said. "Someone who cares about you very much."

"I guess."

She arched an eyebrow. "You guess?"

What was she getting at? "Actually," I said, feeling contrary, "he was kind of pissing me off."

She looked me steadily in the eyes. "By the way he stormed out of here, I'd say he was the one who was pissed." Then she shook her head and smiled. "So what are you going to do now?"

I thought of the list of manic pixie attributes and my realization that the trope had a formula. Had Toile figured that out too? I laughed at the idea. Her flighty quirkiness was the real deal; no way was she smart enough to pull a con like that on the entire school.

But I was.

"I'm going to win back my boyfriend."

My mom looked confused, as if I'd answered a question she hadn't asked. "How are you going to do that?"

Good question. Maybe I could use the Formula as a model and alter it to fit this manic pixie crap. I'd need a new attitude, a new approach to school and relationships, not to mention a new style and wardrobe. These were all things I knew virtually nothing about. I was going to need some help.

"Flordeliza," I said, being careful not to use "mom." "You know how you're always trying to get me to do something more fun with my hair?"

"Yes," my mom said, glancing at me sidelong as if she wasn't quite convinced I was about to make her mother-daughter bonding wish come true.

I smiled and placed my hand on top of hers. "Do you think your stylist has any openings tomorrow?"

Armand, my mom's hairstylist, was able to squeeze me in bright and early Sunday morning. You know, when we were supposed to be at Mass. A Mass we never missed.

Flordeliza didn't care. Within seconds of getting off the phone with Armand, she'd already rearranged her Saturday to squeeze in our weekly obligation at the five-o'clock evening Mass. We never, ever went to that one, which featured a guitar and electric keyboard musical accompaniment my mother loathed ("If I want to bang a tambourine, I'll put on Stevie Nicks!"). But when faced with a choice between folk music and finally sharing her love of elaborate hairstyles with her daughter, she'd gritted her teeth and made it through the service.

I was in Armand's chair at the crack of eight thirty the next morning. He stood behind me and slowly pulled the ponytail holder from my long, wavy brown locks. As my hair was freed from its constraints and hung limply down my back, he pursed his lips, his eyebrows raised so high I thought they might permanently relocate up to his shiny bald head.

"When was the last time anyone worked with this?" he asked, not even attempting to disguise the revulsion in his voice.

"I get it cut every ten weeks," I said. "To avoid split ends and maintain healthy follicles."

"Cut." He snapped the final consonant, practically making a second syllable out of it. "Armand does not cut. He transforms."

I was about ready to transform myself right out of his chair when my mom stepped in. "Bea needs your magic, darling." She rested her chin on Armand's beefy, well-toned shoulder. "She's finally ready."

Armand nodded and reclaimed his eyebrows from the stratosphere of his skull, then ran his fingers through my hair. "Strong. Thick. And I can do something with the wave." He turned to my mom. "What did you have in mind?"

Before she could answer, I handed Armand my iPad, cued up to a photo montage of Ramona Flowers from *Scott Pilgrim vs. the World* and all her multicolored hair goodness. "I want something like this."

The eyebrows shot even higher, wrinkling Armand's head into an elephant's hide. He studied the photos, zooming in and out. "Interesting. Edgy, but I could give it a retro softness. I am not dyeing your whole head that shade of pink, but maybe some pops of color . . ."

"See?" my mom said. "I told you he was good."

It took almost three hours, a painfully boring process of cutting, coloring, highlighting, and blow-drying, most of which I spent facing away from the mirror. So when Armand finally spun my chair around, I gasped out loud at my reflection.

"Holy shit!" I said.

Armand nodded, flashing an enormous set of veneers. "Holy shit, indeed."

In an act of hair-styling prowess heretofore unseen in the greater Fullerton area, Armand's appraising eyes and competent hands had transformed my long, little-girl locks into something at once sassy and sophisticated. My subtle waves were almost curly now, freed from the weight of their length. Soft and supple, the curls hit halfway between my chin and my collarbone, giving me the illusion of a longer, more regal neck, then angled upward toward the back of my head, where they just covered the nape. Choppy bangs grazed my eyebrows, framing my face and accentuating its heart shape. As if the amazing haircut wasn't enough, Armand had artfully placed several magenta highlights—just a stray curl here and there, poking through the brown.

I never in a million years would have chosen a haircut like this unless forced into it by my own Machiavellian designs, yet somehow it suited me. And when I slid from the chair and walked to a full-length mirror, there was a hop in my step that hadn't been there a few hours before.

I looked like I was more fun—it was as simple as that.

Lighter, freer, a girl with a spontaneous streak who wasn't afraid to do something crazy. It was absolutely perfect.

The straight-cut jeans and button-down blouse I was wearing? Not so much. I pulled my notebook from my purse and consulted the extensive formula I'd created the night before, then I grabbed my phone and texted Gabe.

Meet me at the mall in 30?

The Formula 2.0™:

$$\int_f^s F(x)\sqrt[v]{R} = \varnothing$$

If F is a continuous real-valued function defined on a closed interval [f, s] between freshman and senior years of high school, R is the social role previously decided upon, and v is the void created by R, then the radical of R to v degree is equal to the empty set, i.e., "eternal happiness."

Or:

(1) Pick the role you want to play.

(2) Create the void by convincing your environment that it needs you.

(3) Be the niche they didn't know they wanted in the first place.*

*Subheading: "Manic Pixie Dream Girl"
- childlike playfulness
- outlandish clothes, preferably matched with wild hair dye
- exhibits noticeable "wacky" quirks and antics of which she seems wholly unself-aware
- thinks about the world in a new and unique way
- overly friendly, bordering on flirtatious
- spontaneous, especially with displays of affection
- never embarrassed or shy, laughs off faux pas
- single-minded goal: male wish fulfillment

SEVENTEEN

"YOU WANT TO dress like Toile?" Gabe asked. We were in line at the Coffee Hut at the food court, along with Kurt Heinzmueller, who either happened to run into Gabe at the mall or had come with him, I wasn't entirely sure.

"Triple-shot latte," I ordered. I needed to be sufficiently caffeinated for what was about to happen. "Think of it as a makeover," I said, looking Gabe up and down. "Just like yours."

"I hope not," Kurt muttered.

"This makeover," Gabe said, eyeing Kurt, "is going to score me that internship at the *Register* when I finish my article."

"At the cost of playing into every gay stereotype of the last two centuries," Kurt countered. "Is that worth it?"

"Yes."

"If you say so."

Gabe narrowed his eyes. "You could try being a teensy bit more supportive."

Kurt shrugged, then took a sip from his enormous soda.

Gabe took a deep breath and immediately got back into character, which made sense since the odds of us running into classmates at the mall over the weekend were relatively high. But despite his confrontation with Kurt, there was an ease with which he wore his new role today that I hadn't noticed before. He'd also added some new wardrobe components. Cropped linen pants, boat shoes, and a jaunty, short-brimmed fedora completed today's look.

"We're going to make you look fabulous," he said, taking my hand.

"So by changing your hair and how you dress," Kurt said, pausing midsip, "you're going to get Jesse back."

"Yep." Why was he here again? "I've tweaked the Formula. Instead of identifying the need and filling it, I'm going to show Jesse something he didn't know he needed: Manic Pixie Bea."

"Has Spencer seen your hair yet?" Gabe asked as I added fake sugar to my latte.

"No." I hadn't asked him to join us. I told myself that was because he wouldn't be much help on a shopping spree, but part of me had been apprehensive about texting him. What if he was too busy? What if he was with Cassilyn? I kind of didn't want to know.

"I'm sure he'll love it," Kurt said.

Gabe jabbed him in the ribs without comment. "What's the game plan?"

I laid out an overview of my new style: it needed to be

a blend of vintage and modern, mixed together with the kind of reckless abandon that makes you think the wearer is either the edgiest person on the planet or got dressed while blindfolded. Bright colors were a must, as were outlandish patterns. Preferably together. We needed to be on the lookout for items with glitter or sequins, and anything that looked as if your grandmother might have bought it before the war was absolutely golden.

I was nervous about this phase of the Formula 2.0, even more so than I was when Armand chopped off my hair. Clothes shopping highlighted my body insecurity, and my fear that people would stare and point and laugh at me if I wore anything that made me stand out. Which, unfortunately, was the point of manic pixie fashion.

I chalked my clothing self-doubt up to nine years at Catholic school, where everyone wore a uniform and standing out in any way was a punishable offense. I'd been yanked from that extreme and thrown into public school at my most awkward phase, and for the first time in my life I'd had to put together outfits every day. Which was when I'd sort of adapted my own version of a uniform—tailored jeans, a sensible but feminine blouse, and a blazer—which had served me well for three years. My clothes weren't memorable, but being memorable at Fullerton Hills wasn't necessarily a good thing.

Besides, I freaking hated the mall. *Hated.* I didn't feel like I fit in with all the confident, fashionably styled mannequins, to say nothing of the customers. Instead, I shopped almost exclusively online using the credit card my dad had given me. I rarely charged very much—my wardrobe staples weren't exactly designer—and he paid the small balance every month without question.

But today, I didn't have time to wait for two-day priority shipping. I needed brand-new outfits immediately.

Store after store, dressing room after dressing room, I tried on clothes until my fingers ached from rebuttoning my blouse time and time again. Gabe was a trouper. He'd scurry around the racks holding up possible options while I gave my thumbs-up or thumbs-down like Diocletian at the Colosseum. Even Kurt pitched in, though he tended to pick out anything with sparkles, and I wasn't sure if he was being serious or thought this was all one elaborate joke.

Gabe turned out to have a keen eye for my new look. He found some gems: the fifties flare swing dress in a petunia print, the teal cardigan with a ruffled collar, the curry-yellow corduroy shorts, and the flowy polka-dot jumpsuit. Some dusty corner of Gabe's brain had come to life, ignited by the Formula, and I could tell he was really enjoying himself.

And so was I, oddly. I'd been looking forward to this phase of the Formula 2.0 with as much enthusiasm as the average student approaches a surprise math test (not me, of course—I love pop quizzes) but after a half dozen stores and almost twice as many shopping bags, I was beginning to understand the high school ritual of shopping at the mall with your friends. I was actually having fun.

Until we exited the last stop of the afternoon and ran smack into Esmeralda, Dakota, and Noel.

The panic hit me like a bucket of ice water in the face. I wasn't ready to unleash the new me on the general population of Fullerton Hills. I had the haircut, and bags full of new clothes, but I hadn't been able to rehearse how I would act or what I would say, and I hadn't yet compiled a cheat sheet for daily manic pixie life. Beneath the bouncy curls and streaks of brightly colored hair dye, I was still just Beatrice. And to these girls, not even that. I watched Esmeralda's left eyebrow rise a quarter of an inch and I was reminded that to them, I was only Math Girl, unworthy of a proper name, and suddenly I wished I'd never thought of the Formula, or learned about manic pixie dream girls, or taken any sort of steps to win back my ex-boyfriend. I just wanted to crawl into a hole and hide, and I wondered, with a sense of dismay, whether this was how Gabe and Spencer had felt at school last week when they'd arrived in new wardrobes with new personalities and new roles to play at school.

But if Gabe had experienced fear or panic in the face of Fullerton Hills' elite, he certainly didn't show it now.

"Dahlings!" Gabe said, immediately in character. He swooped over to Esmeralda, kissing her quickly on each cheek before repeating the process with the stepsisters. "You look *zoopa* fabulous."

"Thank you . . . ," Dakota and Noel said, their voices trailing off in perfect unison.

Gabe grabbed my hand. "You guys know Beatrice, right?"

"Really?" Kurt said. "You don't want to introduce me to your fancy friends?"

I saw Gabe's armor of flamboyant nonchalance falter. "Kurt, no, it's just—"

"I know when I'm not wanted." He stormed off as fast as his shuffling feet could take him. "Put that in your article."

"Who was *that*?" Esmeralda said.

But Gabe didn't answer, his eyes still fixed on the exit door Kurt had disappeared through. So I piped up, seizing the opportunity to reestablish myself.

"He's no one," I said, noting that Gabe flinched at my words. "Just ran into him. Hanging out at the mall. Because that's what we do a lot." I held up my bags. "Shopping and hanging out and . . . you know."

Esmeralda turned her cold eyes to me. She had an amazing talent for putting your insecurities on display. "No, I don't know. What else do you do?"

I read treatises on linear systems in algebra, calculate percentages for fun, and create mathematical formulas to apply to everyday life. Yeah, no. Even *I* realized I couldn't say that out loud.

"I shop," I began.

Esmeralda never even blinked. "You said that."

"And hang out."

"Said that as well."

Dammit. What else did popular teens do at the mall? "Food court?"

She was having none of me. "You're that Math Girl, aren't you?"

"N-no," I stuttered. But it was too late. She'd dismissed me and my new look. To her, I was the same old loser.

"See you at lunch tomorrow," Esmeralda said to Gabe as she began to leave. "And I think you should seriously reconsider who you hang out with."

EiGHTEEN

AN UNMITIGATED DISASTER. That was the best way to describe my first attempt at rebranding. Not only had I not been prepared for actual conversation with the most popular girls in school, but I had no answer for the inevitable *Aren't you that Math Girl?* question.

"This is a good thing," Gabe said as we took the bus across town.

I felt utterly despondent. "How?"

"Because we still have time to fix you."

"It's hopeless," I said, staring out the window as an endless row of minimalls flew by in a blur. "I don't know how you and Spencer did this. I'm sorry I ever invented the Formula."

Gabe rolled his eyes. "Stop it. You just weren't ready."

"Tomorrow's going to be a disaster," I said. "I should return all these clothes."

"So dramatic," Gabe said. "You're starting to sound like your mom."

My head whipped around, eyes narrow. "You take that back."

But Gabe just smiled. "That's the fighting spirit I want to see."

The bus eased to a stop a few blocks from Spencer's house. "Now, don't stress," Gabe said as he gathered up some of my shopping bags. "The Formula works, and think how awesome your submission for that scholarship is going to be if you pull this off."

"I guess."

"You just need a little practice."

"Practice?" I asked.

"The day you came up with the Formula, I spent most of the night practicing my new role in front of the mirror before unleashing it at school."

"You did?" Gabe had seemed so natural in his new role. I hadn't thought for a moment that it was because he'd practiced it at home. Maybe there was hope for me yet?

He nodded. "And look how well it worked. Those snobs talked to me at the mall just now like we were old friends, even though I was hanging out with two people who they don't consider to be worthy of their time."

He had a point.

"It's fascinating, really," he mused, gazing out the window, "how quickly they've accepted me. It's sort of changed the focus of the article from working to infiltrate their ranks to the disturbing speed at which they've just looped Gabriel into their daily lives."

"You mean it's disturbingly shallow," I said, clarifying.

"Yeah, and now I'm one of them."

"Gabe, you'll never be one of *them*."

He paused for a moment, shook his head, then turned back to me. "You're right. They're just subjects for my article." He laughed. "I'm undercover, like you said."

"Exactly." But I couldn't shake the feeling that not only did Gabe feel like a bona fide member of Cassilyn's clique, but that he enjoyed it.

"Anyway," he said, smiling. "Esmeralda caught you off guard. So we just have to make sure that doesn't happen again."

Half an hour later, I sat curled up on the sofa in Spencer's studio compiling a cheat sheet of the various manic pixie dream girl components I'd need to start incorporating into my new role, as well as examples from the various movies I'd familiarized myself with, translating common manic pixie characteristics into modern high school action points.

"Ready?" Gabe said, peering over my shoulder, impatient as ever.

I took a deep breath. "I think so. I've narrowed it down to five key components."

"Only five?" Spencer asked. He sat beside me on the sofa, one foot resting on his knee as he balanced a sketch pad on his lap. His eyes never left the page.

He'd meant the question sarcastically, but I answered with all seriousness. "Yes, five." I set my notebook down on the table so Gabe could take a closer look. "Some of these we've already got covered; some I'm going to need help with."

"Category one," Gabe read out loud. "Fashion."

"It has to be a mix of cute vintage and eye-catching statement pieces," I said. "Like that French chick in *Amélie*."

Gabe laughed. "We certainly took care of that today."

"No joke," Spencer said. "How many credit cards did you max out?"

I ignored him. "Toile's cornered the market on hats, but I'll still need a signature look. Something outlandish."

"Face tattoo?" Spencer suggested.

Now it was my turn for sarcasm. "Yes, a face tattoo. What a fabulous idea. Thank you for your help."

"Stop being a dick," Gabe said, kicking his leg.

"I'm thinking about mismatched shoes," I said. "They'd show childlike whimsy and prove that I'm not bound by societal restrictions on wardrobe."

"That would certainly make a statement," Gabe said. "But won't they hurt?"

I shook my head. "As long as I make sure the shoes are the same height—or the same style in different colors—I should be okay." I hoped. I certainly didn't want to injure myself in the name of manic pixieness. "I mean, I'm only going to have to do this for a week or two, right? I should be okay."

"A week or two," Gabe said with a nervous glance at Spencer. "Sure."

"You think less than that?" I'd calculated 8.75 school days as the optimal time for my plan to work, but if I could ditch the mismatched shoes before then, even better.

"Category two," Gabe read, instead of answering. "Social interactions." He took a deep breath. "This is where you're going to need some work."

From day one, Toile had seemed ignorant of the societal norms of the American high school. She spoke to anyone, regardless of social rank. She made direct eye contact in the hallways. She spoke loudly, conspicuously so, in order to draw attention to herself, and utilized a head-turning mix of lighthearted laughter, spontaneous compliments, and a total lack of embarrassment to ingratiate herself with the student body.

"I have to outdo Toile on every point. Act more naïve and childlike, let more non sequitur comments come flying out of my mouth. I need to channel that *Annie Hall* 'lah-di-dah.'"

"Lah-di-dah?" Gabe asked.

I flipped to the next page in my notebook, where I'd transcribed a scene from the movie. "Yeah, she has this scattered, stream-of-consciousness style of talking, like she's just saying every single syllable that pops into her head. 'Um, yeah, er, I don't know . . . ,'" I said, trying to mimic the style. "Like that."

"Shouldn't be too hard," Spencer chimed in.

"I realize you're attempting to make a joke," I said snidely, "but you're actually right. I do have all those thoughts in my head, I just keep them inside when I'm at school. But no more!"

He cringed. "I'm not sure I can be seen with you at school."

"Ignore him," Gabe said, as if I needed to be told. "Try it out. Like, we're just hanging out in the cafeteria over lunch. What would you say?"

"I haven't really planned anything out yet," I said, suddenly nervous.

"Just say whatever pops into your head. It'll sound more authentic that way." Gabe morphed into character. "Bea, darling. I just love what you've done with your hair."

Right. Whatever pops into my head. "Really? Thanks! I mean, I wasn't really sure . . . The pink and all. It kinda looks like candy. Oh, have you ever thought about what's in a Skittle? Think about it! Tasting the rainbow could mean a whole lot of different . . . Oh. My. GOD!" I turned to the window, pointing outside. "Check out those clouds! Doesn't it look like a princess riding a pony jumping over the TARDIS?" I dropped the act. "What do you think?"

"Wow." Gabe's eyes were round and unblinking, like he'd just had them dilated at the optometrist's office. "That was insane."

"If those words came out of my mouth, I'd want to cut out my own tongue so I'd be physically unable to articulate them again," Spencer said. "But other than that . . ." He gave me two thumbs-up.

"You're doing great," Gabe said, shaking off his stupor.

"Category four: wacky quirks and crazy antics." He glanced up at me. "I'm afraid to ask."

"You know," I explained. "Like Charlize Theron frolicking with dogs on the beach in *Sweet November*. Or in *(500) Days of Summer* when that Zooey person made her cute boyfriend scream 'penis' at the top of his lungs in the park. Or when the chick from *Friends* stabbed Ben Stiller's pillows."

Gabe pointed at Spencer. "You've created a pop culture monster."

"Short of staging a bank robbery or streaking naked through a school dance," Spencer said, "I'm not sure how you're going to escalate from Toile's cafeteria choreography display on the first day of school."

"I don't know either," I admitted. "But I've come up with an initial list of acceptably wacky antics." I picked up my notebook and flipped to another page. "What do you guys think: (a) organizing a flash mob, (b) singing at the top of my lungs as I skip to and from class, (c) throwing confetti in front of me so I'm always walking on sparkles."

"Excuse me," Spencer said, pushing himself to his feet. "I need to throw up."

"(D)," I continued, "greeting perfect strangers with a Euro-style kiss on both cheeks, or (e) handing out paper flowers to everyone at school. My stepmom's got a stash of paper daisies on wire stems from her short-lived scrapbooking phase. I doubt she'd miss them."

"Those are, um . . ." Gabe grasped for words. "Interesting options."

I slouched back into the sofa. "I know. I'm not in love with any of them."

"Let's just revisit that one," he said, turning back to my categories. "Next up, your name."

"What's wrong with Beatrice?" Spencer asked.

I shook my head, curls whipping past my eyes. "While sufficiently old-fashioned in a hipster baby kind of way, Beatrice isn't quirky enough. I mean, these manic pixies all have hopelessly adorable names: Clementine, Polly, Claire, Sabrina. For God's sake, Toile's named after fabric. How can I outdo that?"

"Silk?" Gabe suggested.

"Sounds like a pimp," Spencer said. "And besides, do you really want to run the risk of direct fabric comparison?"

"Exactly," I said. "But I need something playful, effervescent. The kind of name that you can't help but voice with perky exuberance."

"Why don't you go right at it and call yourself Beapix?" he said.

Gabe laughed. "More like Beatrix."

I caught my breath. That was it. "Gabe, you're brilliant."

"Beatrix?"

"No." A huge smile spread across my face. "Trix. *Trixie*. It's a diminutive of the Spanish 'Beatrix.' I can tell everyone it's a family nickname or something."

"I am not calling you Trixie," Spencer said. "Period."

I waved him off. It didn't matter if he did. Just everyone else. It wasn't as if people at school knew my name anyway.

Trixie was as good as Beatrice when everyone knew you as Math Girl.

I grabbed my notebook, suddenly energized. "Last section. Male wish fulfillment."

Spencer groaned. "I'm afraid to ask."

And all of my positive energy drained away. "This is where I crash and burn."

"Why?" Gabe asked.

"I just . . . I don't know how to make a guy think he's the only person on the entire planet." This was my biggest manic pixie stumbling block. The idea that I was supposed to exist solely to make Jesse feel good about himself? It made my stomach turn. Of course I *wanted* him to feel good about himself. I wanted everyone I cared about to feel that way. But that was a by-product of a good friendship, not the reason for it. And I wasn't sure I was going to be able to put my own wants and needs aside in order to focus exclusively on Jesse's.

"WWMPD?" Spencer mused. "What would manic pixie do?"

"Well," I said, scanning through my examples, "Kirsten Dunst listened to Legolas complain about his life for hours and hours in *Elizabethtown*. Though I'm not sure Jesse's capable of talking for that long."

"He doesn't know enough words," Spencer quipped. I stuck my tongue out at him.

Gabe pointed at Spencer. "Come here, smart-ass. Time to be helpful." Then he grabbed my hand and dragged me to my feet. "You just have to make him feel like you're paying attention. Like you're hanging on every word that comes out of his mouth." He placed me in front of Spencer. "Pretend Spencer is Jesse."

"You've got to be kidding me," Spencer said.

Gabe held his forefinger in front of Spencer's lips. "Shush, you." Then he turned back to me. "This is Jesse. He's your boyfriend. You're Jesse's girl."

Spencer groaned. "I'm going to kill—"

Without looking at him, Gabe slapped his hand over Spencer's mouth, silencing him. "You're just hanging out in the halls after school. What do you do?" He took several steps away, then slashed his arm down between Spencer and me like a greaser opening a drag race. "Go!"

I shifted my weight back and forth between my feet. I could do this. I was a girl, after all. Weren't we all born with intrinsic flirting skills? I'd just misplaced mine along the way.

Spencer stood awkwardly before me, one hand shoved deep in his pocket while the other was pressed against his leg. His body was stiff, his pose practically combative, as if I might punch him in the gut at any moment. I'd seen similar body language from him last week in the cafeteria when Cassilyn asked to have her portrait painted. He'd gone rigid, set his jaw, closed up. But then, within minutes, he'd relaxed. She'd laughed, touched his arm, and his whole body had melted.

Could it work for me?

I looked up and smiled. "So I heard you were in Europe

this summer," I said, opening with a topic that interested him. It seemed the thing to do. "I've always wanted to go. Was it as amazing as I've dreamed it would be?" Good start, and it wasn't even a lie.

Spencer's brows drew together, wrinkling above his nose, and his eyes darted away from my face. "Um, yeah. It was cool."

"The art galleries must have been breathtaking. And the architecture."

He shrugged. "Yeah, you know."

I fought my natural urge to say, *No, I don't know—that's why I'm asking you, smart-ass* and instead took a step closer to him. "What was your favorite thing?"

"I don't—"

"A painting? A sculpture?" My mind raced, trying to recall what pieces he'd been excited to see. "That one by Klimt with all the gold?"

Spencer swallowed. "'The Kiss.'"

I sucked in breath. "Yes! Was it as magnificent as you thought it would be?" He had a print of the painting on the wall of his bedroom. I closed my eyes and tried to picture it in my mind. "I can only imagine. Those colors and patterns." I leaned forward, my head tilted upward, and my fingers found his. "The way he's holding her head to the side as he kisses her. And the way her hand is draped around his neck . . ."

I was surprised how many details I remembered. Art had never interested me in the same way math and numbers had, though I'd always been supportive because it was something that Spencer loved. But when I closed my eyes and pictured that print, it was as if I was discovering it for the first time. The girl's face cupped in the man's hands—there was something sexy and wonderful about it, and I could feel my lips curving into a smile.

I felt breath on my face and my eyes flew open. Spencer's lips were inches from mine, his head bent toward me, his eyes closed. He was about to kiss me.

Yes.

I started, surprised by my own subconscious. "No!" I blurted out.

Spencer's face blanched as if all the blood had been drained from his body.

"I . . . I mean," I said, feeling as if I'd made a horrific blunder but not exactly knowing why, "I think we're done. I've got it."

"Oh yeah," Gabe said, the air whooshing from his mouth like he'd been holding his breath. "You've got it, all right."

I couldn't look at Spencer. What was that all about? We were just playacting, and yet the look on his face, the voice in my head, the feeling deep in my stomach as if I'd experimented with the dreaded Pop Rocks-and-soda combination. The same way I'd felt yesterday when we were wrestling in my room . . .

No, Spencer and I were friends. *Good* friends, but *just* friends. I'd been pretending that he was Jesse, that's why I'd wanted him to kiss me. The only reason.

"I should go." I grabbed my bag and hurried to the door, just daring to cast a look back at Spencer as I yanked it open. He stood at the sink with his back to me, totally unreadable.

NiNETEEN

IT TOOK LONGER than expected to get into costume the next morning due to an unforeseen glitter eyeliner mishap.

Note to self: glitter eyeliner burns.

I'd managed to do my hair (bouncy short curls) and makeup (highlights included said glitter eyeliner, in blue, and bright pink lipstick in a hue so ridiculously over-the-top I looked like a five-year-old who'd gotten into Mom's vanity) to manic pixie perfection, and as I stood before the mirror in my carefully constructed outfit, I had to smile. I'd paired the curry-yellow corduroy shorts with teal tights, a striped boat-neck shirt, and a fuzzy pink sweater with bejeweled buttons. True to category one, I wore a pink skimmer flat on my left foot and a floral one on my right.

Basically, I looked as if I'd gotten dressed in the dark while raiding my grandma's closet.

I was horrifyingly perfect.

But perfectly manic pixie or not, I was nervous. I had

my cheat sheet in my pocket (written in pink glitter ink, just for added authenticity) and a kind of manic pixie peace offering for Jesse to force him to sit up and take notice; I was as prepared for this day as I was for any school exam (which is to say, 110 percent) but unlike exams, which I approached with a mix of excitement and cockiness, I couldn't shake the sinking sense of dread in my stomach. Why? I was going to have to talk to people—people I didn't know—and be nice to them.

God, I sounded like such a bitch for even thinking it, but it was true and I needed to acknowledge it. I didn't really like most of the people at Fullerton Hills, and they didn't like me. But now, I was going to have to go out of my way to be nice to them. All of them. Any of them. And it was freaking me out.

They don't like Math Girl, but they'll like Trixie.

What if they didn't? What if people treated her the same way they treated me, with a mix of negligence and irritation? I'd lose Jesse forever.

But as much as that worried me, the flip side was terrifying. What if people *did* like Trixie? What exactly would that mean? I would still be me, sort of. How could people like and dislike me at the same time?

You're confusing yourself.

My hand drifted to my pocket, where my fingers grazed against the folded piece of paper within. I had a plan, I had a goal. If my calculations were correct, in less than two weeks, I'd have Jesse back and the most kick-ass scholarship submission MIT had ever seen.

I just had to stick to the Formula.

As I stood on the front steps staring up at the chrome facade of Fullerton Hills High School, I fought the urge to chase my mom's car down the hill, run home to change, and forget this entire plan.

I felt utterly naked. I'd traded in my wheelie bag for a patchwork patterned tote I'd found in storage, and somehow I felt less confident without my trusty luggage sidekick. Less me.

But that was the point.

I took a breath, steadying myself. Is this what it had been like for Gabe that first day after we came up with the Formula? Had he been as terrified as I was as he stood in this exact same spot, wearing a bow tie and suspenders, with those heart-shaped sunglasses perched on his head? Had he been having second thoughts about the idea of pretending to be someone else? Someone not quite himself?

But it had worked out for Gabe. Look at him now! He could unleash his snarky wit at will without risk of getting his ass kicked. He was accepted by the popular girls, tolerated by the jocktocracy despite his role in getting their beloved coach fired, and some of them were even soliciting him for relationship help. How much more of a win could that be? If he could trust in my formula, then dammit, I could too.

"Nice shoes," someone said. I looked up and recognized

Milo and Thad, staring as they passed with matching looks of derision.

Ugh. What kind of benevolent God would allow Milo Morris and Thad Everett to be the first two people I encountered today? They hated me. And there was no way they were going to buy into Trixie.

It was too late now. If I hung my head and scurried away, my entire manic pixie plan would be over before it began. All I could do was snap into character and play it to the best of my ability.

So instead of slinking into the shadows, I skitted forward, falling into step beside them. "I know, right?" I said, my voice as bubbly as I could make it without throwing up in my mouth. "My left and right feet just could not agree this morning. Leftie wanted the pink sparkly ballet flat, while Ms. Right insisted on the floral Toms."

Thad looked at me sidelong, eyebrow arched. "Your feet talk to each other?"

An inauspicious start. "Of course." Then I batted my eyelashes as flirtatiously as possible and laughed, loud and carefree.

"Do I know you?" Milo asked.

Well, at least they didn't recognize Math Girl. "You can call me Trixie," I said, without really answering his question.

"Okay," Milo said without question. "Later." Then he and Thad bounded through the front door into the foyer.

I paused by the entrance, my heart fluttering. They hadn't called me out, hadn't threatened me or laughed at me.

Milo and Thad had just accepted Trixie.

Had it really been that easy?

Spencer was already in AP English when I arrived, scribbling in his sketchbook.

"Hey!" I said, dropping into my desk. "You'll never guess what happened."

He didn't look up. "You ran into Jesse and after one look at you he expressed his undying love?"

Ugh. "No. But I did run into Milo and Thad and they totally didn't recognize me. They even talked to me like I was a real person."

"You *are* a real person."

"You know what I mean."

He glanced up at me then. I'd been halfheartedly hoping that yesterday's weirdness would have evaporated overnight, to be forgotten or ignored but certainly not acknowledged. There was a tightness around Spencer's mouth, pulling the corners down into an unfamiliar frown, and his face sagged with fatigue.

I forced my smile to deepen, as if I was willing my good mood on him. *Please*, I practically begged. *Let's go back to normal.*

For a split second, I thought he was going to bring it up, or tell me to go to hell, or that our friendship was over. He looked pained, maybe even a little bit angry.

Please.

"Your eyeliner looks like you head–butted a fairy," he said.

I smiled. My old Spencer was back.

The bell rang, followed by the familiar crackle of the overhead speakers. Principal Ramos's voice filled the room.

"A few announcements," she said after we'd retaken our seats. "We have two new clubs holding their first meetings at lunch today. In the library, the Cosplay Chess Club." Her voice slipped off the mic as if she'd turned her head to speak to someone in the room. "Cosplay chess? Is that a thing?" She cleared her throat. "Right, and in the Activities Center, we have the Free Candy Club. Seriously?" she asked her invisible partner.

"I guess," came the muffled reply.

"Whatever." She cleared her throat. "The back-to-school dance will be next Friday," Principal Ramos continued, stifling a yawn. "No tickets required, just your student ID. And no outside guests."

A groan went up from our class, though I didn't quite understand why. Who were these people who wanted to go to other high schools' dances? I barely wanted to go to mine, but I seemed to be in the minority.

"No guests?" I said out loud, trying to make it sound like I couldn't control the words flying out of my mouth. "That totally blows."

Around me, students laughed. Not at me, with me.

That was new.

"In addition," Principal Ramos continued, "you'll notice that your principal is still doing the school announcements this week. Apparently, our ASB president and vice president decided to move to San Diego over the summer." Principal Ramos *herm*ed into the microphone. "Without telling anyone. So we'll be holding a special election this Friday to fill the open positions. Details and sign-up sheets are available in the office. And last . . ." I heard a rustling of papers. "I'm pleased to announce that we have new coeditors of the *Fullerton Hills Herald*. This year, our school paper will be produced by Gabriel Muñoz—"

I grabbed Spencer's arm, I was so excited to hear Gabe's name.

"—and Michael Torres."

TWENTY

"MICHAEL TORRES IS coediting the school paper?" I repeated, still confused by what I'd just heard.

"Sounds like it," Spencer said.

"Could there be more than one Michael Torres at this school?"

"Possible," Spencer said. "But I doubt it."

The school paper didn't even crack the top ten of Michael Torres's interests. The Cosplay Chess Club would have been more up his alley, and I was relatively sure he'd never even read the *Herald* let alone considered working on it before this semester. What was he up to?

"Moving on from Donne," Mr. Schulty said, leaning back against his desk and loosening his tie. He did this every day, as if he were getting comfortable with us, and I wondered if he did that with every class, retightening it after the bell. "We're going to tackle Milton's masterpiece, *Paradise Lost*. Who wants to read from the first book?"

I had never once offered to read aloud in any English class I'd ever taken, especially not poetry. I'd made my thoughts on the genre pretty well-known, but a manic pixie craved the spotlight and adored romantic things like poetry, so once again, I intensified my energy, plastered an enormous smile on my face, and shot my hand into the air.

Mr. Schulty's eyebrows practically disappeared into his hairline. "Beatrice?" he said, clearly skeptical. "Do you have a question?"

"I'd like to read," I said.

His eyes narrowed. "You realize it's a poem, an art form you've described as a necessary high school evil."

"Yes." I stood up and marched to the front of the room, my English poetry anthology in hand. "Where should I start?"

He blinked, watching me closely as if trying to decide if I was putting him on, then opened his book. "Line two forty-two."

I flipped to the assigned section and threw myself into the part. Milton's early modern English prose was stilted and stiff, but not nearly as bad as I'd anticipated. I wasn't exactly sure what all the words meant, especially in their current arrangement, but I'd learned enough about reading poetry out loud to know that pacing was guided by punctuation, not line breaks, and I tried to interpret it accordingly. Some of the lines I even kind of liked: "The mind is its own place, and in itself can make a Heav'n of Hell, a Hell of Heav'n." I mean, wasn't that what my friends and I were doing with the Formula? Making a heaven of hell with the power of our minds? I could get on board with that.

I read to the end of the section, then paused, unsure if I should continue. I looked up and found every single set of eyes in the classroom upon me.

Not that I hadn't expected to find some people watching me. But most of my classmates followed along in their books when someone was forced to read out loud, or doodled in their notebooks from abject boredom. But everyone was staring at me, eyes wide, as if I'd just done a striptease on Mr. Schulty's desk.

I felt a familiar wave of panic boiling up, and I turned to Spencer instinctively for help. He was watching me too, but instead of the stunned look everyone else wore, he was smiling.

"Was that okay?" I asked, more to Spencer than to Mr. Schulty, who answered.

"Beatrice," he said, "that was—"

My brain kicked in, reminding me of why I'd volunteered to read in the first place. "Trixie," I corrected him. "Call me Trixie."

He shrugged. "Sure, whatever. That was quite good. I'm impressed. Thank you."

He was telling me to go back to my seat. But what would a manic pixie do in this scenario? My brain quickly accessed my brand-new manic pixie film database and retrieved an image of Winona Ryder spinning around on an ice rink in *Autumn in New York*. That would do.

I threw my arms wide and my head back, and spun around in what must have been the world's most awkward pirouette. I lost my balance, staggered into Mr. Schulty's desk, and sent a file holder and pencil caddy careening across the room.

"Crap!" I said. Most of the students laughed at my clumsiness, but it felt good-natured, not derisive, and I smiled at them sheepishly. "Sorry."

I started to pick up the mess. But Mr. Schulty stopped me.

"No, it's fine." He gathered pens and scissors off the floor. "Just . . . take your seat, Trixie."

I flounced back to my desk and dropped into my chair, puffing an errant curl out of my face. This manic-pixie-dream-girl thing wasn't so hard after all.

I take that back. This manic-pixie-dream-girl thing was freaking exhausting.

First off, I'm pretty sure I smiled more during first and second periods than I had in the previous seventeen years of my life. My cheeks ached with the effort to keep my lips curved into an upward arc, and I was convinced my forehead was permanently wrinkled from my perky brows. Meanwhile, my eyes were starting to glaze over, and my lighthearted laugh, which I whipped out for everything from introducing "Trixie" to my second-period Latin teacher to explanations about my shoes, was beginning to sound more hollow and maniacal with every passing second.

The rest of my body felt equally run-down, as if I'd

sprinted two laps around the track without adequate warm-ups or appropriate footwear. I'd spent all morning engaging anyone and everyone in conversation. I noted with some concern that Toile's fashion statement for outlandish hats had spread like wildfire. I saw a variety of sun hats and cabbie hats (even Esmeralda was wearing a snood) on the female denizens of Fullerton Hills. But instead of avoiding it, whenever I saw funky headwear in the hallways, I set myself on a collision course, amping up my energy and perkiness as I introduced myself to the wearer. I had to fight Toile at the source, but keeping my intensity at a fevered pitch all morning had drained my will to live.

That said, my transition from Beatrice to Trixie was going pretty well. A few classmates looked at me strangely, or thought I was new at school instead of just a new version of the nameless Math Girl. But most people, including my teachers, simply noted that I had undergone some kind of radical style transformation over the weekend, and moved on.

Who knew reinventing yourself could be so easy?

It was with equal parts adrenaline high and sugar crash that I trudged out of second-period Latin, smile still plastered on my face, and forced myself to skip down the hallway to my locker like a six-year-old. I really wanted to spend the fifteen-minute nutrition break before third period hiding in the library reference stacks, curled up on the floor, where I could hopefully snag a quick disco nap, but, unfortunately, there was something else I had to do first. I swapped text-books quickly, casting a furtive glance in the tiny magnetic mirror on the inside of my locker door to make sure my glitter eyeliner was appropriately sparkly, then headed off to find Toile and Jesse.

I needed to confront them before lunch in the cafeteria, where the fishbowl effect would be in full force and a thousand pairs of eyes would be witness to the first encounter between Jesse's ex- and current girlfriends, but as I rounded the corner toward the stairs, I bumped into someone who made my entire body tense up.

Michael Torres.

"I know what you're doing, and it won't work." His narrow dark eyes were even narrower and darker than usual, and his spiky hair unfurled like a porcupine on the defensive.

Could he know what I was up to with the Formula? No, that was impossible. Michael Torres was a sneak and a narc, but he was utterly lacking in imagination. I just needed to stay in character.

"Mikey!" I cried, hoping such an adorable nickname for my mortal enemy would throw even the stoic Michael Torres off balance. "Isn't it a beautiful Monday?"

"Huh?"

"The start of a week is so full of promise." I winked at him. "You know, most people hate Mondays, but I always look forward them. You can make anything happen."

Michael Torres stared at me, dumbfounded, as if he'd just discovered that I was the long-lost granddaughter of Albert Einstein, and that NASA had decided to let me skip college and postgraduate school altogether and offered me an exclusive directorship right out of high school. "I . . . guess," he stammered.

Never in my three years at Fullerton Hills had I known Michael Torres to be tongue-tied.

"Oh, and congratulations on the coeditor position on the paper! Sounds super exciting. Anyway," I said, flashing my megawatt grin, "gotta go. See ya!" Then I turned and skipped off.

Breaking eye contact must have snapped him back into reality. "Hey!" he called, scrambling after me. "Bea!"

I kept going, refusing to acknowledge my old name, until Michael Torres blocked my path once again.

"No matter what you do, you're not going to outwit me," he said, "and you're not going to win. Not this time."

Win? I didn't realize we were in competition for anything. Whatever. Fucking with Michael Torres was an unanticipated joy of this whole endeavor. I blew him a kiss, then spun around and continued down the hall.

"I'll be watching you!" he cried after me.

Creeper.

Michael Torres was a nice warm-up: as someone who knew me as more than just Math Girl, he was my toughest audience yet, and despite my general loathing of every interaction we had, I was grateful that he'd given me a momentary boost of Trixie pixie confidence, because when I finally spotted Toile and Jesse at the bottom of the stairs, all of my bravado drained away.

He leaned against the banister, laughing as he held her

hand, then slowly raised it to his lips.

I fluffed my hair, making my curls bigger and bouncier than ever, and pulled one artfully dyed strand forward so it hung lazily in front of my face, as if I'd just been tossing my hair and couldn't be bothered with where it fell. Then I squared my shoulders and hurried down the steps.

"Jesse!" I cried, giving him a quick squeeze on the arm before I turned to his girlfriend. "Toile! I'm so glad I ran into you."

"Bea?"

I didn't look at Jesse (partly because I didn't trust myself to stay in character instead of smacking him across the face, and partly because ignoring him would be the more intriguing, Trixie-like move) but I could hear the bewilderment in his voice, as if he'd just come across a Calculus II Maclaurin Series on the SAT while he was still in Trig I.

But if Jesse was overtly confused by my new appearance, Toile seemed genuinely enthused. "I love what you've done to your hair, Bea," she said, reaching out to finger a curl. "I wish mine did that."

"It's Trixie," I said. Then scrunched up the side of my mouth and puffed upward, coquettishly blowing the errant curl from my eyes.

Toile tilted her head to the side, wide-eyed. "That color is called Trixie?"

Dammit. I'd walked right into that. Score one for Toile.

Thankfully, two could play at that game. I laughed, jiggling my curls. "Oh my God, you're so cute. No, silly. Call *me* Trixie." Then I glanced back at Jesse. "It's a family nick-name."

"It is?" Jesse asked.

I ignored him. "Look!" I pointed at one of the windows that framed the main door of the school. Toile and Jesse immediately turned. "Oh, no. Sorry. I thought I saw a rainbow outside." I gripped Toile's arm. "Can you imagine? A rainbow without any rain? What if we saw them everywhere? Every day? Wouldn't that be the most magical thing ever?"

"Wouldn't it?" she cried. "I would totally just about burst my—"

"Oh, Jesse!" I said, cutting her off. That was the surest way to curtail her natural flightiness. "I have something for you. I was just doodling, you know, in class, and I thought of you."

I pulled a brightly colored paper daisy from my tote bag. About two inches in diameter, made of magenta and orange construction paper glued together over a wire "stem." On the center disk of the flower, I'd written a formula.

$$j = \sqrt{-1}$$

Jesse stared at the paper flower. "What is it?"

"It's an imaginary unit," I said, pointing to the symbols. "See, *j*—that's you—represents a quadratic polynomial without a multiple root, which means the equation has two distinct solutions." I glanced up at Toile.

"Cool," he said.

I wanted to further explain the poetic brilliance of the imaginary number in relation to our current situation, how the two distinct solutions to the underlying equation "$x^2 = -1$" are directly inverse, i.e., total and complete opposites, but that was something Math Girl would do, not Trixie.

"It made me think of you," I said instead.

"That is really awesome." The corners of his eyes softened and his lips curled into a tiny smile. "Thank you."

I could have pressed my luck, but I knew it was better to get out quickly and let him think about me. "It's been lovely chatting and sharing with you guys. You're adorable together. See you at lunch? *Ciao*, ta-ta, and *adieu*!" I chirped, making up my new catchphrase on the spot.

I noticed with immense satisfaction that Jesse stared after me as I skipped off down the hallway.

"And that, my dear Toile," I muttered, "is how you manic-pixie in the big leagues."

TWENTY-ONE

WHEN I ARRIVED at the cafeteria for lunch, I was doubly happy that I'd already orchestrated my initial meeting with the new couple. Jesse and Toile were sitting with Cassilyn.

Fine. Whatever. Toile's popularity with Cassilyn and her friends wouldn't last long. Those girls had the attention spans of Tasmanian fruit flies, who are born, breed, and die all in one twenty-four-hour cycle, and where the time allotted to individual thoughts is less than a nanosecond. Okay, not that Tasmanian fruit flies have cognitive reasoning skills, and even by insectoid standards, they're low on the IQ scale. Then again, so were Dakota and Noel.

Point being, I needed only to shift the spotlight in my direction and Toile's notoriety would fade.

So I made sure I was in perky form as I walked across the cafeteria, swinging my tote bag before me as if I were just traipsing through a field of flowers without a care in the world.

"It's going to take me a while to get used to this," Gabe said as I spun onto the seat beside him.

"The hair or the clothes?" I asked.

He pumped his eyebrows. "The perk."

"I'm not *that* different."

Gabe's jaw dropped in faux shock. "Have you lost your mind?"

"I don't know," Spencer said, swinging his long legs onto the bench next to me. "I kind of like Trixie."

"Do you?" I asked, confused. He'd been the one most adamantly against my transformation.

He smiled tightly. "She's so much nicer than Bea."

"Ha–ha." Behind me at the other table, I heard a peal of laughter. I glanced over and saw Toile leaning her head against Jesse's shoulder, laughing hysterically at something. Cassilyn, Dakota, and Noel were also twittering in unison, and Jesse beamed down at his new girlfriend as if sunshine were emanating from her eyeballs.

Time to make a move.

I laid my hand on Spencer's arm, threw my head back, and let out a shriek that pierced the live acoustics of the cafeteria like feedback from a speaker system. I'd wanted to imitate uninhibited laughter, but instead the dissonance that emerged from my mouth sounded like a bird of prey going in for the kill. All around us, people stopped and stared.

Well, at least I had their attention.

Spencer smacked me on the back, hard enough that it set me coughing.

"What the hell?" I said as the people around us returned to their regularly scheduled lunch conversations.

"Sorry," he said, grinning wickedly. "I thought you were choking on something."

"I hate you."

"I know."

A figure appeared behind Gabe, blocking the sunlight. "Is there room for me?" Kurt asked.

So now just anyone was welcome at this carefully curated lunch table? Great.

Of course, I couldn't say that. Bea might have wanted to, but Trixie had to be welcoming to everyone. I stood up and cleared my throat loudly, hoping to catch Jesse's attention. "Oh my God, yes! Kurt, our table is always open to kindred spirits."

He blinked. "Um, okay."

I made room, and he slid his tray onto the table.

"So," he said, his gaze shifting between the three of us, "are you really all doing research for Gabe's article or is there something else going on?"

"Something else going on," Spencer said.

I elbowed him. "Like I said at the mall, it's all part of the same experiment."

Kurt seemed unimpressed. "Is it working?"

"Well," I said, gesturing around us, "we're sitting here. So there's that."

"And Spencer's painting a portrait of the hottest girl in school," Gabe added. "So there's that."

"Who?" Kurt asked.

I nodded toward Cassilyn. Was he really so oblivious?

"Oh, Cassilyn. Right." Kurt shrugged and turned his focus to his lunch.

"What did you say about Cassilyn?" Thad had spun around on his bench to face us, but instead of addressing the question to Kurt, he was pointing his meaty forefinger at Spencer.

"Nothing," Spencer said honestly. But he maintained eye contact, and his voice didn't falter.

"Yeah, you did," Milo chimed in. "I heard her name."

Spencer wouldn't back down. "But not from my mouth."

Gabe attempted to diffuse the mounting tension. "Such a sexy mouth too." He reached over and smooshed Spencer's cheeks. "I just want to kiss it."

Cassilyn laughed, appearing behind Gabe. "You're so cute." I wasn't sure if she meant Spencer or Gabe.

Thad wasn't taking any chances. "I have a sexy mouth too." He turned to Gabe. "Don't you want to kiss it?"

For an instant, I saw Gabe's character drop. "Um . . ."

"Yeah." Kurt laughed. "Do you?"

"No one asked you, idiot," Milo barked.

I saw the dilemma on Gabe's face: defend Kurt and ruin this new persona he'd so carefully curated, or let his friend get insulted. He'd never failed to come to my or Spencer's defense, and as I saw his eyes narrow on Milo, I realized that he wasn't about to start now.

What would a manic pixie do?

My brain spun, like the reels on a slot machine, and each settled on a different manic pixie: Kate Hudson's groupie from *Almost Famous*, Sabrina Fairchild, and Ruby Sparks.

What did all of those characters have in common? They all spoke French. Captivating, romantic French. Just like Toile on the first day of school.

"Idiot!" I sprang to my feet. "From the French *idiot*," I said, affecting a French accent. It was utterly charming, and hopefully, disarming.

"What?" Milo asked, his anger already ebbing.

I grabbed his hand. *"Oui, oui, monsieur! Idiot! Qu'est-ce que c'est?"* I covered my mouth with my hand and giggled as if I'd made the most hilarious joke in the world.

"You speak French?" Cassilyn said.

I curtsied. *"Oui!"*

"That's so coo . . . ," the stepsisters whined.

"*So* cool," Jesse echoed.

Cassilyn turned to Spencer. "Do you speak French too?"

"No," he said. Then he grinned at me. "Just Trixie here. Go on. Say some more."

Spencer knew damn well I didn't speak a word of French and was just parroting phrases I'd picked up over time, but in that moment, with half the cafeteria staring at me, I slipped into some kind of fugue state, channeling every French phrase I'd ever heard in my life, from Sheri's short-lived foray into Cuisine Bourgeoisie to when my mom dated Hubert from Montreal to my dad's love of old Hercule Poirot movies. *"Crème brûlée à la mode,"* I continued. I tapped Milo on the arm, as if he were in on the joke. *"Laissez-faire nom de plume. N'est-ce pas, soup du jour, mon ami? Tout de suite!"*

"Fibonacci's balls," Spencer said under his breath. But out of the corner of my eye, I saw he was smiling.

And while Milo and Thad might not have been, they'd also completely forgotten (a) that they'd been angry, and (b) if they'd been angry, what they'd been angry about. Manic pixie distraction technique for the win!

While all eyes were still on us, I grabbed Kurt's hand and hauled him to his feet. *"Tour de force haute couture film noir, garçon."*

"But I'm not done with my lunch yet," he complained.

"Take it with you," I whispered. And as he gathered up his tray, I winked at Gabe. He looked so grateful I thought he was going to throw his arms around my neck and squeeze until my head popped off. *"Mais oui? Mais non."*

Then I looped my arm through Kurt's and escorted him across the cafeteria and out of harm's way, crying back over my shoulder, *"Ciao,* ta-ta, and *adieu!"*

TWENTY-TWO

AFTER SCHOOL, SPENCER was waiting for me at my locker, hands shoved deep in the pockets of his jeans, his hair hanging shaggy in front of his eyes. "You made quite a splash at lunch."

"WWMPD?" I said. "Just like you told me."

He smiled. "You made the manic pixies proud."

A dark figure hurried toward us, hood pulled up over his head. As he passed, he looked up and I saw the suspicious features of Michael Torres glaring at me. *Watching you*, he mouthed, then disappeared down the hall.

"What was that all about?" Spencer asked.

"Oh, you know. Just my number one stalker who isn't exactly sure why he's stalking me."

"Great."

"Hey, Trix!" someone yelled from down the hall.

I turned and saw a girl from my AP Physics class. I waved. "Hey, Giselle!" As soon as she was out of earshot, I dropped my voice. "She knows my name. Isn't that awesome?" Before today I could have counted on one hand the number of students at Fullerton Hills who knew my name.

"Actually, I'm more surprised that you knew hers."

I laughed, a real laugh this time, not the forced display I'd been using all day. "Right? It's amazing what happens when you start talking to people." I hurriedly pulled textbooks from my locker, piling them into my tote bag. "They talk back, in case you were wondering. Like, in a nice way instead of a douchey way. I didn't realize there were so many non-asshats at this school."

Spencer's eyes drifted over my head. "There are plenty of real asshats too."

"Hey, Bea."

My heart stopped at the sound of Jesse's voice on the other side of my locker door. My face was hidden from his view, so I took a deep breath, then plastered a smile on my face before I swung the door closed.

"Jesse!" I squealed, a little too loudly. "How was your day? Full of beauty and wonder, I hope."

Beside me, Spencer started to cough. "Sorry," he sputtered. "Allergies."

"I really liked that thing you gave me this morning," Jesse said, leaning in.

"Thing?" I asked.

"The flower with those numbers. You said it was a formula just for me, right?"

Holy crap, in the lunchtime craziness, I'd completely

forgotten about that silly flower. "Yeah. You know how I am with numbers. I was just thinking of you and doodling on the page, and out it came."

Spencer's coughing erupted again, more violently this time. "Sorry." He covered his mouth and looked away, which barely disguised his laughter.

"And in the cafeteria today you were totally . . . I don't know. Everyone was watching you." Just like everyone was watching Toile last week. "The French and everything. It was really cool."

"*Mais oui?*" Spencer mocked. *"Mais non."*

But Jesse's attention was locked on me. "Hey, do you need a ride home? Your dad's, right?"

I gritted my teeth through my smile. My mom's. Despite Jesse's inability to remember where the hell I lived on any given day, I really wanted to say yes.

"WWMPD?" Spencer prompted in a singsong voice.

He was right. The manic pixie move would be to keep Jesse off balance and leave him wanting more.

"Sorry!" I stood on my tippy toes and pecked Jesse on the cheek. "Gotta run. See you tomorrow on another wonderful school day!"

Spencer draped his arm over my shoulders as we left the building. "Just making him jealous," he whispered. Then he slid his hand down my back and pulled my body close.

"Good idea." If jealousy had made me totally reinvent myself, maybe it would jump-start Jesse's brain and remind him who he really wanted to be with.

When we reached Spencer's car, I glanced back to see if Jesse was following us down the stairs, but he was nowhere in sight. I raised my right hand for a high five. "That. Was. So. Awesome!"

Spencer smacked my hand halfheartedly. "Looks like you're getting exactly what you want."

"Yeah." That's what I said, but that's not what I felt. I mean, yes, I wanted to get Jesse back. But as quickly as he'd dropped me for Toile, he'd seemingly dropped her for me. What kind of a guy did that?

We drove in silence, lost in thought. New hair, new clothes, new attention from the popular kids. That's all it had taken for Jesse to sit up and take notice of me again. But it was still me, wasn't it? Trixie wasn't a completely different person.

Or was she? I thought about Giselle from AP Physics. I'd been in science classes with her for two years and yet I'd never actually spoken to her until today. She'd always seemed aloof in class, surrounded by her friends at lunch, and I'd categorized her as one of the bitchy girls who looked down on me. On Beatrice. But when Trixie piped up before class, Giselle was friendly and talkative and not at all the kind of person I'd expected her to be. Had I misjudged her all these years? Or was she different with Trixie from how she'd been with Beatrice?

I winced, realizing I'd made a serious miscalculation with the Formula. I'd only taken into account the outside factors, but hadn't really considered how the Formula would affect the user.

"Cassilyn's coming over tonight," Spencer said from out of the blue.

"Oh yeah?" I glanced at him sidelong. He kept his eyes straight ahead, hands at two and ten on the steering wheel, and his face was absolutely placid.

"Doing the last set of sketches."

"You've been spending a lot of time with her." It was a statement, not a question, and I realized as the words came out of my mouth that I'd voiced them more for me than for Spencer, as if I was having a tough time grappling with the idea that my best friend might have a crush on the most popular girl in school. And that the feeling might be mutual.

"I guess so," Spencer said. "She's nice. Not nearly as vapid as the stepsisters, or as bitchy as Esmeralda. I was . . . surprised."

I turned in my seat to face him. "Good surprised?"

He shrugged, but his eyes never left the road. "Yeah, I mean, I assumed she was kind of an idiot, but she's really not."

"Oh."

He was interested in her. That was pretty clear. How did I feel about that?

"I was thinking maybe I'd ask her to the back-to-school dance."

"What?" I blurted out. "You can't do that."

"Why not?"

Well, for starters, he and Gabe and I had gone to every single school dance together since freshman year, and I had a panicked reaction at the thought of him breaking up our ritual. But that sounded selfish.

"I think Thad already asked her," I said instead.

Spencer was quiet for a moment. "She told me she didn't have a date."

I wondered if Thad knew that. "I guess you could, then. If you wanted to." I paused. "Do you want to?" Why did I want to know so badly?

"We don't have a lot in common," Spencer said by way of an answer, "but she's interested in learning more about art."

Unlike me.

"I'm taking her to LACMA Saturday," he said. "For the Fauvism exhibit. I've been dying to see the Van Dongens . . ."

I didn't hear much after that. So he'd already asked Cassilyn on a date? When was he going to tell me that? And to the Fauvism exhibit. Spencer had asked me last week if I wanted to go with him, but I'd gotten sidetracked by Jesse at lunch. Now he was taking Cassilyn? I was his go-to museum buddy. We'd seen every major exhibit to come through Southern California since we'd gotten permission to ride the train unaccompanied, and now he was taking her?

Isn't this what you wanted?

Oh, shut up, Brain. Sure, when I'd come up with the Formula for Spencer's social situation, I'd envisioned his eventual acceptance by the A-listers at Fullerton Hills, but somehow that had meant painting Milo and Thad in football poses, not dating Cassilyn Cairns.

You're doing the same thing with Jesse.

Okay, yes. If Jesse and I got back together, he'd be the person I'd want to do things with: movies, concerts, museums. Although I wasn't exactly sure what kind of movies Jesse liked. Or music. And I wasn't sure he'd ever been to a museum. Still, we'd work those things out. This was what it meant when you and your friends started dating. Things changed.

"We're here," Spencer said. I noticed with a jolt that we'd stopped in front of my mom's town house.

I climbed out of the car stiffly and closed the door, but stood with my hand on the open window. I wanted to say something, but I couldn't quite figure out the words. Was I happy Spencer was dating Cassilyn? No, not really. And the old Beatrice would have said that. Blurted it right out. *You and Cassilyn only have a 13 percent chance of a lasting relationship, based on factors including, but not limited to, interests, relative intelligence, and social standing.*

But that was the old Beatrice. Trixie saw the world in a positive light—this was the ultimate test.

"I'm glad Cassilyn's not as dumb and bitchy as I thought," I said, realizing as I said it that though my tone was upbeat, my word choice was still caustic.

The corners of his mouth drooped. "I wish I could say the same for Jesse."

Then he peeled away from the curb.

TWENTY-THREE

MY SENSE OF victory over Toile lasted exactly sixteen hours, and died the instant I walked into school the next morning. Draped across the entrance hallway, rippling gently in the breeze, was an enormous banner, hand-painted in garish green and gold—Fullerton Hills' school colors—advertising "Jesse Sullivan for ASB President."

I froze dead in my mismatched Mary Janes. Toile's fingerprints were all over the banner, literally and figuratively. First off, there was no way Jesse's handwriting could have been that neat and legible. The letters were bubbly, evenly spaced, and outlined in gold glitter. Plus, the banner was decorated with shamrocks and daisies—also with glitter centers—which reeked of Toile.

She'd upped me on "Category five—male wish fulfillment" by giving Jesse his much-coveted "thing." Instead of Hammock Guy or Poetry Guy, he was going to be School President Guy. My sad little paper flower with the imaginary unit couldn't compete. Once again, Toile was in the lead.

"I didn't see that one coming," Gabe said, materializing at my elbow, his flamboyant act at full throttle.

"I can't believe she got him to run for office," I said. "I'll never beat her now."

Gabe snorted. "You mean you'll never get Jesse back now. That's the goal, right?"

"Right. Yes. Getting Jesse back is my goal." Why did I repeat it? As if I needed to remind myself. Maybe I was angry with him, my ego wounded in a way that would take a while to heal. Not that I wouldn't—I was relatively sure the moment Jesse looked at me with those deep brown eyes and said, *I love you, Bea, and I want you back*, I'd melt into his arms and forget all the crap he'd put me through. Like 73 percent sure.

Okay, maybe 63.

"Hey, Trixie!" Annabelle, a bespectacled redhead from AP English, waved as she and her friends passed us in the entrance hall. I waved back, smiling big, and noticed that she was wearing two different Doc Martens boots: a white one on the left and a black one on the right.

"Do you think she borrowed that from you?" Gabe asked.

I glanced down at my own feet, where I sported a blue Mary Jane on one foot and a silver one on the other. "Maybe." It had taken Toile's hat fetish five full days to start popping up around school. If Annabelle's shoe expression was truly Trixie-inspired, as opposed to just an early morning, pre-coffee wardrobe malfunction, then I'd upped the manic pixie–fication by at least ninety-six hours.

Gabe rested his chin on my shoulder. "Maybe you should run for president? Take this Trixie thing to the next level."

I shook my head. "I'm not popular enough. We'd need someone in with A-list support in order to inspire complete strangers to—"

"Hi, Gabriel!" someone called from above.

He blew a kiss to the upper balcony. "Hello, dahling!" The girl giggled and waved, then disappeared over the railing. "That blowing-kisses thing works every time," Gabe said under his breath. "Who knew girls were so susceptible? I swear, I've learned so much about your gender using the Formula."

My eyes were still fixed on the balcony. "Who was that?"

"No idea."

A gaggle of sophomore girls waved at him in unison as they passed us. "Gabriel!"

"Kisses!" he said, wiggling his fingers at them. Then he whispered to me. "See? Every time!"

Complete strangers. I turned to Gabe. "You."

"What did I do?"

"You should run for ASB president."

"Me?"

I nodded, curls flying around my face. "You're friends with all the popular girls now, and in less than a week even students you've never met before know your name. You're a rising star, which makes you the perfect candidate."

Gabe just stared at me, dumbstruck.

"Think about it," I continued, talking quickly. I was getting excited by the idea. "If you got elected, you could do a lot of good around here. Not to mention what it would mean for your article."

"I *have* been struggling with a conclusion," he admitted, patting the notebook in his breast pocket. "But ASB president is a lot of responsibility."

"I can't think of anyone else at this school who I'd rather see in charge of things."

Gabe shook his head. "I don't know . . ."

Just then, Cassilyn, Esmeralda, and the stepsisters strode across the foyer toward us. No better time to test the waters.

"Mention it to the girls," I told Gabe under my breath.

"Now?"

I nodded.

Gabe heaved a sigh. "Fine." The moment the girls approached he was back in character.

"Dahlings, I was just telling Trixie here," he said, linking his arm through mine, "that I think I'd make a fabulous ASB president. Don't you think?"

"Oh my God!" Cassilyn cried, not waiting for her friends to answer. "I think that would be my favorite thing ever."

"*Zoopa* idea," Esmeralda said, mimicking Gabe's German accent perfectly.

"*Zoop* . . . ," Dakota and Noel echoed, the final vowel dissipating into matching vocal fry.

"Right?" I said, playing off their enthusiasm. "He'd be so much fun."

Cassilyn grabbed his hands. "Oh, you *have* to run. We'll totally vote for you."

Esmeralda eyed her closely, ready to one-up her. "Campaign for you."

That's all I wanted to hear. "What do you think, Gabriel?"

"I think," he said, his eyes bright, "that I'll have to sign up in the office today."

"Awesome!" Cassilyn squealed, then kissed Gabe on the cheek. "See you guys at lunch."

Gabe waited until they had rounded the corner before he took me by the shoulders and dropped his act. "Please tell me you're not just asking me to do this because you want to beat Toile."

"Well," I said, unable to lie to my friend, "I'm not *just* doing it for that reason. But seriously, Gabe, if you don't want to do this, tell me."

He paused for a moment, as if contemplating all the factors, then smiled. "No, you're right. I would be good at this job. Like *really* good."

I arched an eyebrow. "Like *zoopa*?"

"Exactly." He scanned the foyer, which was already dotted with flyers and banners touting a full range of candidates. "What about campaigning?"

The first warning bell rang, signaling that we had ten minutes until first period. "I'll come up with a plan," I said. It's what I did best, after all. "We'll meet at Spencer's after school. And make magic."

TWENTY-FOUR

"OKAY, I SIGNED up for the election," Gabe said the instant he burst through the door of Spencer's studio after school. He dropped onto the sofa, crossed his right leg over his left, and folded his hands over his knee, which was a totally in-character pose even though he was just hanging out with us. "Let the fabulousness begin."

Kurt hesitated in the doorway, a soda cup in his hand. He must have driven Gabe over from school and wasn't sure whether or not he was welcome.

I bowed at the waist, ushering him in. "Welcome to Spencer Preuss-Katt's magical clubhouse."

"Shit, Bea," Spencer said. "Leave that Trixie crap at school, okay?"

"I did," I said, glaring at him.

He lowered his chin. "'Magical clubhouse'?"

I guess Spencer was right, but it hadn't felt like part of my Trixie routine while I was doing it. "Can't I just be naturally whimsical sometimes?"

"I don't know," he said, "can you?"

"So, do you even know what you're supposed to do as ASB president?" Kurt asked, pausing between sips.

"I do." Gabe pulled a crumpled piece of paper from his bag. "I'd run weekly meetings of the executive board, read the daily announcements, and—this is my favorite—I would be the face of the Fullerton Hills student body." He dropped the page to his lap. "Isn't that absolutely, positively perfect for me?"

Spencer laughed. "Sounds like an extrovert's paradise."

"It's more than just the spotlight," I said, feeling like Spencer was chiding Gabe. "Gabe could make some huge changes at our school."

"Exactly," Gabe said, leaning against me. "Tolerance, understanding. I can squash the culture of elitism and bullying, and really make Fullerton Hills a place where everyone feels safe."

"Amen," I said.

"If you can get elected," Kurt said, musing into his straw.

"Good point." Gabe turned to me. "What's the campaign plan? Most of the good advertising spots around school are already taken. Hallways, stairwells, cafeteria."

"And the theater, library, and gym are booked for rallies tomorrow and Wednesday," Kurt added.

"I really want to make an impression with this campaign," Gabe continued. "All eyes on me, you know?"

I snorted. "Oh, we know."

"I mean for the article," he said, wagging his chin at me.

"Mmhm."

He ignored me. "How are we supposed to get any traction?"

"I'm going to give you the same advice I gave Bea," Spencer said. "Face tattoo."

Gabe gazed at him coolly. "I'm so totally drawing on your face with a Sharpie the next time you fall asleep."

"What's your plan, Bea?" Spencer said, getting us back on track. "Since you convinced Gabe to do this."

"I'm not five," Gabe said, his forehead wrinkled in frustration. "No one convinced me to do anything. I *want* to be ASB president."

Kurt stole a glimpse at him. "You'd be really good at it too. I mean, of everyone running, I feel like you could actually bring the student body together."

Gabe flushed pink. "Thank you."

"The Formula hasn't failed us yet," I said, pushing myself forward on the sofa. "So I say we stick with it." As I pulled a pen and notebook out of my bag, I caught Spencer mouthing *the Formula* while he wrinkled his nose as if the toilet had backed up. I poised my pen over the page and turned to Gabe. "How many days until the election?"

"Speeches are Thursday at lunch," Gabe said. "I've already got the perfect outfit planned."

"Outfit," I said, not entirely sure how that would help his campaign. "Check."

"And voting is open online from then until nine o'clock

that night. Which is perfect timing because Mr. Poston wants me to submit the article on Friday."

I nodded. "Plenty of time."

"Two days is plenty of time?" Kurt asked.

I did a few quick calculations, weighing the benefits of various campaign strategies. The traditional high school model consisted of:

(a) in-school advertising, in the form of banners, flyers, and handouts;
(b) virtual advertising, utilizing photos, text, and video, on various social media platforms;
(c) traditional glad-handing.

As far as I could tell, everyone followed the same model, trying to come up with a "new" way to get their name bigger, brighter, and more memorable than anyone else's on election day, but always utilizing these same strategies.

Because that's what got people elected in high school: name recognition. That needed to be our focus.

I drew a quick graph, plotting the traditional buzz arc over time. "Here's what I think," I said, hastily inking a bell curve to connect my plot points. "Candidates start strong, unleashing their campaigns on day one and then doubling down on their tactics as they get closer to the election. Using this method, they see a sharp spike in name recognition during the first twenty-four to forty-eight hours, then fall off sharply."

"It's true," Gabe said. "Polls we did at the *Herald* last year showed that early leads faded by the election."

"The average American teenager has an attention span of approximately seven seconds," I said. "I think it's actually to your advantage that you haven't started campaigning yet."

"How?" Spencer asked.

The boy had no vision. I pulled a red pen out of my bag and drew another curve on top of the first one. It started later in the timeline, but peaked right at Thursday's election, and almost twice as high as the original. "By delaying your 'launch,' we're beginning your ascent later, when the initial noise of the other candidates has died down."

It was a brilliant strategy, if I did say so myself, and I pictured the final triumphant conclusion of my scholarship submission: Gabe elected ASB president, Spencer with a portrait exhibition, and me beating Toile to get Jesse back. Early admission, here I come!

"Won't Gabe just get lost in the rallies and giveaways?" Kurt pressed. "By tomorrow, half the school will be wearing buttons and swag from other candidates."

"Not if we make a game out of it," I said.

Gabe tilted his head. "I don't get it."

"Who else have you told that you're running for student body president?" I asked.

"Just you guys, plus Cassilyn, Esmeralda, and the stepsisters."

I wasn't worried about the girls, who'd probably forgotten about Gabe's candidacy twenty seconds after they learned of it. "Perfect. So here's what we're going to do: tease a secret candidate."

Gabe bit his lip. "Is that ethical?"

I shrugged. "Sure. Why wouldn't it be?"

"Journalists strive to be accountable and transparent. It's one of our statutes."

"Which we're not violating. This is simply a campaign strategy. We're not lying to anyone."

"I guess you're right," Gabe said.

"And when we finally reveal your name," I said, "we'll do it with a bang."

Gabe's eyes grew wide. "Oh yeah?" I knew he'd like that idea.

Spencer looked skeptical. "So you campaign without using his name at all, then wait until the speeches to out him?" He held his fist out to Gabe. "No offense, dude."

"None taken." Gabe returned the bump.

"Exactly," I said. "A huge unveiling of the secret candidate in front of the entire student body. A captive audience, forced to pay attention. They won't even remember the other candidates after you walk out onto that stage. That's a ninety percent efficiency rating on your campaign."

"Okay, I can see how that might work," Kurt said. "But how do we spread the word about a candidate if we can't even use Gabe's name?"

"I'll design a flyer." I made a few notches on my bell curve, marking off campaign milestones. "Which we shove in every single locker tomorrow before school. Drop a clue, then promise more. It'll be like a giant scavenger hunt. Significantly more effective than banners and posters with Gabe's name, which have a max efficiency rating of thirty-three percent."

"You know what?" A smile spread across Gabe's face. "This could work. We might actually pull it—"

A knock on the door startled us. Spencer shot to his feet.

"Who's that?" I asked, noting the flush in his cheeks.

"Client. I mean, it's Cassilyn."

Gabe waited until Spencer was at the door before he beckoned Kurt and me to lean in. "I've got gossip."

My head snapped up. "Yeah?"

"Thad is pissed off that Cassilyn won't go to the dance with him," Gabe whispered. "She told Esmeralda she wasn't interested in dating jocks anymore. Said she wants someone more artistic, and everybody knew exactly who she meant."

Suddenly, Gabe's intimacy with the A-list wasn't so appealing. I didn't really want to hear that Cassilyn was telling everyone she was interested in Spencer.

"So Esmeralda immediately told Thad," Gabe continued, "right before *she* asked *him* to the dance. He said yes, of course, but then he told me that he really only agreed to go with her because he wants to make Cassilyn jealous."

"Thanks for inviting me over again," Cassilyn said. The word "again" jabbed at me, as if she'd laid special emphasis on it.

"Do you think Spence's really interested in her?" I swallowed, feeling a strange lump in my throat. Going to the dance together was one thing. A long-term relationship was something else entirely.

Gabe shrugged. "Who wouldn't want to date the hottest girl in school?"

Kurt tilted his head to the side. "But I thought you said Spencer was in love with—"

"Cassilyn!" Gabe rocketed to his feet. "Darling, how are you?"

"Gabriel!" She floated across the room and kissed him on both cheeks. "What are you doing here?"

"Campaign stuff," he said. "Remember? I'm running for ASB president."

"Duh, of course! You're going to be my favorite prez ever."

I gritted my teeth. Anything new was her favorite thing ever.

"Can you believe I'm getting my portrait painted by a real artist?" she continued.

Spencer's face, still pink from the initial flush of Cassilyn's arrival, deepened to an unbecoming shade of fuchsia. "Oh, I'm not a real artist. I mean, I don't actually sell anything. It's just a hobby."

"Bullshit!" I blurted out. I know it wasn't very Trixie-like, but I couldn't help it. I hated the way he discounted his talent in front of other people. Why was he always trying to pretend that his art wasn't the most important thing in his universe?

"Trix . . . ," Spencer said, his eyes pleading with me to

stop. But Spencer wasn't that scrawny kid getting picked on in gym class anymore. There was no reason for him to hide what he loved.

"Art is not your hobby," I said, narrowing my eyes at him. Then I turned to Cassilyn. "He's had interest from a half dozen galleries in LA." I wasn't even lying. His moms had submitted a few of his acrylic and plaster pieces to their gallery friends downtown, who had offered to see a full range of pieces for a possible showing as soon as he had a larger body of work.

Cassilyn's gaze lingered on Spencer's face as I spoke, then gradually trailed to me. "You and Spencer are good friends, right?"

She'd asked me that same question just last week. Was she seriously that airheaded or was her forgetfulness intentional? "Yes."

"*Just* friends?"

So that was it. She was fishing to see if Spencer was single. "We're . . ."

Just as I was about to confirm Spencer's bachelorhood, I paused. An image popped into my head: Spencer and Cassilyn getting hot and heavy on that very sofa. That's where it was headed, if it hadn't happened already, and the thought momentarily paralyzed me.

"We're just friends." Only the words didn't come out of my mouth. Spencer had said it, his voice so concretely dismissive it startled me.

"Right," I said, forcing a smile. "Just friends."

TWENTY-FIVE

GABE, KURT, SPENCER, and I showed up early for school the next morning with a half dozen boxes of flyers. The plan was simple: shove one in each locker and then post the extras wherever we could find the space.

The task was slow and involved a variety of paper cuts and wonky creases before I discovered a folding and stuffing system that didn't leave me with bloody fingertips. We split up and worked in silence, focused on the job at hand. Fold and stuff, fold and stuff. Each flyer had the identical message:

WHO WILL BE YOUR NEXT ASB PRESIDENT?
IT'S A ZOOPA SECRET!
FIND OUT THURSDAY!
YOU DON'T WANT TO MISS THIS!

By waiting until the general assembly to announce Gabe to a captive audience of the entire student body, there was a

91 percent chance that his would be the only name people would remember when the polls opened. Jesse would lose the election, then lose interest in Toile, and I would win.

You mean you'll get Jesse back.

Yes, of course, Brain. That's what I meant. I'd "win" Jesse back. That was the whole reason I was doing this. It wasn't a competition with Toile: this was just about my relationship with Jesse.

I was lost in thought, finishing up the last row of lockers upstairs at the end of the math-and-sciences floor, when one of the locker doors flew open. I screamed, dropping my box of flyers, as Michael Torres squeezed his skinny frame out of the tight metal interior.

"Beatrice Giovannini," he said, his voice slimy.

"What the hell were you doing in there?" I panted, my heart in my throat.

"It's my locker."

As if that made it better. "You didn't answer my question."

"I told you," he said, his nostrils flared. "I'm keeping an eye on you."

"You're stalking me an hour before school starts from the interior of your locker?"

"Maybe I am and maybe I'm not," he said with a grin that he probably thought looked enigmatic but came off as super creepy. "Maybe I'm doing something so amazing you can't even imagine its scope. Maybe I'll—"

I cut off his rant. "Boldly go where no man has gone before."

Michael Torres gasped, horrified. "How dare you quote *Star Trek* to me? You don't get to do that. I quote *Star Trek* to you."

We were getting nowhere. There was only a 3 percent chance Michael Torres could have known that I would be at school that early, less than 1 percent that I'd be in the hallway with his locker, but I kinda didn't want to know what he was actually doing in there.

"What do you want, Michael Torres? I have work to do."

"I see." He crouched down and picked up one of the scattered flyers. "Secret candidate, eh? So that's what this Trixie business is all about. You're running for ASB president."

The last thing I needed was Michael Torres ruining Gabe's campaign. "No, I'm just—"

He stepped forward, his eyes locked onto mine. "Well, I'm going to tell everyone what you're up to. Totally going to blow your secret. At first I thought those notes your friend Gabe is always scribbling in his book had something to do with it, but now I know better. If you think you're going to beat me by using information theory to get elected to school office, you're wrong."

I froze. Information theory? What did that have to do with the election? Unless . . .

"You read about the scholarship in *MIT News Magazine*." Coeditor of the school paper. Why hadn't I realized it before? Michael Torres was going to use the *Herald* as his information theory project.

Which was a good idea, but not nearly as good as the Formula.

"I don't know what you're talking about," he said, his eyes darting back and forth across my face. He was a horrible liar.

"Mmhm."

So we were both going after the same scholarship and he thought I was going to use the election as my research. Clearly, he had no idea about the Formula. And I planned to keep it that way.

"You caught me," I said. "Red-handed. That's exactly what I'm up to."

He arched an eyebrow. "Really?"

I nodded enthusiastically as I gathered up my remaining flyers. "Trixie, the campaign—it's all part of my plan to get that scholarship for myself."

Michael Torres looked confused, as if his concept of reality had just exploded in his face. "Oh. Okay."

"But you were just too smart for me, so now I'll have to think of something else." I hugged the mostly empty box of flyers to my chest and hurried down the hall toward the stairs. As long as he continued to believe he'd figured out my plan, he might stop spying on me.

Might.

"Good job, Michael Torres. *Ciao*, ta-ta, and *adieu!*"

I was leaning over the balcony searching for Gabe or Spencer to tell them about my encounter with Michael Torres when I spotted Toile and Jesse in the foyer.

They were also plastering the school with flyers: green

and gold with sparkling shamrocks, just like the enormous banner that was draped below me. It looked as if they'd hand-glitter-glued every single one. As I watched, Toile did a little pirouette, then mimicked a ballet dancer *en pointe*, flitting around the empty foyer. She wore a baby-doll dress that flared as she spun, exposing the bare skin above her thigh-high striped stockings. The tiny top hat that was secured under her chin by an elastic strap flopped back and forth.

Try as I might, I could never totally be *that*. Toile was so effortlessly carefree, as if the only ideas in her head were of the here and now: no worries about the future, no calculations of percentages of probable outcomes based on her actions. She thought of something and did it. As simple as that. And no manic pixie cheat sheet or forced whimsy could compete.

Jesse was delighted by the display. He took her hand and twirled her around while she giggled.

Just kill me.

"Aren't you guys cute," I said, traipsing down the stairs. The words could have sounded sarcastic, but I kept my tone light and perky.

"Oh, hi!" Toile said, pausing midtwirl. Jesse's arm knocked her tiny top hat askew, and she fumbled with the strap to straighten it. "We're just putting up more flyers for the campaign."

I stepped onto the tile floor and help up my stack. "Me too!"

Jesse's eyes grew wide. "Are you running for office?"

I took the opportunity to break into my boisterous Trixie laugh. "Oh, no. I don't have time for that." Then I dropped my voice to a whisper. "I've been recruited to help a secret candidate."

"Seriously?" Toile said.

I started. For an instant, her voice was neither light nor perky. Her lips weren't smiling, and her violet eyes weren't sparkling with childlike wonder. She sounded sarcastic and looked skeptical. Totally, 100 percent un-Toile-like, and just for a second, a new idea crossed my mind.

Could Toile's manic pixieness be just as much of an act as mine?

Then Toile clasped her hands together and cooed, "I mean, seriously how exciting. I love a good mystery." She grabbed Jesse's arm, bouncing up and down on her toes. "Don't you?"

Or I could be completely wrong about that.

"Who's it for?" Jesse asked. "Someone popular?"

I handed him a flyer. "I have *no* idea."

He stared at it blankly. "What if it's someone horrible and not cool at all?"

"But that's the amazing, sublime cosmic mystery of it all," I cried, then I mimicked Toile's pirouette from before. "Isn't that awesome?"

"You almost done down there?" Spencer called from the balcony.

I glanced at him, and just caught sight of Michael Torres slinking into the shadows of the upstairs hallway. Had he been watching my interaction with Toile and Jesse? "No," I said, shaking off Michael Torres's stalkiness. "Got sidetracked. Come help?"

Spencer hurried downstairs and, after casting some serious side-eye at Jesse, began plastering his leftover flyers around the room. Students were arriving, and in a matter of minutes the foyer had gone from empty to bustling. I had a big stack of flyers in my hand, and decided the most manic pixie move would be to hand them out. To strangers. Who I'd have to talk to.

You can't make omelettes without breaking eggs.

"Secret candidate running for president," I said, confronting the first group of students who passed within my orbit. "You'll have to wait until tomorrow to find out who it is!"

"Cool," a couple of girls said, each snatching a flyer from my hand.

That was easy. "Secret candidate," I said, accosting another group. "Find out who it is on Thursday."

An upperclassman wearing a letterman jacket pursed his lips. "You sure you can't tell me?" He almost sounded flirtatious.

I batted my eyelashes playfully. "I would, but then I'd have to kill you."

Damn, I was good at this.

As I approached more and more students, I got bolder in my spiel. Louder and more outgoing. It was fun, actually. Like I was playing a role I'd always wanted to play but was too afraid to try. Talking to people wasn't so bad when you had nothing to lose.

Spencer kept his eyes on me, his face a mix of surprise and annoyance, darkening whenever I flirted with a group of guys. He didn't approve, of course, of Trixie or of this campaign or probably of me talking to anyone who wasn't him or Gabe. But I was having fun. At high school. For the first time ever in a setting that didn't involve an exam paper and a ticking clock. How could my best friend possibly disapprove?

But Spencer wasn't the only one watching me. Jesse kept glancing in my direction, his eyes lingering longer than was appropriate for mere curiosity and once, right as the warning bell rang, I could have sworn I saw him smile at me.

Then Toile took his hand and pulled him down the hallway to show choir.

The crowd in the foyer began to thin. I shoved the last few flyers in my tote bag and started toward first period when I saw Jesse trot back to me. "Hey," he said, his voice low. "Do you want a ride home?" Three days, two offers. I was winning again.

This time, I decided to accept. "Sure."

"Meet me in the lot right after the bell, okay?" He glanced over his shoulder, probably looking for Toile. I half wondered how he was going to ditch her after class.

Whatever. Not my problem! "Will do." Then I blew him a kiss and flounced off to class.

* * *

Jesse was waiting for me at his car after school as promised. As soon as he saw me hurrying down the stairs, he slipped into the driver's seat, leaned across, and pushed open the passenger door.

"Thanks," I said, climbing inside. I realized he was rushing because he wanted us out of there before Toile appeared, and I wasn't going to argue the point. I needed some alone time with Jesse, not a scene with Toile where she might sway the momentum back in her favor.

"So, the campaign," I began as we sped down the hill away from campus. "How's it going?"

He shrugged. "Fine, I guess. Toile's doing most of it."

As I suspected. "Yeah, but are you having fun? That's the point, right?"

"Toile is fun," he said, not answering the question. "Sometimes."

That seemed like an opening. "Sometimes?"

"Yeah, you know. She's wild and does crazy things. That's fun." We stopped for a light and Jesse turned to me with a little smile on his face. "But not as much fun as you are." Then he laid his hand on top of mine.

"Oh."

Okay, so that should have been exactly what I wanted to hear: that I was out-pixie-ing Toile, that I was reminding Jesse of our relationship, that I was winning him back. But something about the gleam in his eyes—like we were about to do something naughty—made me want to smack him.

He stopped the car in front of my dad's house, and I let

out a yelp of surprise. "You remembered!" I was relatively sure it was the first time he'd gotten it right.

He cut the engine. "How could I not remember where my girl lives?"

Your girl?

"Um, thanks for the ride," I said, suddenly irritated. Hadn't he just been blissfully happy with his girlfriend that morning? One minute he was twirling her around, enthralled by her little-girl antics, and the next he was sneaking back to talk to me, practically begging for the chance to drive me home. It was almost as if he was trying to date both of us at the same time.

He unlatched his seat belt. "I can think of a better way for you to thank me." He half closed his eyes and leaned over as if he was going to kiss me.

Maybe it was the weirdness, or maybe I was subconsciously playing by the manic pixie rule book, but instead of letting him kiss me (or even kissing him back) I opened the door and practically catapulted onto the sidewalk.

"See you later." I grabbed my tote bag, then slammed the door and ran up the steps to the house.

TWENTY-SIX

I STARED DOWN the street long after Jesse's boxy Scion had disappeared around the corner. What the hell had just happened?

I could feel a tightness spreading through my stomach, accompanied by an unfamiliar nausea. Panic.

Why was I panicking? I should have been elated that Jesse wanted to kiss me again. Wasn't this what I wanted?

I remember the first time I'd felt this way: the day my dad had sat me down and told me he was moving out, that he still loved me, but that he and my mom needed to try "living apart" for a little while to see if it could help their marriage. It had seemed so strange to me at the time. How could spending less time together improve their relationship? Sure, they fought all the time, but even seventh-grade Beatrice had realized that a separation was just a trial run for divorce.

I'd felt the same knot in my belly, the same queasy feeling as if I were going to hurl rocks. I'd tried to steady myself, hang on to my dad's words as if they were scientific facts instead of white lies told to ease a child into the idea of divorce. My mom had done a great job of toppling my tenuously built house of cards. The instant my dad's Lexus, packed to the roof with books and clothes and a smattering of other cherished personal items, pulled out of the driveway, she launched into a rant.

"Lying, cheating . . . Do you know what your father did? With that *puta* secretary?"

The knot had tightened. Fear and panic had swamped me, wave upon wave, until I couldn't do anything other than curl up in a ball on my bed and cry until there were no more tears. My mother had been able to channel her hurt into anger—anger that she'd never been able to get over, which was odd because, well, what the hell did she expect? She'd been my dad's legal secretary, and he'd cheated on his first wife with her, so was it really such a shock that he'd cheated on her with Sheri? Of course, I didn't know that at the time, and while my mom could hide behind her rage, I was merely left with the sharp pain of loss and a desperate, haunting sense of my own helplessness.

Only I wasn't helpless anymore. I was in charge of my destiny, or at least of my love life. Wasn't I?

I heard the crying the moment I walked through the front door, and it banished all thoughts of Jesse. It sounded like a cross between an overly tired child and a puppy with separation anxiety. "Sheri?"

I waited a few seconds for a response, but all I heard was

the continued whimpers coming from the back of the house. I left my bag by the door and slowly crept down the hallway. "Sheri, are you home?" The whimpering turned into a moan, which got louder as I knocked on the bedroom door. "Sheri? It's Bea."

"In . . ." Sheri sniffled, her voice crackly. "Here."

I crossed the soft carpeting of the expansive master suite, decorated in light oak and ecru with pops of lavender and green, passed his-and-hers walk-in closets and a conjoined dressing area, and poked my head into the bathroom. Sheri sat in the middle of the tile floor—legs crossed, face buried in her hands as she wept quietly. Around her lay a dozen discarded pregnancy tests of every brand and variety on the market, and each one showed a single blue or pink line across its face.

Poor Sheri. She and my dad had been trying for two years to supply me with a half sibling, but to no avail. And now her life was a mélange of fertility doctors, hormone injections, blood tests, ultrasounds, and vitamin cocktails.

"Hey," I said from the doorway. "You okay?"

She heaved a jagged breath, her frosted ponytail jostling. "No."

I stepped onto the tile floor, picking my way past Clearblue Easies and First Responses, and crouched down beside her. "It's going to happen, Sheri. Eventually."

Her head jerked up. Black mascara and liner streaked down her cheeks like she was a rabid fan at an Alice Cooper concert, and her eyes were puffy and bloodshot. "You don't know that."

"You're with the best fertility doctor in Orange County. He's got like an eighty-nine percent success rate with women your age." She knew this as well as I did, and had repeated Dr. Aaronstein's statistics to my dad and me over the dinner table on more than one occasion, but every time she peed on a stick and got a negative result, she was crushed by disappointment.

Sheri stared at the ceiling. "This is hopeless." I fought to keep from rolling my eyes. She'd only just started fertility treatments and had a long way to go before actual hopelessness set in. She grasped my hand. "What if I never give your father a child? He'll leave me for sure."

What was this, *Downton Abbey*? "Sheri, my dad isn't going to leave you if you can't have his kid." I forced a laugh. "He left my mom, remember?"

Sheri caught her breath. "That's right!" Her face brightened, the cloud of fear and disappointment lifted, and she hugged me. "Oh, Bea. Thank you."

I couldn't believe I was comforting my stepmom by reminding her that she broke up my parents' marriage.

A door slammed at the back of the house. "Sheri? Sheri, are you okay?" My dad's footsteps pounded down the hallway. "You said it was an emergency."

Sheri bolted to her feet and stared wild-eyed into the mirror. "Stall him while I fix my face, will you, Bea? I don't want him to see me like this."

"No problem."

I intercepted my dad in the bedroom, where he'd dumped

his briefcase and jacket. "What's wrong?" he asked.

I nodded. "Just bad news on the . . ." I dropped my voice, hoping Sheri couldn't hear me over the gushing faucet. "Pregnancy tests."

"Oh." He tilted his head to the side. "Did you do something different to your hair?"

So much for the lawyer's attention to detail. "I cut off six inches and added streaks."

"Oh, good. I thought I was going crazy for a second." His face relaxed. Not completely, though. Never completely. I wasn't sure if it was his lawyer nature or the fact that he was carrying around a history of lying to his wives, but there was always a cloaked look in his eyes. "Is she okay?"

"She'll survive," I said.

He loosened his tie. "I'll be happy when this is over."

"We'll all—" Something caught my eye as my dad unbuttoned the top of his shirt. A smudge on his neck that had transferred to his collar, hot pink and shimmery, like an opaque lip gloss. And not the color Sheri wore. "Dad, seriously?"

"What?"

I turned him toward the mirror and pointed at the evidence. "Let me guess—Tonya's shade?" His new secretary, only four months on the job, was a buxom redhead that strutted around the offices of Kelger & Giovannini as if she'd just left a *Mad Men* casting call.

"Mrs. Akers," he said sharply, naming the elderly part-time receptionist no one had the heart to force into retirement.

He rubbed the spot off his neck with his thumb and quickly removed his button-down, stripping to his undershirt. He looked sadder this way, less important. "She was just thanking me for her birthday gift."

"I see." I didn't entirely buy it and was about to tell him so when my phone buzzed with a text from my mom.

Have another hot date tonight with Benjamin Feldberger, Esquire!!!!
Glad you're at your dad's so I'll have the house to myself.

Ew.

You should maybe mention this to your dad? Just in case he knows Ben?

"Anything important?" my dad asked, pulling a polo shirt over his head.

"No." I slipped the phone back into my pocket, leaving my mom's texts unanswered. She'd probably send a dozen more, but suddenly I was too exhausted to deal with my parents' ridiculousness. The sound of running water stopped, and I turned to leave. "Be nice to Sheri, okay? She's kind of a mess."

TWENTY-SEVEN

I FLED TO my bedroom, quietly closing the door. I just needed to shut everything out: Jesse, my parents, my friends, the election. Everything.

This bedroom was easily twice the size of my third-floor room in the town house. The sprawling ranch-style McMansion was brand-new when my dad bought it a couple of years ago, with four bedrooms including dual masters, two offices, formal living room, informal living room, formal dining room, informal dining room, and a massive back-yard swimming pool that belonged in a music video. The four bedrooms had been Sheri's request: room for me, guests, and her own theoretical children. She'd given me the larg-est bedroom other than the master, and taken great pains to "help" me decorate it, which basically meant presenting me with paint samples in such indistinguishable shades as "sand," "sandstone," "paradise sand," and "tropical sandstorm," and asking for my opinion.

197

Don't get me wrong, the room was lovely. My queen-size, pillow-top bed with a half dozen heavily stuffed pillows sheathed in cream shams could have been photographed for a design magazine, and the chrome and ecru lines of the dresser and armoire matched both the vanity mirror and the enormous flat-screen TV that was embedded directly into the wall. Sheri's attention to detail when it came to decorating her house on my dad's credit card was meticulous, and though her minimalist style didn't necessarily fit my tastes, I could appreciate the continuity of the decor.

Plus my room was quiet. Back of the house and on a corner lot meant no street or neighbor noise. It was my own little sanctuary.

Except for my things. I wasn't a particularly "stuff"-oriented seventeen-year-old, to be honest. The divorce had purged me of the permanency of physical belongings. When you're being shuttled back and forth between residences every 3.5 days, it's kind of hard to care about things that can't fit in a single carry-on. I kept a stash of clothes and a full range of toiletries here, but I'd never fully embraced this place as a home. No personal trinkets other than what my dad or Sheri had supplied—a framed photo of the three of us, for example, that Sheri had given me last Christmas. I kept all my keepsakes at my mom's, mostly pinned to my corkboard. Things that meant a lot to me. Memories I shared with Gabe and Spencer.

Usually the sparse, barely personalized nature of this room didn't bother me, but for some reason it felt utterly barren today. For the first time since I was twelve, I wanted my stuff. Something bright and fun and *me* in the room. Maybe I had something in my bag? I yanked my patchwork tote off the plush carpet and dumped its contents unceremoniously on the bed.

Everything tumbled out onto the pristine duvet cover: textbooks, my iPad and laptop, pens and pencils, scientific calculator, a pack of gum, the tube of sparkling pink lip gloss I'd adopted as Trixie, a dozen brightly colored leftover flyers from this morning, a couple of tampons whose wrappers had seen better days, and a candy-apple-red flash drive.

Flash drive? That's right. A gift from Spencer the day after Jesse dumped me. I'd completely forgotten about it in the midst of all the manic pixie mayhem.

I snatched it off the comforter and examined it for clues as to its contents. Nothing scrawled on its flat surface. No labels or numbers other than the gigabyte capacity. What had Spencer put on it?

I reached for my laptop and lifted the clamshell case, sparking the screen to life. I was about to plug the flash drive into my USB port, when my browser window, which was open to my email in-box, refreshed itself and I found myself staring at a message from Toile Jeffries.

Fibonacci's balls.

I dropped the flash drive onto my bed and opened the email with a shaky hand. I was expecting to see an angry rant, accusing me of stealing Jesse from her or something equally as dramatic, but instead, I found myself staring at the cartoon image of a white rabbit.

It wore a cowboy hat with an Old West gun holster slung around its waist. The rabbit had been Photoshopped onto the front steps of Fullerton Hills High School. A hoedown song played as a short animation clip kicked in. The rabbit winked and with a cheeky smirk on his face, planted one three-fingered hand on his hip and outstretched the other, giving an exaggerated thumbs-up. Above him, bright green letters scrolled across the screen as if painted by a brush, spelling out "'Jesse James' Sullivan," and below, "He'll clean up our school!"

Toile's newest campaign strategy was quintessential manic pixie. Adorable cartoon character, fun Photoshopping, even referring to Jesse as a classic Old West outlaw (which made no sense, but whatever) was all in line with her quirk.

Barf.

I mean, it was cute. And as it looped back to the beginning and replayed itself, I actually found myself bopping along to the old-timey music. Which was bad. If it was sticking in my head after just two plays, how many Fullerton Hills students would remember it come election day?

I paused the animation, staring at that smirking bunny. Toile had blind copied me on this email, so it was impossible to know how many people it had gone out to. But factoring in her status as the new kid at school and Jesse's relative lack of friends and contacts, I had to assume, for the moment at least, that the damage was minimal. Still, people might forward the email, spreading it far beyond its initial reach. And that could be a problem.

I hadn't considered using the internet for Gabe's campaign: it felt too conventional. And email seemed like an especially weak avenue. A quick Google search gave me an impressive statistic on the internet usage of the average teen: 92 percent of high school students went online daily, and nearly three-quarters of them used a smartphone to access the internet at any time of day or night. Not only that, but a staggering 71 percent of teens used multiple social networking websites, with Facebook, Instagram, and Snapchat as the overwhelming favorites.

Facebook, which Toile didn't use.

That was my opening.

I grabbed a notebook from my bag and quickly sketched out a plan of attack:

(1) Build up social media networks.
(2) Friend everyone I could find at school.
(3) Carpet bomb sites with an ad campaign teasing our secret candidate.

The first two steps were relatively simple, though time-consuming. I already had Facebook and Instagram accounts, but my list of friends on each was basically limited to Gabe, Spencer, my mom, and Jesse. I'd refused to answer friend requests from anyone at school, ignoring them for years, but that was Beatrice, and this was Trixie. Time to network.

I quickly changed the name on my Facebook profile

from Beatrice Maria Estrella Giovannini to Beatrice "Trixie" Giovannini, and opened my friend request page. Thankfully, Facebook had kept all of them for me, dozens and dozens, which I quickly accepted, scrolling through without even looking at who I was approving. Next, I skimmed through the "People You May Know" section and added anyone who went to Fullerton Hills, or whose multiple friends in common included a majority of my classmates. Finally, I started opening the friends lists of my new connections, perving through and adding all potential Fullerton Hills students.

It took forever, and after doing the same for Instagram and Snapchat, I broke for dinner. While my dad related the not particularly exciting details of his workday, I contemplated the more complicated third step of my plan.

If I created an animated cartoon gopher, I'd be viewed as a copycat. Besides, I didn't want to explicitly reveal who our secret candidate was. Not yet. So I needed something catchy and fun, but still mysterious.

What would be totally original and capture people's attention? I wasn't an artist. Not at all. Nor was I particularly proficient in animation, though I could probably string some images together in iMovie if I needed to. But what?

I needed to play to my strengths. What was I good at?

Math.

Math.

More math.

I sat up straight in my chair, Sheri's meat loaf forgotten. The formula I'd made for Jesse. That was it.

"Bea, are you okay?" Sheri asked, interrupting my dad, who was still rambling full throttle about depositions and mediation agreements.

"Do you still have those paper flowers?" I asked, knowing full well she did. "The ones you used in your scrapbooks."

She nodded. "I think so."

"Can I borrow a few?"

Her face lit up. She was pleased that I'd taken an interest in something she liked or, more probably and also more pathetically, happy that someone needed her for something. "As many as you like. They should be in my supply drawer in the office."

"Is this, uh, for a school project?" my dad asked, attempting to be parental.

"Kind of." I stood up and bussed my plate to the counter. "More like an extracurricular activity."

He arched an eyebrow. "But it won't interfere with your classes or homework, will it?"

Seriously? I'd done just fine at high school without him taking an interest in my studies. "I have a weighted four-point-eight grade point average. I think I'll be fine."

Back in my room armed with a stash of brightly pigmented paper daisies in a variety of color combinations, I got to work. I needed a formula, and the first thing that came to mind was the general theory of curvilinear coordinates.

Which was created by the mathematician Gabriel Lamé.

And while I knew that no one else would ever get the joke (except possibly Michael Torres, although he completely lacked imagination in that regard), it made me smile.

A few quick tweaks (and substantial mathematical liberties) later, I had a working model.

$$\left|\frac{FHHS}{a}\right|^g + \left|\frac{ASB}{b}\right|^m$$

I was pretty sure Lamé had just rolled over in his grave, but the formula didn't really need to make sense—it wasn't like I was actually plotting a superellipse—it just had to be eye-catching. In this case, g and m were thinly veiled references to Gabriel Muñoz, the number one candidate, while Fullerton Hills High School and ASB president were easily recognizable.

This was so going to work.

I grabbed a black marker and wrote the first part in the center of one flower, then grabbed another and added a few more symbols, and so on and so forth until I had twelve different flowers showing the progression, as if someone was writing them out. Then, in order, I snapped a photo of each with my phone. Some creative photo editing and a little color correction to make them pop, and I was ready to load them into iMovie.

An hour later, I had my final product. Matched with the "Mahna Mahna" song from an old Muppets sketch my mom used to play for me when I was a kid, I had twenty seconds of what looked like stop-motion animation, building out the formula, and one final flower that said, "Who's the #1 candidate? Find out tomorrow!"

Ready for upload.

I logged into Facebook and saw that, in addition to all the people whose invitations I had accepted, I had four more, plus a ton of people had accepted my requests.

Who knew my manic pixie Trixie would be such a hit at school? I was practically popular.

Each new contact got a post on their timeline with my animation. Then I posted to Instagram and Snapchat, tagging as many people as I could.

It was almost eleven o'clock when I finally closed my computer.

If that didn't beat Toile at her own game, nothing would.

TWENTY-EIGHT

BY THE NEXT morning, I had the entire student body of Fullerton Hills whipped into a frenzy. The "surprise" candidate was all anyone could talk about, and it was all because of Trixie.

I estimated Trixie's social media outreach at 737 Fullerton Hills students. Almost half the student body. And it made me feel kind of badass.

In less than a week, I'd gone from the nameless Math Girl to someone with a hundred Facebook friends and dozens of Instagram reposts. People knew my name, said "hi" to me in the hallways. They were even copying my mismatched shoes. It was as if I'd been reborn.

And now I was going to use that newfound notoriety to get Gabe elected ASB president.

The plan was simple. During the election assembly, I'd take the microphone and unveil the surprise candidate, ushering onto the stage Gabe, who would then give a charming, utterly adorable speech that would win the hearts and votes of the entire audience and propel him to victory. Seemed like a total no-brainer to me.

To Spencer? Not so much.

"Don't you think you went a little overboard?" he asked as we wove through the hallways on our way to the assembly.

A group of underclassmen I didn't recognize passed us, and one of the guys pointed at me. "We got you, Trixie!"

I smiled, big and shiny, though I had no idea what he was talking about. "Thanks!" Then I turned back to Spencer. "What do you mean?"

Spencer shrugged, shoving his phone into his jeans pocket. "You're trying to get Gabe elected, right? Not Trixie."

I hated the fact that he spoke about Trixie as if she was someone else. "I'm not running for ASB president."

"I know," he said with a tight smile. "That's my point."

"Feeling you, Trix!" someone yelled from down the hall.

"Thank you!" I called. "Are you accusing me of something, Spencer Preuss-Katt?"

"Don't be so dramatic, Bea."

I stopped short. "Trixie."

"*Bea*," he said emphatically. "And I'm not accusing you of anything. I know you're trying to get Gabe elected. But that formula came from you, from Math Girl, not from Gabe. Don't you think people will get confused?"

"I put his initials in the formula!" I threw up my hands. "People would have to be idiots not to get it."

"And what about all these people?" he said, gesturing to a group of girls who had just waved at me from down the corridor. "Why do you think they're screaming your name in the halls?"

I rolled my eyes. "They love Trixie. What can I say? She's a hit."

Spencer sighed. "I just think maybe this whole election thing has gotten out of hand. You wanted to get Jesse back, fine. Whatever. But now you've got Gabe actually excited by the idea of being ASB president. He's already submitted the article detailing his rise from nobody to school president."

"I know," I said. "Isn't it great?"

"Only if it works."

"It'll work." My plans always worked.

"I just think," Spencer said with a weary sigh, "you need to take a look at why you're doing all this. What do you really want?"

My friends' happiness, a strong submission to MIT, rubbing Toile's face in it.

"Is it really about Jesse?" he continued. "Or do you just want to beat Toile?"

Before I could respond, I felt a tap on my arm and turned around to find Michael Torres's glowering face. "We need to talk."

"No, we don't."

He ignored me, shifting his glare to Spencer. "In private."

Spencer arched an eyebrow but didn't say anything, just

pointed at the water fountain on the other side of the hall. "I'll be over there."

Michael Torres waited until he was out of earshot before he dropped his voice. "I just want you to know that when you lose the election tomorrow, it's all because of me."

"Seriously?" I blurted out. This was completely ridiculous.

"Yes."

"For once in your life, Michael Torres, please listen to the words that are coming out of my mouth. I was joking yesterday. I am not running for ASB president."

He laughed. "You expect me to believe that?"

"It's the truth!"

"Sure it is." He smiled knowingly. "So you won't mind that I told every single person I've crossed paths with in the last two days that they shouldn't vote for you because you're a big fake."

I could not for one second imagine anyone at Fullerton Hills taking Michael Torres's advice on anything. In fact, they'd be more likely to do the exact opposite.

I caught my breath. *We got you, Trix! Feeling you, Trix!* Those were cries of support from people I didn't even know. Could Michael Torres's plan have backfired so horrifically that he'd actually convinced people to vote for me?

"Oh no," I said out loud.

"Exactly," Michael Torres said, misinterpreting. "And if you're ever at MIT—visiting, of course—be sure to look me up." Then he turned and scurried down the hall.

"Bea, we're going to be late." Spencer took my arm and guided me toward the back door to the theater. "What was that all about?"

I looked up at him, a cold wave of panic washing over me. "People might think I'm the secret candidate running for president."

"Duh, that's what I've been trying to tell you. Cassilyn mentioned it last night after you left. She thought it was weird that, and I quote, 'that geek said Trixie was running for president,' since Gabe was running too and she thought you were friends."

Michael Torres's unpopularity had counterbalanced Gabe's newfound popularity. This was not good.

"I had no idea what she was talking about," Spencer continued, "but I told her you weren't even running. Thank God your name isn't on the ballot."

"Yeah," I said, forcing a laugh. "Thank God."

We ducked into the stage door for the theater, where I was supposed to meet Gabe before the assembly. No damage had been done yet. Gabe had Cassilyn and her friends on his side, plus we were about to get a microphone and the rapt attention of the entire Fullerton Hills student body.

"It's going to be fine," I said, more to myself than to Spencer.

"If you say so," he muttered.

I stepped around Spencer's tall frame and peered around the backstage curtains, looking for Gabe. I wanted to make sure his speech was spot-on. The wings were filled with potential candidates. Most of them held crumpled-up pages in their hands and were rehearsing their speeches in mumbly voices as they wandered in aimless circles, while a few chatted among themselves, nervous small talk in hushed tones, eyes flitting around to see who was watching.

I was still searching for Gabe when I saw Toile and Jesse emerge from behind one of the tall black curtains at the back of the stage. Toile eased the sleeve of her dress back up to her shoulder as Jesse pawed at her waist. Then he pulled her body into his, wrapping his free arm around her back as he kissed her.

Right there. Backstage at the theater in front of all the candidates, less than twenty-four hours after he'd tried to kiss me in his car.

Rage was an emotion I tried to keep under wraps. I'd seen what it had done to my parents—continued to do to them, in fact—and it was one more of those irrational, unpredictable emotions I wanted nothing to do with. They made you do stupid things, things you regretted.

Things like what I was about to do.

"Kiss me," I said to Spencer.

Beside me, I felt his body go rigid. "What?"

No time. I had to make a statement, needed to show Jesse that I didn't care. Without thinking, I reached up and grabbed Spencer on either side of his face, pulled him down, and kissed him.

It should have felt like kissing my brother, if I'd had a brother. I mean, that's how I'd always imagined kissing

Spencer would be. Well, no, not that I'd *imagined it* in a romantic-fantasy kind of way, but he's a guy and I'm a girl and we'd been hanging out for a couple of years, so it was really only natural at least once in all that time a fleeting thought would cross my mind about his lips meeting mine. And yeah, I'd always thought it would be brief, closed-mouthed, and entirely clinical. Which was why I could do things like hang out with him alone in his studio without it getting awkward or tense.

But as I stood there backstage, pressing my face into his, I felt something else. Something weird and strange and kind of uncomfortable was simmering inside of me, and when Spencer's tongue flicked across my lips and his arm slipped around my back, I shivered.

"What the hell is this?" Gabe said.

Spencer's arm fell away and I pulled back. "Nothing." My voice sounded shaky.

Kurt stood beside him. "That didn't look like nothing."

I felt my skin growing hot as a blush deepened. "I was just trying to . . ." I was about to say *make Jesse jealous* because, you know, it was the truth, but it sounded so painfully pathetic, I stumbled over the words.

"Trying to fish something out of Spencer's larynx?" Gabe asked.

"Jesse and Toile were—"

"What the fuck, Bea?" Spencer's words exploded from his mouth. His face was pale, his lips pressed together until they practically disappeared. I'd never seen him that pissed off before, and it was so startling, I involuntarily took a step away from him. He pushed by me, heading for the door. "Leave me out of your bullshit. It's fucking pathetic."

I should have gone after Spencer, should have stopped him and apologized and . . . Well, shit. What was I supposed to say? *I'm sorry I kissed you. Let's pretend it didn't happen.*

Did I mean either of those things?

The point was probably moot because at that moment, Principal Ramos took the stage and began introducing the candidates. Showtime.

"You're last on the list," Kurt said, holding a crumpled piece of paper in front of Gabe's face. "Right after Jesse. Is your speech ready?"

Gabe patted him on the cheek. "I'm fine, Mom."

Kurt wrinkled his nose at Gabe. "You're going to be *zoopa*," he said, mimicking Gabe's German accent to perfection.

Gabe arched an eyebrow, then they both burst into laughter. I was glad they were so relaxed about the election. I wished I could feel the same.

The speeches proceeded slowly. Most were met with polite applause from the audience, but as we made our way through the vice presidential candidates, you could feel the tenor of the room heighten. By the time the ASB president speeches began, even from backstage I could hear the twittering antsiness of the audience crescendo. Could it have been because of me?

Jesse's speech was pretty good, actually. Surprisingly. Not

that I was hoping he'd stutter and stumble and look generally unpresidential. I mean, it wasn't Jesse I was trying to ruin; it was Toile. But still, I wasn't expecting that he'd take the stage and deliver his speech with such easy confidence.

"In conclusion," he said, folding up the paper in his hand and shoving it back in his pocket, "I just want to thank my amazing girlfriend, Toile Jeffries." My stomach clenched and I felt every muscle in my body tighten with a mix of anger and disgust. "She's the reason I'm here and she makes my life better in every possible way." He turned toward the wings. "I love you."

Toile stood near the edge of the curtain, her face tinged with the glow of the bright stage lights. Her shimmering hair peeked out from the top of her newsboy cap, crowning her head like a halo, and her perfect alabaster skin practically glowed with happiness as Jesse strode across the stage, swept her into his arms, and kissed her.

Once again, I fought the urge to punch someone, only this time, I imagined my fist connecting with Jesse's crotch instead of Toile's face.

"And now," Principal Ramos said, "our final candidate for ASB president . . ." She paused, and even through the haze of Jesse and Toile, I noticed that the entire theater quieted down. "Gabriel Muñoz."

Instead of applause, a subdued murmur simmered in the audience as Principal Ramos waited for Gabe to take the stage.

"Why aren't they applauding?" Kurt asked. "Wasn't this supposed to be the big reveal?"

"What do I do?" Gabe asked.

"Gabriel Muñoz?" Principal Ramos repeated. She turned toward the wings, a plastic smile plastered across her face with eyes like daggers that said, *What the hell are you waiting for?*

I ignored the nagging voice of fear in the back of my head that suggested I'd colossally screwed up this whole campaign, and squeezed Gabe's hand. "I'll fix this." Then I took a deep breath and hurried onto the stage.

The moment the hot lights blinded me, I heard a roar of applause in the audience. It took me several seconds to realize that they were reacting to me, Beatrice Giovannini. They knew who I was.

"About time," Principal Ramos muttered as she shoved the microphone at me, clearly not caring that my name probably wasn't Gabriel Muñoz.

"H-hi," I stuttered, my voice booming through the speaker system.

"Trixie!" someone shouted from the crowd, igniting a smattering of claps.

I smiled. "That's me!" Sorta. Whatever. It felt good to finally have a face at this school. "So I'm guessing that you've all seen the ads, hinting at a supersecret candidate for student body president? Well, I'm here to introduce him!"

"Him?" someone near the front asked.

I ignored the comment. "Your next president—the one you should *all* vote for—is . . ." I gestured to the wings. "Gabriel Muñoz!"

Gabe trotted onto the stage to a round of polite applause, but mostly there was a rumbling of confusion in the audience. Gabe's face looked pained as he took the microphone. "Thanks, Trixie," he said, holding his prepared speech in his hand. I noticed that the paper was trembling. "My name is Gabriel Muñoz, and I want to be your president. Why? That's a good question. I think Fullerton Hills is made of awesome and I want to show the rest of this city that we're the best high school around."

I didn't hear the rest of his speech. The only sound was the pounding of blood in my ears. You could feel the energy in the auditorium dissipate, draining away the longer Gabe spoke. He noticed too, because as the audience got quieter and quieter, Gabe spoke faster and faster, rushing through his speech like a movie on fast-forward.

Finally, the bell. A reprieve.

Principal Ramos took the microphone and reminded everyone that voting would be open until nine o'clock, then barren silence was broken by the rumblings of the entire student body exiting up the aisles.

Maybe it wasn't as bad as I thought it was? After ten speeches, everyone was probably bored. Maybe Gabe still had a chance?

"Vote for Trixie!" someone yelled as students were filing out of the auditorium, followed by a few enthusiastic cheers.

Yep. I'd completely screwed up.

TWENTY-NINE

"I DON'T KNOW what happened," I said when we were all backstage again.

"No big deal," Gabe said, but his body language said otherwise. His shoulders sagged, his über-fey persona forgotten, and he was just my nerdy friend watching his dreams go up in smoke. "I can just rewrite the article, I guess."

"I'm so sorry," I said.

He smiled sadly. "It's not your fault."

"Oh my God!" Kurt cried. "Don't defend her!"

"Her"? Like I'm just some nobody in Gabe's life? "I'm his best friend," I said, "and I was just trying to help."

"Right," Kurt said. "Like you 'helped' him become this flaming queen that all the popular girls fawn over? Like you 'helped' him get excited about this election, then stabbed him in the back?"

Whoa. "Gabe asked me to help him be more popular.

Okay? I didn't put a gun to his head and force him to do anything."

Kurt's face was bright red, a zit about to pop. "No, you just gave him his first taste of the drug, then let it do its thing."

"Hey," Gabe said, laying his hand gently on Kurt's shoulder. "Bea's right: I asked for her help."

Kurt shrugged off Gabe's hand. "And what did it get you, huh? Popularity? But what did it lose you?"

I was officially confused about what was happening, though I got the distinct feeling that we were no longer talking about the election. "Are you guys together?"

"No!" Gabe said quickly.

"Exactly," Kurt said, his voice catching. "Can't let anyone see you with a nerd like me, right?"

Gabe's face paled. "Kurt . . ."

Kurt drew his arm across his face, wiping away a flood of tears. "Leave me alone." Then he disappeared behind the curtain.

How long had that been going on? And why hadn't Gabe shared it with me?

"Why don't you come over after school and I'll see if I can fix this election thing?" I offered.

Gabe didn't look at me. "I can't. I need to . . . I just need some time."

"About Kurt?"

He glanced up at me, and what I saw in his eyes, a mix of confusion and hurt, told me that even though he said he didn't blame me for this election fiasco, deep down, he did. "I need some time away from Trixie."

As soon as I got home from school, I morphed into damage-control mode.

I plastered Gabe's name all over social media. I replaced formula flowers with pictures of Gabe and a speech bubble that said, "Vote for me, Gabriel Muñoz!" and put them everywhere. That would do it. It totally would.

It had to.

Meanwhile, Gabe hadn't responded to my texts. I'd sent a half dozen of them already, and I could picture him in his room, organizing his Warhammer armies, refusing to look at his phone. I hadn't heard from Spencer either, but that was on me. I'd typed him twenty texts, then deleted them without sending. I still had no idea what I was supposed to say to him, and every time I thought about our kiss, a vaguely uncomfortable feeling stirred inside my stomach that I immediately suppressed. Whatever it was, I didn't want to know. It couldn't be good for our friendship.

Maybe I deserved the silent treatment. I'd pushed them pretty far, I realized. I mean, they'd asked me to, but I do have a tendency to go overboard with things. It's just that I want everyone to be happy. And I'd gotten so excited about the Formula, this amazing masterpiece that brought my love of mathematics into my everyday life. The siren song of the MIT scholarship was ever present. I needed Spencer and Gabe to gain popularity because of my calculations. I needed

Trixie to be a success, to win back my ex-boyfriend in a sweeping display of mind over matter. But everything had gotten muddled.

Spencer was right. I needed to ask myself what I really wanted.

And on the eve of the election, that answer was simple: I wanted Gabe to win. Not for the Formula, not for his article, but because he really wanted to be president.

I reloaded Instagram and posted another round of Gabe photos.

It had to work.

I was in homeroom a full ten minutes before the bell Friday morning, hands clasped in front of me so tightly my fingers had turned white. The seconds ticked by slowly, tortuously. I felt like an inmate on death row, waiting for a reprieve before the midnight deadline. Had I done enough? Had I reached enough people to undo the damage from my epic fuckup?

Deep down, I knew the answer was "no," but hey, a girl could dream, right?

Spencer arrived a few minutes early, his head bowed as he entered the classroom. I half expected him to take a seat on the opposite side of the room, considering what had gone down between us yesterday, and I was pretty certain I detected a momentary pause as he stood in the doorway, as if debating where he should sit. But to my surprise and relief, he ambled around the back of the room and dropped into the seat behind me, as usual.

"Hey," I said softly, trying to sound contrite. I didn't want to fight with Spencer, though it seemed like all we'd been doing lately. But if he noticed the olive branch I was attempting to extend, he didn't act like it.

"Hey." He wouldn't look at me, and the bite in his voice conveyed a clear subtext: *I haven't forgiven you.*

My stomach clenched. Okay, I probably deserved that too.

To compound matters, Toile and Jesse arrived just seconds before the bell, hand in hand. She was laughing, as usual, a burgundy felt fedora perched jauntily on her head, and Jesse beamed at her as if literally the meaning of his life emanated from her lips.

If he won the election, that would be it. Toile would have Jesse forever. It would be my own fault. I was too arrogant, too enamored of the glamour of being Trixie, of feeling important for once in my high school life, as opposed to just being the nameless Math Girl lurking on the fringe of society. I'd gone too far, trying to use the Formula for personal gain. Helping my friends was one thing. Selfishly helping myself? Yeah, the law of averages was not in my favor. And now I was dealing with the consequences.

The bell rang, and everyone fell instantly silent in anticipation. Announcements. The Pledge of Allegiance. The room seemed to crackle with excitement as Principal Ramos took the microphone and began reading off the election results, beginning with vice president. I held my breath.

"And for ASB president . . ." She paused, and I heard a

rustling of papers. Fibonacci's balls, get on with it already! "Well, that's new," she said, obviously surprised. "It appears we have a dead tie in this race. Have we done a recount already?"

From the background, a muffled voice said, "Twice."

"Huh," Principal Ramos said. More rustling. "But neither of these people were official candidates."

Shit.

"Write-ins?" she said. "They can do that?" Whomever she was talking to must have giving her the affirmative. "Okay, then. It looks as if we're going to have a runoff election for the first time in Fullerton Hills history. The two candidates who have tied with the most votes via write-in are . . .

"Toile Jeffries and Trixie Giovannini."

THIRTY

IN MY SEVENTEEN years on this planet I had never been as thankful for anything as I was that Gabe wasn't in my homeroom when the election results were announced. I'm not sure I could have looked him in the eyes.

Toile wasn't so lucky.

"I didn't win?" Jesse asked, turning around in his chair to face her.

She shook her head.

Jesse wasn't getting it. "But you weren't running, were you?"

All Toile could do was to stare at him, dumbstruck. "I don't know what happened."

You can say that again.

I mean, write-in candidates? Seriously? In the last one hundred years of US history, only seven congressional races have been won by write-ins, establishing the statistical probability of a successful write-in campaign for the United States

House of Representatives at approximately 0.03 percent, and yet here at Fullerton Hills High School, the student body overwhelmingly voted for not one but two write-in candidates for ASB president.

What the hell was wrong with our school?

"Will the runoff candidates please report to the school office?" Principal Ramos continued. Then she shifted away from the mic. "How the heck are we supposed to do this?"

Toile slowly rose to her feet, her burgundy felt fedora askew, and walked out of the classroom in a daze. I followed, no less horrified but significantly less confused about how I'd gotten there. Michael Torres's plan to sabotage me had backfired. But what about Toile? There was a piece of me that bristled at the idea that we'd gotten the same number of write-in votes. Shouldn't I have won?

One thing I knew for sure: I didn't want to be ASB president.

It was time to step aside.

Principal Ramos was on the phone when we arrived, so Mrs. McKee, the school secretary, directed us to a couple of chairs outside her door. Toile sat down primly, with her back erect, and stared straight ahead.

"So this is weird," I said, breaking the ice. I wondered if Toile felt the same way I did about the prospect of getting elected. Maybe we could both drop out?

"Yes," she said without looking at me.

"I really don't want to be president," I said, forcing a

laugh. "And I was thinking that maybe—"

"You should drop out of the race?" she suggested, glancing at me sidelong.

"Me?" More like "we."

Instead of answering, she turned to face me. Her features were unreadable, blank and benign, the way my mom looked at me when she asked a question she already knew the answer to. But her eyes were cold and, just like in the hallway yesterday, totally un-Toile-like. "You don't want the job. So why not?"

She had me there. "Maybe we should both drop out."

Her upper lip flattened, her eyes pinched as she stared down at me with a seemingly limitless supply of contempt. It wasn't the first time I'd seen a crack in her cheerful facade, but it was the first time I'd seen it up close and personal. And as she glared at me, I had the funny feeling that I was seeing something real, something that had been buried deep beneath that bubbly layer of whimsy.

"You just don't want me to win. You're jealous." Then she went for the jugular. "It's not my fault people at this school like me better."

My temper ignited, and all I saw was red. Ten seconds ago I was ready to drop out of the race, and now I would have sold my soul to win it.

I plastered my best manic pixie smile on my face and met her glare. "Let's see if they still feel that way after the runoff."

Her nostrils flared, and she sucked in a sharp breath. I knew that look: anger. Toile, our resident happy-go-lucky sunshine-and-rainbows girl, looked as if she wanted to claw my eyes out.

Was this the real Toile Jeffries?

Principal Ramos opened her office door, breaking our standoff. "Toile and Trixie?" She sounded about as welcoming as a prison warden.

"I'm Toile," she said, rocketing to her feet. Her voice was perky and high, a complete one-eighty from the murderous glare that had been directed at me.

Principal Ramos gave her the once-over then turned to me. "You must be Trixie. I assume that's short for Beatrice? Since we don't actually have a Trixie Giovannini registered at this school."

"That's me!" I repeated my by-now-well-rehearsed line. "It's a family nick—"

"Don't care," Principal Ramos said, cutting me off. "I don't know what you two pulled, but a runoff based on a write-in campaign is, in my opinion, a disgraceful miscarriage of democracy."

I cocked my head to the side. "Isn't it actually the ultimate expression of democracy?"

She ignored me. "So we'll do a runoff at the waste of school budget and my time." She raised an eyebrow. "Unless one of you would like to graciously step aside?"

"Nope," I said, smiling at Toile. "How about you?"

"Jell-O monkeys!" she squealed, and wiggled her fingers in front of her mouth.

"Is something wrong with you, Ms. Jeffries?" Principal Ramos asked.

You have no idea.

Toile shook her head. "Yes. I mean, no." She bit her lower lip. "I just . . . I feel like I'm in a rut, you know? Like I'm not living each day to its full and unique potential, and whenever I feel that way, I do something that I've never done before, like shout, 'Jell-O monkeys,' in the principal's office, and then I can feel unique again even if it's only for a second."

My body stiffened. *And then I can feel unique again even if it's only for a second.* Where had I heard that before?

Principal Ramos sighed. "My time is valuable, Ms. Jeffries. Are you dropping out of the race or not?"

"Oh," Toile said with a small smile. "No. I'm not."

"Of course not," Principal Ramos muttered. "Why would anyone want to make things easy on me?" The bell for first period rang, and Principal Ramos spoke quickly. "Runoff will be Thursday. Posters and banners—heck, all campaign materials—are prohibited." She was clearly making this up as she went along. "I'm not dealing with the cleanup a second time. This will be a one hundred percent virtual election. Understood?"

"Yes, ma'am," Toile said.

"Good. Now get to class. I'm not writing late passes for either of you."

Toile grabbed her bag and dashed out of the office before I'd even gotten out of my chair. I'd barely heard Principal Ramos's instructions. My brain was racing to access my manic pixie database.

I wandered into the bustling halls. That line. I'd heard it recently. I was positive.

I fished my phone out of my bag and typed in a few words from Toile's weird monologue in Principal Ramos's office. A video result popped up immediately: Natalie Portman in *Garden State*.

I stood outside AP English and watched the short clip, completely oblivious to the press of bodies around me. About thirty seconds in, Natalie Portman uttered the line I remembered, and which Toile had practically quoted verbatim.

The slip in character. The anger. The combative response when I suggested we both drop out of the race. A manic pixie dream girl line lifted from one of the most famous manic pixie dream girl movies.

Toile's manic pixie act was just as phony as mine.

She was following a formula.

THIRTY-ONE

GABE WAS ALONE at our lunch table when I hurried into the cafeteria; Spencer sat with Cassilyn at the adjacent table. He had his sketch pad, and his pencil was flashing around the page while Cassilyn leaned in, watching his progress with rapt attention. And she wasn't the only one. Esmeralda was watching Spencer from beneath her fluttering lashes, and across the table, Milo and Thad glared at him. Only unlike the adoration on Cassilyn's face and the envy in Esmeralda's dark eyes, Milo and Thad just looked pissed off.

"Hey!" I said softly, sliding onto the bench next to Gabe. "You aren't going to believe what happened in Ramos's office. Toile dropped her act. Right in front of me. Can you believe it? And then she quoted a line from *Garden State* as if she were just making the thought up out of thin air. Gabe, she's totally faking this manic-pixie-dream-girl crap. Isn't that awesome?" I held up my hand for a high five.

Instead of reciprocating, Gabe shifted his body away,

boxing me out with his shoulders.

"Come on," I said, realizing I was—literally—getting the cold shoulder. "The election wasn't my fault."

Gabe opened a yogurt container and picked up a spork, but didn't say a word.

"I thought it would work," I continued, talking to the back of his head. "I thought everyone would realize I was campaigning for you."

Spencer rounded the table and sat down next to Gabe. "You would have made an amazing ASB president." His eyes never even flitted in my direction.

Gabe smiled at him. "Thanks."

"I said I was sorry!" I threw up my hands. "I don't even want the job."

"But your article submission for the *Register* is awesome," Spencer said. "Even if you have to change the ending."

"You read it?" I asked Spencer, then turned to Gabe. "Can I—"

"Thanks," Gabe said to Spencer. "Nice to know I have at least one good friend."

"Fuck." I planted my forehead against the lunch table. So this was what it felt like to be a ghost haunting your old neighborhood, listening to people talk about you like you weren't even there.

"Are you going to the dance with Cassilyn next Friday?" Gabe asked, nodding at the table behind us. "Or do you want to meet up at the diner beforehand?"

The diner. Our traditional pre-dance meal. We'd load

up on junk food, then all roll into the dance together. Safety in numbers.

"Haven't decided yet," Spencer said.

"Well," he said, arching an eyebrow. "We'll only need a table for two. Since *someone* won't be with us."

I sucked on my bottom lip, trying to stave off the tears. I wasn't a crier. But to sit there and be ignored by my friends, and to listen while they cold-heartedly cut me out of their lives, even if I deserved it . . . I couldn't take it. I stood up, shoved my lunch bag back into my patchwork tote, and fled the cafeteria.

It was a warm and sunny day per usual, almost too warm, but thankfully I found an unoccupied, semishady spot halfway down the stairs to the parking lot where I could wait out the lunch period.

Things would blow over. I knew they would. Everyone was raw from yesterday's assembly and the unexpected election results. Gabe's pride was wounded, and Spencer . . . well, that was something else entirely.

Honestly? Their reactions were more than a little dramatic. Flat-out ignoring me was childish, a punishment reserved for a six-year-old pariah on the playground, not one of their closest friends. They should have just told me to my face that they were angry. Then we could have discussed it like rational, civilized pre-adults. I could have explained the innocence of my actions and the victim-of-circumstances nature of the entire ordeal.

Still, as much as I could justify my actions as being above-board and having only everyone's best interests at heart, there was a nagging little voice in my head that said otherwise. It reminded me that I had enjoyed the name recognition, of feeling like I was actually somebody at this school instead of the nameless Math Girl. I'd gotten a thrill out of that assembly, a shot of adrenaline and power as I'd taken the microphone and had the entire student body cheer for me. I'm not exactly an introvert, but I'm not a performer either. But at that moment, I had felt like the center of attention at a school that had barely known I existed two weeks ago, and I had to admit I loved every second of it.

So maybe I had something to apologize for after all?

I pulled a spiral notebook and mechanical pencil from my bag, took a deep breath, and leaned against the banister. I needed to make amends, show my friends how much I cared about them.

I needed a new formula.

Thε Formula 3.0™:

$$\int_{t}^{m} F(x) \sum_{n=x}^{3} V^{n} = \varnothing$$

If F is a continuous rεal-valuεd function dεfinεd on a closεd intεrval [t, f] bεtwεεn Thursday and Monday, V is thε void crεatεd by F, thεn thε εmpty sεt, i.ε., "Εtεrnal happinεss," is thε summation of grand gεsturε x appliεd ovεr thrεε intεgεrs.

Or:

(1) Find thε void in my friεndships.
(2) Idεntify thε fix.
(3) Find a way to show thεm I'm sorry.

THiRTY-TWO

I SAT BACK and reviewed my calculations. Honestly? It might have been the best formula yet. Elegant and simple, yet detailed and specific. I mean, sure, I could have just apologized, but I'd said I was sorry in the cafeteria and they hadn't listened. This formula would help me target the precise issues they had with me and come up with a fix.

I was doodling on the page, my mind focused on how to make amends to my friends, when a shadow blocked out the fuzzy rays of sunshine penetrating the foliage overhead.

"Can we talk?"

I craned my head around and found Michael Torres two steps above me.

I was surprised to find him (a) not glaring at me, (b) not insulting me, and (c) not sneaking around spying on me. Plus, his entire demeanor had changed. For starters, he was smiling—a real smile, not an evil mastermind's leering grin—and instead of hands on his hips or arms folded across his chest, his hands were tucked casually into the pockets of his chinos, the epitome of a friendly classmate.

"What about?" I said, immediately on my guard.

Michael Torres took my response as an invitation and squatted on the step next to me. "Look, I give up," he began. "You win."

"What are you talking about?"

He shrugged sheepishly. "I tried to prevent you from getting elected, but you beat me. I miscalculated how popular you've become."

Why was he admitting this to me?

"I think we both know what this is about," he continued, eyebrows raised. Then he paused as if waiting for me to fill in the blanks.

"Our mutual dislike for one another?" I suggested. "The fact that you're a pompous jerk? Your inability to accept that I'm ranked higher in our class than you are?"

He clenched his jaw and I could see him fighting to remain calm. "No," he said through gritted teeth. "I meant the MIT scholarship."

Ah, so he was finally admitting it. Michael Torres had invented an entire drama in his head, one in which I was running for ASB president in order to thwart his own efforts to win the scholarship by infiltrating the school paper. But he wasn't going to believe me if I told him the truth, so I decided not to bother.

"I joined the *Herald* to test my theory on the mathematical dissemination of information via the press, and you reinvented yourself in order to be popular enough to get elected to the student government. I'm sure you're working on a formula and backing it up with research, same as me."

Michael Torres understood only part of what was going on, and while I had no plan to enlighten him, I couldn't help but laugh. At the moment, the MIT scholarship was the least of my worries.

"What's so funny?" he demanded, his forced affability beginning to crumble.

"Nothing," I said, suppressing a giggle. "Sorry."

"I'm trying to be nice," he said. "I thought maybe we could help each other out."

It would be a cold day in hell before I'd accept help from Michael Torres.

"I'm willing to collaborate with you," he continued. "Share my research and submit for the scholarship together."

I snorted. "Seriously?"

He missed my sarcasm. "Yes. You just have to drop out of the runoff election."

Alarm bells went off in my mind, and all I could hear was the sound of the lobster-looking guy in that *Star Wars* meme yelling, "It's a trap!"

I was about to point out that his motivations made absolutely no logical sense, when I noticed that Michael Torres wasn't looking at me anymore. Instead, his attention was focused on a grassy tier of the hillside leading down to the parking lot, where two figures sat eating their lunches. I recognized the navy beanie and burgundy fedora right away.

Toile and Jesse.

Why was Michael Torres so interested in them?

"Hey!" I said, snapping my fingers in front of his face. "Why do you want me to drop out?"

"I . . . I just . . . ," he stammered. Then he cleared his throat and turned back to me. "You should leave the school government to someone who'll do a good job."

So that was it. "Toile?"

"Yeah."

"Toile would not make a better president than me."

Michael Torres laughed as his eyes trailed back down the stairs. "Um, yeah, she would. She's fun and she's nice to everyone. That's exactly what this school needs."

Unbelievable. Toile was just as big a fake as Trixie, and yet half the school had bought into her bullshit. She'd charmed Cassilyn and her friends, weaseled her way onto the A-list, and even had Michael Torres eating out of her hand. But it was all make-believe, and it was about time this school knew it.

"Toile doesn't care about this school," I said, shooting to my feet. "She only cares about herself."

Michael Torres popped up beside me, his face instantly red. "That's not true."

"Yeah, it is. She's a fake. I've seen the real Toile Jeffries, and trust me, she ain't sunshine and rainbows."

"You're just bitter," Michael Torres said, spit flying from his mouth. "Because she stole your boyfriend. You don't care about the election. You just want to beat Toile."

I winced. First Spencer, then Michael Torres. They'd both accused me of wanting to get back at Toile for stealing my boyfriend. Were they the only ones who believed it? Were other people thinking the same thing?

"See?" Michael Torres said, taking my silence for agreement. "You can't even deny it."

I pushed my finger into his chest. "You know what, Michael Torres? You can take that offer and shove it up your ass."

"I was trying to help you," he said, nostrils flared.

He was so full of shit. "Really?" I countered. "Like when you helped Milo and Thad find Gabe in the cafeteria? Did you think he might be intimidated into dropping out of the paper so you could take over?"

His eyes faltered, proving that I'd hit the nail on the head. "No, I . . ."

"You've been nothing but a dick to me since the first day of school," I continued, backing him down the stairs. "And going after my friend so you could have a chance at that scholarship is truly pathetic. Not only am I not dropping out of the race, but I'm going to win. Not just the election, but the scholarship too."

"Fine," he said, hiking his backpack up on his shoulders. "But just so you know, this is war."

Then he turned and marched back up the stairs toward campus.

THIRTY-THREE

IT WAS A long, lonely three-day weekend.

As much as I hated to admit it, Michael Torres was right. Sort of. Somewhere along the way, my goal of getting Jesse back had shifted to a competition with Toile. Things had gotten out of hand, and I'd ended up hurting the people I cared about the most: Spencer and Gabe.

Thankfully, I had a formula for that.

There were two things I could do to make amends to my friends. First up: I needed to talk to Kurt.

I was at Hidey Hole Comics at the crack of eleven on Sunday, when they opened. My mom had driven me over after Mass, but thankfully waited in the Prius while I walked up to the front door. I was pretty sure she was texting with Benjamin Feldberger, but at least that kept her occupied.

At exactly 11:02, a familiar figure approached the glass door from the inside of the store and unlocked it. Kurt pushed open the door to admit the lone customer, but didn't realize it was me until I stepped inside.

"Hi, Kurt."

He stared at me, blinking slowly, as if I could have been a hallucination. "Gabe doesn't work today."

"I know."

He continued to hold the door open. "Then why are you here?"

I had to give him points for consistency. He definitely disliked me. "I wanted to talk to you."

"What about?"

"Gabe." Duh.

"Oh." Kurt let the door swing closed and turned to a tiered comics display in the window, busying himself with straightening each pile. I appreciated his attention to detail despite the fact that he'd opened two minutes late.

"Gabe really likes you," I said, getting straight to the point. "And I know you like him."

"Really?" Kurt said without looking at me. "Did your formula tell you that?"

Ugh. "No," I said, smiling. "My eyes."

"It doesn't matter." Then he sighed, slow and deep. Which told me it did matter. Very much.

I just needed to be honest with him. Maybe he'd see that we both had Gabe's best interests at heart. "I know how you feel about me, and about Gabe's new look."

He paused and glanced at me, eyebrow arched. "Do you?"

I snorted. "Yeah, you hate us both. But you know as well

as I do that how he acts at school is just that. An act."

"Exactly." Kurt stepped away from the display case and stared down at me. "It's an act and it's totally ridiculous. It sets LGBTQ gains back thirty years and makes me feel ashamed every time I don't speak up about it."

"I didn't even think of that." I felt awful. I'd never meant to insult homosexuality or make anyone feel uncomfortable. Gabe was my best friend, and I loved him and accepted him no matter what. I was just trying to protect him. "You weren't here our freshman year to see Gabe get his ass kicked at school once a week. It was brutal. And that first day of school when you saved us in the cafeteria? That was going to be the beginning of Gabe's worst year of bullying. I had to save him from that. And now, for the first time since we started high school, the jocks are leaving Gabe alone."

Kurt didn't respond. He may not have agreed with the Formula, but he couldn't deny that it had protected Gabe.

"I know he can be a little bit much," I continued. "With his *zoopa*s and his need to be in the spotlight."

"That formula released the crazed attention whore that was hiding inside of him," Kurt said. "I don't like how New Gabe is starting to replace Old Gabe. It's like he's not the same person anymore."

"Of course he is."

Kurt arched a brow. "Are you blind?"

"Look, maybe you could just roll with the New Gabe for now?" I suggested. "There are only eight more months of school. I know that seems like forever, but in the great scheme of things, it's not that long at all. And after that, there will be no more Cassilyns and Esmeraldas to impress, and no more Milos and Thads to avoid."

Kurt laughed dryly. "There will always be Milos and Thads."

I sighed and turned toward the door. He was probably right, but a part of me was hopeful that once we were all out of the clique-controlled cesspool of Fullerton Hills, things would be different. "I just wanted to clear the air. I hope you and Gabe can work it out."

"Me too."

Maybe Kurt and Gabe's problems were more than I could fix, but at least I'd tried.

My mom turned off her phone screen the moment I got into the car. "Is everything okay, Beatrice?"

"Yeah."

"Mmhm."

She booted up the hybrid engine and we drove in silence. I could see her glancing over at me every few minutes and I knew she wanted to say something. Probably itching to relate all the details from her most recent date with Benjamin Feldberger, and as much as I loved my mom, I just couldn't handle an intensive conversation about her love life today. Maybe if I just stared out the window she'd leave me alone.

"How is Spencer?" she asked, catching me off guard.

Instantly, I could feel Spencer's lips pressed against mine, his arm pulling my body close. I recalled every detail of that moment: the backstage murmurs, the glare from the stage lights, the fluttering in my stomach, the spicy-sweet scent of Spencer's cologne. I could feel my heart racing, and the heat rose to my face as if it were all happening again, right there in my mom's car. And I realized with a sinking sensation that I couldn't recall my first kiss with Jesse in the same amount of overpowering detail.

"Beatrice?"

"I . . ." I swallowed, my mouth suddenly dry. "He's fine." I guess.

"I haven't seen him around lately." She cast another side-long glance in my direction. "And I thought maybe things weren't okay between you two."

"He's been busy," I said. With Cassilyn.

"Ah."

More silence.

"And what about your plan to get Jesse back?" she asked. "How is that going?"

"It's . . . fine."

"Fine," she repeated. "Spencer is fine. Jesse is fine. You're fine." She stopped at a traffic light and turned to face me. "Only I am your mother, so I know that everything is *not* fine."

There was no point in denying it. Momtuition had won again.

"You're right," I said. "Nothing is fine. Spencer's not speaking to me and Jesse can't decide who he wants to date." *Can't or won't?*

"I see." She smiled at me. "I think you cannot change what Jesse wants, no matter how hard you try. He has to figure that out for himself."

I doubted very much if Jesse could figure anything out for himself at this point.

"But Spencer, well, I'm sure you can find a way to smooth things over. He cares about you very much, after all."

Part two of the Formula 3.0: I'd drop out of the runoff. It would show my friends that I cared more about them than about beating Toile or even getting Jesse back. And at that moment, I desperately needed Spencer to know that.

I pulled my phone out of my bag and quickly typed a text:

Dropping out of the runoff. Beating Toile isn't worth it.

And unlike the twenty other texts I'd composed to Spencer over the last few days, I actually sent this one.

Not that it mattered. By the end of the holiday weekend, he still hadn't responded.

THiRTY-FOuR

AFTER SPENCER HAD ignored my text, I had steeled myself for school days full of lonely lunches and general ostracism, so I was surprised when I found my friends hurrying toward my mom's car when she dropped me off Tuesday morning. Gabe's face was ashen, Spencer's jaw was clenched, and I knew right away that something was wrong.

"What happened?" I asked as soon as I closed the passenger door behind me. No need for Flordeliza to get involved.

"Bea," Gabe said, placing his hand on my arm. "Is there any way you could go home sick?"

This didn't sound good.

"*Anak*," my mom called, rolling down the window. "Is everything okay?"

Momtuition. It's real. "Fine, Mom," I said, only half turning back. "I'll see you tonight." I waited until her Prius pulled away before asking again. "Seriously, what's going on?"

Gabe sighed. "It's the election."

Oh, good. An opening. "Gabe, about that. I've decided to drop out. Beating Toile isn't worth our friendship. So I'm just going to let her have it."

I smiled, hoping he and Spencer would realize I was serious and things could go back to normal between us, but instead, they exchanged a worried glance.

"I think Toile already let *you* have it," Gabe said.

"What?"

"She put up some flyers."

"Toile *and* Jesse," Spencer said, emphasizing the conjunction. "She had help."

I was confused. "But Ramos said this was supposed to be a virtual election. No campaign materials."

"It's worse than that." Gabe swallowed. "They're . . ." His voice trailed off, and he looked to Spencer for help.

"They're attack ads," Spencer explained.

I froze, a chill running down my spine. "What do they say?"

Carefully, Spencer removed a flyer from his messenger bag and handed it to me. I recognized the graphics immediately: brightly colored daisies, just like the animation I'd done for Gabe's campaign. Only instead of formulas written in their centers, these flowers had photos. The first was my sophomore yearbook photo—pre-Trixie, of course, and not particularly flattering. I'd been up late the night before, absorbed in a new book on statistics and their application with the behavioral sciences, and had slept through my alarm.

With no time for contacts or a shower, I'd thrown on my glasses and pulled my hair up into a bun at the top of my head, completely forgetting it was school picture day. The result was cringe-worthy.

The second flower held a current snapshot of Jesse, and the third had Toile. There was a minus sign between my photo and Jesse's, a plus sign between his and Toile's, and then an equal sign led to the fourth and final photo: Toile and Jesse kissing.

Below, a single line of text: "Jesse chose Toile over Math Girl, and so should you."

My hands shook as I stared at the page. Campaigns were campaigns, and of course they could get serious. But this was hitting below the belt, a sucker punch to my gut, and I couldn't believe that Toile would sink this low.

"How many?" I asked, my voice raspy.

"A . . . a lot," Gabe stammered.

"They're everywhere," Spencer added. "All over school."

Spencer was right. Toile couldn't have done this on her own.

Jesse.

I felt a sharp pang of sadness as I realized someone I had cared about had intentionally hurt me, but that emotion was replaced almost immediately by red-hot rage. I crinkled up the flyer, scrunching it into a ball in my hand, then I threw it aside and practically ran up the steps to the main entrance. I needed to find Toile and Jesse.

Spencer had been right: there were flyers everywhere.

Like every two feet down the hallways, on the front and back of every door, up and down the staircase. Some had been removed, and I could see people huddled around them, whispering in hushed tones as I passed. I didn't care. I could sense Gabe and Spencer following behind, and though I was relatively sure they were calling out my name, I couldn't hear anything other than the pounding of blood in my ears.

I sprinted upstairs, pushing through packs of students as I went, aiming for Jesse's locker. I saw the white sailor's hat on Toile's head even before I spotted my ex-boyfriend at her side, his hand resting possessively on the small of her back.

"You bitch!" I roared. Around us, the halls fell silent.

The color drained out of Toile's face as I stormed down the hallway.

"Bea!" Spencer cried. I felt his hand on my arm, but I shook him free. "Bea, wait!"

"How dare you?" I got right up in her face, backing her against the wall of lockers. "This is dirty, even for you. Couldn't beat me fair and square so you had to drag Jesse into it?"

"I . . . ," she stammered. "I didn't do it . . ."

"You're full of shit, Toile. I know this whole manic-pixie crap is an act."

Her eyes darted back and forth. "What?"

"And I'm going to expose you. Understand? I'm taking you down."

"Break it up!" a voice boomed. Mr. Poston pushed his way through the gathered crowd. "What's going on here?"

"Nothing, sir," Jesse said, taking Toile's hand in his.

"Sure." Mr. Poston spotted Gabe. "Muñoz, you want to tell me what's going on?"

But I wasn't going to force Gabe to cover up for me. "It's my fault," I said, stepping forward. "I was angry about those flyers."

Mr. Poston looked from me to one of the posters and then to Toile. He pointed at both of us. "You two come with me."

Principal Ramos stood behind her desk and pulled at the lapel of her vesty pantsuit. "Do you want to explain to me again what the problem is?"

I pointed at Toile. "She completely ignored your rule about no campaign materials."

"I didn't do it," Toile lied.

I snorted. "Plus this flyer is in violation of rule number two of the Fullerton Joint Union High School District campaign bylaws: 'Posters must not contain any of the following—references to sex, drugs, or alcohol, or personal attacks on other candidates.'"

Principal Ramos raised her eyebrows. "And how does this attack another candidate?"

"She's dating my ex-boyfriend," I said, feeling more disgust than anger. "That's what the flyer references."

"But I swear," Toile began, "I didn't . . ."

Principal Ramos held up her hand for silence. Toile froze midthought, then Principal Ramos whisked the piece of paper off her desk, holding it between her thumb and fore-finger, and let it flutter into the wastebasket. "Toile, you are responsible for removing all of these by five o'clock today. Now, unless there's something else, I think we're—"

"You're not going to punish her? How is that fair?"

Principal Ramos's stare was icy cold. "Isn't that the ultimate expression of democracy?" she said, throwing my words back into my face.

Ugh. Did *everyone* like Toile better?

"The election will continue as scheduled on Thursday. Now get to class."

Toile scurried out of the office and down the hall with unexpected speed. Not that I blamed her. If she wanted to play dirty and Principal Ramos wasn't going to lay down the law, then Toile wanted to stay as far away from me as was humanly possible.

An hour ago I was going to drop out of the election and let Toile have the ASB president job, but now? No freaking way.

Things were about to get ugly.

"Dah-ling!" Gabe's sunny tenor rang out over the blanket of white noise in the cafeteria. "I see you haven't been expelled yet. Too bad. I hear prison is hot."

Spencer followed behind him. "Don't be ridiculous. Bea would look horrible in orange."

Gabe arched an eyebrow playfully. "Says you." He slid his tray onto the table, then threw his arms around my neck from behind and hugged me so fiercely I choked. "I'm sorry," he whispered. "For what we did at lunch on Friday."

Despite the depths of social humiliation to which I'd been subjected, I smiled. I'd go through it all again if it meant Gabe and Spencer forgave me. "It's okay," I said. "I deserved it. And thanks, you guys, for looking out for me."

Gabe squeezed my shoulders. "You'd do the same for us."

"I just can't believe Toile did that," Spencer said.

Gabe motioned for us to lean in. "She swore to Cassilyn that she didn't."

I rolled my eyes. "She's full of shit."

"What did Ramos say?" Gabe asked.

I shrugged. "She refused to do anything. Toile has to take down the flyers today. That's all."

Gabe gaped. "That's so fucked-up."

"Right? I mean, I didn't even want to win this election."

"Didn't?" Spencer asked. "Or don't?"

"I *don't* even want to win this election," I said, correcting myself. *I just want to get even with Toile.*

"So what are you going to do now?" Gabe asked.

I was about to tell him that I was going to fight fire with fire, to go after Toile with everything I had and make her wish she'd never set foot at Fullerton Hills, when Spencer answered for me.

"She's not going to do anything."

Gabe tilted his head to the side. "She's not?"

I'm not?

"She said it herself," Spencer continued. "She's dropping

out of the race. If Toile wants it so badly she's willing to rub victory in her boyfriend's face, let her."

I bit my lower lip. Spencer was right, as much as I hated to admit it. I didn't want to be president, and no matter how desperately I wanted to beat Toile, it wasn't worth risking my friendships. Doing nothing was the best option.

"Exactly," I said. "She can have it."

Gabe slipped his arm around my waist and gave me a quick hug. See? Letting Toile win was worth it. Even if losing went against every fiber of my being.

THIRTY-FIVE

WE ALL HUNG out at Spencer's after school, just like old times. And by "old times," I mean last week. Yet it was amazing how fast life could change.

Between Toile and the election (and Jesse, and Kurt, and Cassilyn, and Michael Torres, and my parents, and the formulas) our friendships had been strained. I realized, of course, that most of it was my fault, even though I'd just had everyone's best interests at heart.

But hanging out in Spencer's studio again was amazing. So despite what had happened at school, I was feeling pretty good about myself when I arrived back at the town house in time for dinner.

A feeling that lasted all of 3.5 seconds, the time it took to open and close the front door.

"Mom, I'm . . ." I froze in my mismatched shoes.

My mom was in the kitchen, perched on the edge of the counter. Her legs were crossed, skirt hiked so far up her thighs I felt the need to avert my eyes, and she balanced a three-quarters-empty wineglass in one hand while the other grazed up and down the micro-check business shirt of the man leaning into her. He was on the short side, probably not much taller than my mom, and slight of build, with a thin spot in his salt-and-pepper hair just at the back of his head. His hands gripped my mom's waist tightly and his lips pressed almost as tightly against hers as the two of them made out like middle schoolers in a game of Seven Minutes in Heaven—a sloppy, tongue-happy display that was equal parts fascinating and gross.

"Mom!" I repeated loudly. "I'm home!"

Benjamin Feldberger, Esquire—which is who I assumed our visitor was—broke away from my mom and spun toward me, wiping her lipstick off his face with the back of his hand. Meanwhile, my mother didn't even slide off the counter or put down her wineglass. Instead, she bounced her top leg back and forth like a gangster's moll in a Prohibition-era movie, swirling her bathtub moonshine in her glass and looking utterly self-satisfied.

"Beatrice," she cooed, smiling from ear to ear. "You're home."

"Yeah, I just said so. Twice." I hitched my tote bag up on my shoulder and headed for the stairs. "I'll just eat in my room tonight."

My mom clicked her tongue in disapproval. "That's no way to treat our guest. I'd like you to meet Mr. Benjamin Feldberger," she said, relishing every syllable. "I've told him so much about you."

Fibonacci's balls. I plopped my bag down at the foot of the stairs, plastered my best happy-daughter smile on my face, and turned to meet him. I wasn't even sure why I bothered. This guy, like all the others, would be running for the hills when he realized that my mom expected to see a ring on her finger before the end of the year, at which point he'd be replaced with a newer model. "Nice to meet you."

Benjamin Feldberger, Esquire, was nervous. I could tell straightaway. He didn't know whether he should look me in the eyes (or look at me at all, for that matter) and so instead, he focused on a spot about a foot to my left when he stuck out his hand for a shake, as if we were business associates at a mixer. "Pleased to meet you."

He was about my dad's age, but without Andrew Giovannini's imposing presence and cocky swagger, and I guessed that he was more of a behind-the-scenes legal mind than a rock-star litigator like my dad. He wasn't much to look at either—thin lips, watery eyes, rosacea on his cheeks and forehead, and his wispy, thin hair was less than a decade away from total baldness.

Still, when he turned to look at my mom, his entire being lit up, as if she ignited some deep, secret passion of his soul that he didn't even know existed. I knew that look. It was familiar.

It was the way Jesse looked at Toile.

Did I have a manic pixie dream mom?

She slid off the counter and readjusted her skirt. "Benjamin is joining us for dinner tonight. Will you set the table, *Anak*?"

"I . . . I hope I'm not interfering with your studying," Benjamin said nervously as I retrieved silverware from a drawer. He spoke in quick little spurts, gasping for breath between them, as if assessing the impact of his words after each flurry. "Flordeliza has told me all . . . about your academic successes . . . and your plans for MIT in the fall."

My mom opened the oven door and retrieved a bubbling casserole dish. "Beatrice is a mathematical genius," she said. "She's applying for early decision."

"Very impressive." He took a quick gulp of air. "Do you know . . . what you'll study? Theoretical . . . or applied . . . or—"

He was interrupted by the doorbell. At seven thirty on a Tuesday night? Had I left something in Spencer's car?

"I wonder who that could be?" My mom's voice practically sang, and her face was bright with excitement as she eyed the door. Suddenly, I knew exactly who was ringing our bell.

"Mom . . . ," I said. "You didn't."

"Flordeliza," she corrected me. Really? We were still working that ruse? "Could you answer the door, Beatrice?"

I stomped across the floor with more force than was necessary and pulled the door open to reveal the face I'd already known I was going to find. My dad.

"Hey, BeaBea," he said.

"Hello, Andrew," my mom cried from the dining room. "Won't you come in?"

"No," I whispered. "You don't want to." She'd intentionally

invited my dad over while she had her new boy toy in the house so she could show off. Would my mom ever grow up?

"Andrew?" she repeated more urgently.

My dad edged past me. "I don't want to be rude, Bea-Bea."

My mom was leaning on Benjamin's arm, her head resting languidly on his shoulder. "Oh, Andrew!" she said, sounding surprised by his entrance as if she hadn't just been demanding he come inside. "How good of you to come."

"Well, you said Bea needed the books she left Sunday, so—"

"I asked Mom to pick them up on her way home from work," I said, refusing to play along.

"I didn't have time, Beatrice." My mom's voice cut like steel.

Benjamin cleared his throat. "If I'm interrupting something, I can . . ." He started toward the door.

"Don't be silly." My mom yanked him back to her side. "My ex-husband was just dropping off some of Beatrice's things. Andrew, I'd like you to meet Mr. Benjamin Feldberger." She paused and cocked an eyebrow. "Esquire."

My dad strode across the dining room and extended his hand. "Ben, good to meet you. You're starting up the new patent law practice group at Dwyer Hartmann, right?"

Despite the nearly twelve-inch difference in height, Benjamin Feldberger, Esquire, took my dad's hand firmly in his own and looked him straight in the eye. "I am." All traces of the excited nervousness he'd exhibited when talking to me had vanished. Apparently, when it came to business, Benjamin Feldberger was in his element.

"It made quite a stir when they poached you from Knobbe Martens down in Newport."

Benjamin laughed. "I just hope I can live up to the faith they've put in me." Then he gestured toward the open bottle of wine on the counter. "Care for a drink?"

I'd been watching my mother keenly throughout this exchange and as her brow lowered and her smile faded, I realized that this was not the outcome she'd been hoping for.

"He can't stay," she snapped.

"Flor is right. My wife's been under the weather while I've been out of town, so the sooner I'm home the better."

"Oh!" Benjamin piped up. "Were you at the ABA Conference?"

My dad swallowed. "Er, yes."

"Old buddy of mine from Boalt runs that thing each year. Mel Yukimori? You must have met him if you were there."

"Yes, yes," my dad said, clearly flustered. "Great guy." He hurried toward the door. "Enjoy your dinner. Nice to meet you, Ben."

I excused myself early from dinner, pleading homework. Realistically, I could have said I wasn't feeling well, because I was totally and completely sick to my stomach.

And while literally a million different elements of my life could have caused my nausea, tonight my parents were the cause. First my mom, who for reasons I couldn't fathom had insisted on parading her new lawyer beau before her lawyer ex-husband. I felt sorry for Benjamin Feldberger, Esquire, who clearly wasn't an idiot. He'd held his own with my dad, and had soldiered on through dinner, keeping up the conversation despite my reticence to speak and my mom's obvious pouting.

I also felt sorry for Sheri. The instant my dad heard the words "ABA Conference," his entire demeanor had changed. His eyes shifted around the room, his brow glistened with sweat, and he literally couldn't wait to get out of the house. It didn't take a mind reader or a superstar litigator to know he'd been caught in a lie.

And if he hadn't been at the conference, then where had he been?

I shuddered to think.

My parents were overgrown teenagers, unable to control their attention-seeking behavior and throbbing loins. Seriously, how exactly was I expected to engage in anything remotely resembling a healthy romantic relationship with the two of them as role models? It was a miracle I'd found Jesse at all.

Jesse. Maybe I'd been wrong about him. About us.

I thought of the photo on the campaign flyer of Toile and Jesse kissing. They'd looked happy, but how blissful could Jesse have been in that relationship if he'd been trying to hook up with me just last week?

I was surrounded by men who cheated, if not physically, then emotionally. Had I been subconsciously attracted to that in Jesse because I'd been conditioned to seeing the same behavior in my dad?

That was so fucked-up.

I thought of my formulas, the intersection of information theory and everyday life, the effects of statistics on behavioral sciences. What if I could fix this? What if there was a formula that could keep people from cheating?

I needed to know. I needed to know why my dad cheated on his wives, needed to understand the psychology of it, the mental and emotional thought processes. A serious, no-bullshit conversation.

But I couldn't exactly call him up and ask him, not in front of Sheri. It was time for a field trip to Kelger & Giovannini.

THiRTY-SiX

THE ELEVATOR DOOR opened onto the fifteenth-floor offices of Kelger & Giovannini at three fifteen, exactly thirty-five minutes after I left school. My dad should have been done with his lunch meetings and back in the office for the afternoon, but Mrs. Akers, the longtime receptionist, greeted me with a mix of elation and disappointment.

"Beatrice!" she cried, rising from the plush leather chair that seemed built for someone twice her size. "It's so lovely to see you." Her face immediately fell. "But your father isn't back from lunch yet."

Helluva lunch. "That's okay, Mrs. Akers. Do you think it would be okay if I waited in his office?"

"Of course, of course. He should be back any moment." She smiled as she waved me through the glass doors that opened onto the half-floor office, her lips heavily lacquered with a peachy nude matte lipstick.

"I like the new lipstick shade, Mrs. Akers."

"New? Oh, child, I've been wearing the same color for forty years!"

I don't know why I made the comment about Mrs. Akers's lip color. I guess I'd known since that day my dad came home with lipstick on his collar that he'd been cheating on Sheri. I'd wanted to believe what he'd told me, wanted to think that my dad had changed. But he hadn't.

Which is why I was there in the first place.

Why did people lie? Why do something that you weren't willing to fess up to? It seemed so ridiculous to me. So childish.

I slid into my dad's oversize executive chair and spun it around like I used to do when I was a kid. I was midrotation when the office door burst open.

Two people tumbled into the room: my dad with his back to me, and a freckled, sinewy-armed woman who had her face stuck to his. They were lip-locked, pawing at each other like crazed lunatics, and it took the woman loosening my dad's tie and going for his belt buckle for me to snap out of my daze and say something.

"What the fuck?"

Tonya, my dad's legal secretary, pulled away, and I caught a glimpse of her lipstick: shimmery hot pink.

The second my dad saw me, his face flushed crimson.

"Tonya—er, Ms. Steevers," he said. "Can you step outside?"

"Don't bother," I said through clenched teeth. "I'm not staying."

I shot Tonya a withering glance as I marched past her, but I couldn't even look my dad in the eyes.

I was four blocks away in Fullerton's busy downtown district, still marching at a rage-fueled pace, when I heard the car pull up beside me.

"Bea, can we talk about this?"

"No." I sped up, tote bag bouncing off my hip.

A horn blared, and an angry driver shouted an expletive out the window at my dad, who was crawling in the slow lane.

"Please?" my dad begged, ignoring the commuter behind him.

I stopped dead and turned to face him. "If you're afraid I'm going to tell Sheri, don't be." The charming douche in the BMW roared around my dad's Lexus, giving us both the finger as he passed. I didn't blame him. I kind of wanted to flip my dad off too.

He leaned over into the passenger seat so he could see me through the open window. "I just want to explain."

"I'm not sure how you can explain this, Dad."

Another irate blare of a horn and this time two cars veered dangerously around my dad's stopped car. As much as I didn't want to talk to him, I didn't want to cause a massive pileup either. So with a sigh, I reluctantly yanked open the passenger door and dropped into the seat.

"Thank you." My dad pulled away from the curb but didn't initiate conversation. Neither did I. If he wanted to explain his infidelity, I was all ears, but I wasn't going to make it easy on him. The irony of the situation wasn't lost on me. I'd gone to his office to ask him why men cheat, only to catch him in the act. Now I hardly cared what his explanation was—I just wanted to be out of his sight.

The silence continued until my dad veered onto a quiet, residential street and cut the engine.

"I know what you're thinking, Bea," he began, still staring ahead as if he were driving.

I doubt it.

"I could tell you that you were mistaken, that it wasn't what it appeared. But I'm not going to lie to you."

Good, because I'm not an idiot.

"When I have a new secretary . . ." He sighed. "I don't know what happens."

I turned to him in disbelief. "Really? That's your excuse?"

"Guess it's not a very good one."

"It's not even an excuse, Dad." I held up three fingers, counting off his marriages. "A trio of wives. Isn't that enough for you? I thought you really loved Sheri."

His head whipped around. "I do love Sheri. And your mom. And Irene," he said, mentioning his first wife, "though perhaps not as much."

"Then why do you cheat on them?"

"I don't know." He hung his head, staring at the steering wheel.

This was ridiculous. My dad was almost fifty years old. He wasn't some teenager who couldn't control himself.

"Get your shit together, Dad."

He jolted. "Beatrice Maria Estrella Giovannini, how dare you—"

"No," I said, cutting him off. "No more talking out of you. If you're going to act like an idiot sixteen-year-old, then I'm going to treat you like one. You need to grow the hell up and take some responsibility for your actions."

He opened his mouth to respond, then paused as his anger cooled. "You're right."

His shift in mood placated me. "Look," I said, more kindly than a moment before, "you and Mom were a mess, and even though I never thought I'd live to say it, your divorce was the best thing that ever happened to you. You're both so much happier now." For the most part. "But you and Sheri? She's good for you, Dad."

"I know."

"And if you break her heart, I'm never going to forgive you."

He looked up at me, and for the first time in my life, instead of a strong, dominant father figure, I saw a tired old man. "I understand."

We fell silent again. My anger had mostly dissipated, replaced by a sense of sadness and loss. I wasn't a little girl anymore, looking up to her dad, trying to make him proud. Instead, I was the defender of morality, doling out tough love. When had I become the parent to my parents?

"Do you want me to take you home?" he asked.

Ugh. It was Wednesday, which meant "home" was the Giovannini house, and Sheri. She'd been a mess with all the fertility treatments, and the stress of it had knocked her on her ass with a nasty stomach virus. How could I go there and look her in the eye now that I knew my dad was cheating on her?

I could have gone to my mom's, since she was still at work. But eventually I'd have to explain why I was there and not at my dad's. Would I tell her? Would she be gleeful that Sheri had "gotten what was coming to her"? Or would she commiserate with her? After all, they'd both been mistress and wife. It was a selective club.

I felt badly for everyone: Sheri, my mom, even my dad, whose issues with fidelity seemed utterly pathetic. Intellectually, I'd understood my mom's anger when she'd found out about my dad's infidelity, but emotionally, my response had always been "What did you expect?" Not that I was giving my dad an excuse, but my mom's overly dramatic episodes had grown tiresome after a few weeks and I'd kind of shut her out. Now, for the first time, I was internalizing her betrayal. And it sucked.

"No," I said at last. I needed a break, a chance to sit and think about everything. And home wasn't the place for that right now. I craned my head, trying to figure out where we were, and saw that we were right across the street from D'Caffeinated, a place I usually avoided like the plague. But anything was better than spending another moment in that car. "I'm going to grab a coffee. I'll . . . I'll see you at home tonight."

"I love you, BeaBea," he said as I opened the door.

I sighed. "I love you too, Dad."

THIRTY-SEVEN

DESPITE THE HEAVY conversation with my dad, I felt lighter as I crossed the street to D'Caffeinated. I'd been suppressing my anger with him for far too long, and it was good to finally let it out, just like at school yesterday, when I'd finally unloaded on Toile.

I grabbed a double latte and a chocolate chip cookie from the counter (ignoring Flordeliza's voice in my head telling me I should really have picked the fat-free blueberry antioxidant muffin) and tucked myself away at the table in the corner. I didn't know whether to feel sorry for Toile or continue to hate her. Yeah, no. That wasn't really an issue. I hated her. She'd insinuated her way into our school under false pretenses, masquerading as someone she wasn't. Hell, maybe her name wasn't even Toile. I hadn't executed a particularly thorough internet search for her, but her name hadn't popped up during a rudimentary Google search. Maybe that was because she didn't exist?

Suddenly, I had to know.

I pulled my iPad from my bag and quickly logged into the coffee shop's Wi-Fi.

I'd already Googled "Toile Jeffries," so I knew there was no point in walking down that road again. Maybe Toile was a nickname? Middle name? Nom de guerre? If so, "Jeffries" might be her legal surname. But that was a relatively common one, and without a first name, I'd be looking for a needle in a haystack.

Hold up. Not entirely. What had Jesse said that first day of school?

She lived in Hawaii before she came here. Honolulu, I think.

Honolulu would have a limited pool of high schools, so I started there, searching for any students my age named Jeffries.

A hit came up almost immediately.

Sybille Jeffries.

Once I had her name, Sybille Jeffries wasn't terribly difficult to track down.

And I did mean track. Literally across the country. Toile aka Sybille had been enrolled at seven different schools in as many states over the last seven years. Each school had a different version of Toile, none of which was the perky manic pixie who had arrived in Fullerton.

She spent fifth grade at a private Christian school in South Carolina, where she sang in church choir and attended youth Bible study meetings religiously (pun intended). Her hair was light brown then, and she dressed like a tomboy, not in the retro girlie dresses she wore now.

During that summer, her family apparently moved to Pensacola, Florida, and the Sybille Jeffries who turned up at Warrington Middle School was a gung-ho athlete. She played soccer, softball, and basketball, chopped off her hair, and appeared to have a wardrobe that consisted entirely of warm-up pants, sports bras, and hoodies.

But that didn't last long. Her next stop was Corpus Christi, Texas, where, as I would have assumed from the state, Sybille showed up for the first day of seventh grade as a cowgirl. She never played a sport, never even tried out for a team, as best as I could tell, but she wore cowboy boots every single day, had an impressive array of plaid shirts and jean shorts, and loved to country line dance.

I saw a pattern forming. In Bethesda, Maryland, Sybille went dark and goth. In Groton, Connecticut, she was a straight-up preppy. Honolulu got the surfer, and now, in bright and sunny Southern California, we had the bright and sunny Toile.

I had discovered Toile's secret: she was a chameleon who adapted to whatever environment in which she found herself. Now what was I going to do with this knowledge?

The good angel on my shoulder, which oddly enough sounded a lot like Spencer, said to leave it alone. I knew I was right, that her manic-pixie crap was all a calculated act, just as Trixie had been. That should be enough for me. I'd let Toile win the election, let her keep Jesse, and just move on with my life.

The bad angel, which kind of sounded like Flordeliza,

was telling me some long, roundabout story about people in the Philippines I'd never met and generational wrongs that needed to be righted, that would inevitably end with the words "eye for an eye." Because that's how my mom rolled. Bad angel voice was definitely urging me to humiliate Toile in the same way she'd humiliated me.

The thought of that made me smile.

I guessed I was my mother's daughter after all.

But then I thought of Spencer. I could already see the disappointment on his face, and I hated the way that made me feel. And he'd be right: outing Toile's past was a dirty thing to do. But was it any dirtier than what she'd done to me, mocking my breakup with Jesse in front of the whole school?

Two different choices, two very different outcomes. There was only one way to figure this out.

I pulled out my notebook and a pen. Tucked away in my brain somewhere, there had to be a pros-and-cons formula for getting revenge.

I was halfway through some preliminary calculations when a nearby conversation caught my attention.

"I can't believe Cassilyn's going to the dance with that homo," a voice behind me said. A familiar voice. Thad's voice.

"Are you sure?" Milo. I glanced over my shoulder, hardly daring to move, and spotted the two of them a few tables away, sucking on frozen coffee drinks capped with whipped cream, a strange anathema to the machismo coming out of their mouths. I quickly hunched over my notebook, moving my pen as if I were deep in thought, and listened carefully.

"Esme told me. Said that Cassilyn asked him yesterday. Dude's too much of a pussy to even ask a girl out." Thad paused to take a sip, ignoring his hypocrisy. "If it were you, I wouldn't be nearly as pissed."

"Me neither, bro."

"But that pansy-ass painter? Makes me want to punch him in the face."

My stomach dropped. So it was true. Spencer was going to the back-to-school dance with Cassilyn. A real date.

Milo laughed. "Heh. Maybe we should."

"Kick his ass?"

"Exactly. Teach that asshole a lesson. He needs to stay with his own kind."

"Like Faggot Gabriel."

I winced. Faggot Gabriel. Is that how they referred to him behind his back?

"I'd kick *his* ass too," Thad added, "if it weren't a hate crime. But whatever. When should we do it?"

I heard a sucking sound; Milo's thought process apparently involved whipped cream and caffeine. "Are you taking Esme?"

"Yep."

"Good," Milo said. "Tell her that you're driving Cassilyn and Homo too."

Thad pounded his fist against the table. "Brilliant, dude. Then after the dance, I'll take him to the park up on

Bastanchury. You and the boys meet us there."

"And we'll pound him," Milo said. "Right in front of Cassilyn."

I sat there, my heart racing in my chest. This outweighed both Toile and my dad in terms of emergency crisis level.

I needed to warn Spencer.

I heard Cassilyn's laughter before I'd even opened the door to Spencer's studio. Light and joyous. I listened intently at the door, waiting for Spencer's baritone to join her soprano. It did. His laughter was embarrassed at first, but he loosened up.

I opened the door, half expecting to see the two of them in a tangle of limbs and sweat on the sofa. Instead, they were standing in front of Spencer's easel, staring at one of his canvases. "You're right." He laughed. "It *does* kind of look like a hair dryer."

I froze, not quite believing what I was seeing. For years I'd been asking to see some of Spencer's art, but he'd never shown me. And now here he was explaining a piece to Cassilyn?

"What the hell?"

"Bea!" Spencer said, clearly surprised to see me. "Where were you after school? I waited—"

"What are you doing?" I demanded.

"Um . . ." He glanced at Cassilyn. "Cass wanted to see what else I was working on."

Cass? He was calling her Cass now?

"So I know what kind of style my portrait will be," she said, as if she were the foremost expert in portraiture.

I was annoyed and hurt that Spencer valued her opinion over mine, and felt more comfortable baring his soul to her. I wanted to tell him, but that wasn't why I'd come over. "We need to talk."

He pulled his head back as if he'd been slapped. "Oh."

"It's okay," Cassilyn said, her voice still tinkly with happiness. "I have to go. See you at school tomorrow, Spence?"

Spence?

"Yeah. Of course."

Then Cassilyn gave him a hug that lingered longer than I felt was appropriate, and breezed past me to the door.

"Spence?" I said after the door closed behind her. "She's using your nickname now?"

He turned away, grabbing a tarp to put over the canvas. "You call me Spence too."

"I've known you longer," I snapped.

Spencer noted my anger, which was clearly unappreciated. He turned to me sharply, arms folded across his chest. "What did you want to talk to me about, Bea?"

Right. I was here for a reason. "I was at D'Caffeinated," I began, speaking quickly. "And Milo and Thad were there. I overheard them and . . ."

"Yeah?"

"And you can't go to the dance with Cassilyn Friday night."

Spencer snorted. "Why not?"

I snatched a breath. "Because Thad, Milo, and their

douche brigade are going to kick your ass afterward."

He was quiet for a moment, his jaw wiggling back and forth as he ground his teeth. "And you think I should back down? Cancel the date and run like a coward?"

"It's not cowardice." Why were boys so concerned with saving face? "It's self-preservation."

"Why don't you just admit what's going on here?" Spencer said.

"Huh?"

He took a step toward me. "You don't want me to go to the dance with Cassilyn."

"Yeah, that's what I just said." Was he not listening? Had the paint fumes finally gotten to his brain?

He dropped his hands to his sides. "Why can't you just admit you're jealous?"

The word stung like an angry wasp. "Jealous?" I said, forcing a laugh. "Of Cassilyn?" The idea was ludicrous, insulting. Cassilyn may have been pretty and popular, and rich, but that was all she had going for her, whereas I was looking forward to a glorious college career on the East Coast, full of honors and accolades and people who really understood me. Cassilyn would graduate, perhaps even do some token college classes, and then fade into my memories, just like all the kids who were living their best years right now.

I jutted my chin out in defiance. "Why would I possibly be jealous of her? Because you showed her your art?" I forced a laugh. "If you want to show her but not your friends, that's your choice."

He came closer, slowly, as if he were approaching an unbroken pony, and looked down at me. "You're jealous because she's interested in me."

Once again, the fact that Spencer thought he knew my feelings better than I did royally ticked me off. "Hanging out with the popular kids has gone to your head, and now you just expect everyone to be in love with you, just like they do."

"I never said you were in love with me," he said quietly.

I rolled my eyes. "You implied it! I shouldn't have used the Formula on you. You can't handle it."

Spencer's face flushed red. "You're sorry you used the Formula? Are you fucking kidding me? I regret ever asking for your help."

"I saved you from getting bullied," I yelled.

"By ruining my life!"

I gestured around the studio. "How is your life ruined, huh? You've got everything you ever wanted. Art, social stability, a fancy girlfriend."

Spencer pointed to the door. "That girl who just left? She wants me. She's the most popular girl in school, and I can barely keep her hands off me."

I felt a wave of coldness wash over me, as if all the blood was draining from my body. It was sickening, nauseating, and only made me fight back harder. "Yeah? Then why are you trying to stop her?"

"Maybe I won't anymore."

"Fine."

"Fine."

We stood on opposite sides of the room, each breathing heavily, Cassilyn's unfinished portrait witnessing the death throes of our friendship.

"Then I guess there's nothing more to say." Spencer turned away and lovingly re-covered the portrait. I couldn't watch anymore, so I collected my tote bag and left.

THiRTY-EiGHT

"BEA, IS THAT you?" Sheri called from the living room as I let the front door bang closed behind me. "Is everything okay?"

"Fine." It was all I could do to keep my voice from shaking.

"Have you heard from your dad? I've been texting him but haven't gotten a—"

I closed my bedroom door, shutting her out. Shutting everyone out. I couldn't take them anymore.

My world was falling apart. My boyfriend had dumped me. My best friend hated me. My entire school thought I was a joke. And don't even get me started on my parents. Just two weeks ago, I had senior year by the balls, and now it was a complete disaster. How had it gone so horribly wrong?

Toile.

The nightmare that had become my life started the day she showed up at Fullerton Hills with her perky attitude and her *I always see the bright side* quips. And it was all an act, all make-believe. She'd figured out a formula and created this Toile persona to charm everyone around her. It was insidious, really. A deeply subversive plot to take control of our school, and I was the only person who saw it.

The only person who could stop her.

And someone had to. She'd already managed to practically get herself elected ASB president. Perhaps that had been her aim all along? Perhaps promoting Jesse was just a ruse so no one would see that she was plotting a landgrab? It was the perfect cover: the doting girlfriend accidentally makes herself so popular that half the school votes for her. Jesse had never seen it coming.

Spencer and Gabe would understand. In stopping Toile, I was helping everyone.

I thought of the photos I'd found online, the many incarnations of Sybille Jeffries. They were all part of the same pattern. In Texas, the cowgirl. In New England, the preppy. In Hawaii, the surfer. She'd pinpointed a specific personality type that would result in instant societal integration, and played it up. The goal? Friends, romance, popularity: the building blocks of personal power in the American high school. How many other schools had been laid to waste by her machinations? How many unsuspecting girls had had their boyfriends ripped away? How many student governments had been infiltrated and gutted by her scorched-earth policies before she pulled up her stakes and moved on to the next town? Well, I sure as hell wasn't going to let that happen to my school. No way.

And yet, I paused. I remembered how I'd felt when I saw those flyers with Toile and Jesse kissing with my terrible sophomore year photo alongside. It was a punch in the gut, a cold panic at the thought of the entire school laughing at me. Was I really willing to inflict that same level of humiliation on Toile?

But if I didn't, she would win. I couldn't let that happen.

I fired up my iPad and started editing photos together before I could second-guess myself. A collage of Sybille was slowly taking shape, complete with a text box in the middle that said, "Will the real Toile Jeffries please stand up?" After half an hour, I sat back and admired my handiwork. It wasn't the most brilliant composition, but it got the point across. Each photo exquisitely represented Sybille fully embracing her myriad personalities: at Bible camp, holding the softball MVP trophy, country line dancing, dressed in black, on a yacht, holding a surfboard. In each photo, despite alterations to hair and makeup, to fashion and attitude, it was crystal clear that you were looking at the same girl.

I uploaded the collage to every social media network I belonged to, blasting it to several hundred classmates. I may have lost the election, but I was pretty sure I'd just won the war.

"What did you do, Bea?" Spencer was waiting for me at my locker the next morning. I was surprised to see him, considering our blowup was still a fresh wound, but I could tell from his combative stance and glaring eyes that he wasn't here to make peace.

"If you've come to tell me I'm a horrible person," I said coldly, "or some other insight about my psyche that I'm apparently too stupid to see, you can save your breath. I've heard enough."

He shook his head. "I thought you were bigger than she is."

I opened my locker in his face. "For your information, Toile's approximately three-point-two-five inches taller than I am."

He whipped the door all the way open so it banged against the metal wall. "You know what I'm talking about. How could you, Bea? I know what she did to you was awful, but I thought—"

"It wasn't just awful," I said fiercely, all the anger of yesterday igniting again in an instant. "It was humiliating. You wanted me to sit there and take it, like it was okay that she'd ripped my heart out in front of the entire school. If she'd done that to you, I wouldn't have told you to turn the other cheek. I'd have fired up the bazooka and helped you take aim."

"What's that going to do, huh? Prolong the war? Do you even know why you're fighting with her?"

I took a deep breath through my nose. "Because I hate her."

He shook his head. "I thought it was about Jesse."

"It was." I swallowed. "Is." I rested my forehead against

my locker door, suddenly exhausted. "I'm tired of arguing with you, Spencer."

He took a deep breath. "Then why don't you admit that this is all about beating Toile?"

It was, and I knew it. But I couldn't say it out loud. "Why are you on her side?"

"I'm not."

I slammed my locker door so hard the whole wall of them shook. "You've never defended me. Not once. All you've done is tell me how I'm wrong, how I'm a bad friend or a horrible person."

"You're right."

I hadn't been expecting that. I'd been revving myself up, picking up this fight where we'd left off yesterday afternoon. But I'd never thought Spencer would agree with me.

"Oh," I said lamely, the wind taken out of my sails.

"I should have been more supportive." His eyes drooped at the corners like a sad puppy's. "But those photos of Toile you sent out . . ." He looked at the floor. "I'm disappointed in you."

He might has well have stabbed me in the gut with a hunting knife. I felt physical pain as all the air was sucked from my lungs. *I'm disappointed in you.* They were the kind of words your parents used when you'd done something so heinous that punishment seemed inadequate, and though I still hated Toile with every fiber of my being, for a split second as I watched the sharp features of Spencer's face harden, I regretted posting those photos and desperately, desperately wished I could take it all back.

"Spencer," I started. But he held up his hand.

"Good-bye, Bea."

I hadn't gone home sick from school since I'd had the chicken pox in first grade. I prided myself on exemplary attendance, and attributed my academic success in part to the fact that I was in class every single day.

But after my conversation with Spencer, I couldn't stand one more minute at school. Especially not first period, where I'd have to sit behind him for fifty minutes, trying to focus on Mr. Schulty's latest lecture on long-dead English poets while my metaphorical guts spilled out onto the floor in front of me. No freaking way. So instead of the liberal arts building, I turned toward the nurse's office.

Thirty minutes later, Sheri picked me up from the office. She looked green—clearly not over her stomach bug—and I felt horrible that I'd dragged her out of bed to come sign me out of school for the day. But she seemed more concerned with my health than with her own, and when we got home she insisted on warming me up a mug of chicken broth and putting me to bed.

I turned off my phone and tried to sleep. I didn't want to hear from Spencer. And I certainly didn't want to see all the comments on my social media posts with the pictures of Sybille. The thought of it made my fake nausea real.

As much as I hated to admit it, Spencer was right. I shouldn't have embarrassed Toile like that in front of the whole school. Even if she'd deserved it. I had sunk to her level, and did that make me any better than she was? No. In fact, it made me worse because I knew what it felt like to experience that kind of humiliation and I'd gone ahead and inflicted it on her anyway.

So instead of sleeping, I just tossed and turned in bed, occasionally flipping through bad daytime television, or attempted to focus on some current articles in *Mathematics Magazine*.

But I couldn't hide from the world forever. I'd have to go back to school tomorrow and face everyone. It was my penance.

I hardly slept Thursday night, and the next morning, the world was a muted background moving in slow motion around me. I felt sluggish and exhausted when I got to first period, noting with relief that Spencer wasn't in class. I did notice a slight uptick in chatter when I entered the room—I could only imagine the stories that had been going around between my post about Sybille and my subsequent absence from school yesterday.

Then Principal Ramos took the microphone for the morning announcements and the room fell silent.

"We have the exciting result from our runoff election." Her voice sounded anything but excited.

The election. I'd completely forgotten.

"Your new ASB president is Trixie Giovannini."

THiRTY-NiNE

"I CAN'T SAY I'm thrilled that you're going to be ASB president," Gabe said for like the dozenth time that night. "But you know I'll support you when you make your acceptance speech on Monday."

I patted him on the shoulder. "I appreciate it."

Our pre-dance ritual of burgers and fries at the diner had felt a little strange with just the two of us, but it was nice to still have at least one friend. Gabe was quieter than usual, more subdued, clearly still processing my election win (who wasn't?) and had brought it up repeatedly. It made me feel horrible, to be honest. Thanks to me, he'd really wanted the gig, and thanks to me, he hadn't gotten it. To make matters worse, I didn't want to be ASB president. Not even for the pleasure of beating Toile or to round out my research to submit for the MIT scholarship. In fact, it seemed more of a burden than a reward: my focus this semester should have been on college applications (hey, everyone needed a safety school) and ensuring my early acceptance at MIT, and instead, I'd be spending my spare time planning pep rallies and listening to grievances about cafeteria food options and whether or not upperclassmen should be allowed off campus for lunch.

"Have you talked to Spencer?" Gabe asked as he pulled his mom's minivan into the school parking lot.

I tensed up. "I don't want to talk about him."

"He's going to be here with Cassilyn," Gabe reminded me.

"Yeah, I know."

"Are you okay with that?"

What was with the inquisition? "Spencer can date anyone he wants. I don't care."

"If you say so," he mumbled.

We climbed the stairs from the parking lot in subdued silence. Gabe, though utterly dapper in a powder-blue blazer with a contrasting plaid lapel and pockets, looked on edge. I felt dumpy in comparison. My war against Toile over, I'd ditched my Trixie-ness and donned the same old black strapless A-line I wore for most special occasions. It was my favorite dress, or at least it had been. But as I'd gotten dressed that night, I couldn't help but notice how drab it was. Boring. My thoughts kept returning to the petunia-print swing dress I'd bought during my shopping spree. Maybe Trixie had worn off on me in more ways than I'd realized.

Gabe fidgeted incessantly as we waited in line, like a child hopped up on sugar, and he kept double-checking his coiffed pompadour in every reflective surface we passed. Mrs. McKee checked our IDs at the door, and then we headed through the main hallway, back around to the gym. I always loved walking through campus during school dances. Most of the halls were closed to prevent students from slinking off to get busy in the home ec room, and though that thought had never crossed my mind, I enjoyed the dim lighting, the absence of slamming lockers and squeaking sneakers, the all-around calmness in a place that, during regular business hours, was bustling with life.

That relative calm was broken as we approached the gym. I could already hear the thumping of the bass from the DJ's subwoofers. Groups of freshmen loitered in the gym lobby, clustered together for support and safety as they experienced their first high school dance. I envied them in a way. They hadn't made any mistakes yet, and still had their whole high school careers in front of them, where they could make and remake themselves into whoever and whatever they wanted. Even if they never found a formula to help them transform, they'd meet new people and forge friendships that would help them navigate the treacherous waters of high school.

I thought of Spencer and Gabe and me at our first dance freshman year. We'd sat together in the bleachers the whole time, laughing, joking, and despite our total social isolation from the rest of the school, we'd had a great time. We'd come so far since then: Gabe was popular, Spencer was dating Cassilyn, and I was ASB president. And yet, somehow, I still felt like the awkward freshman who'd hidden in the bleachers that night, and I kind of wished I was her again.

"Helloooooo!" a voiced cooed, interrupting my thoughts. I turned, and saw Kurt crossing the lobby toward us. At least, I thought it was Kurt. Instead of his usual baggy jeans, over-size T-shirt, and flannel tied around his waist, he was wearing cropped pants in a pastel madras check, paired with a scoop-neck three-quarter-sleeve shirt and leather boat shoes. His usually shaggy hair, which just that day had dangled in front of his eyes, had been styled off to the side, and his patchy two-day beard scruff had vanished, exposing baby-smooth cheeks.

Had Kurt been using the Formula too?

"What the hell are you wearing?" Gabe's voice was flat.

Kurt's face fell. "I thought you'd like it. That I'd fit in more with your new friends."

"You look ridiculous," Gabe said.

"Oh, so it's okay for you to make yourself over into some-one cooler, but it's not okay for me?"

"This isn't you at all."

"Which you'd know all about." Kurt planted one hand on his hip and laid the other gracefully on his chest, mimick-ing Gabe's favorite pose. *"Zoopa!"*

"I did this for a reason, and you know it."

"Please," Kurt said. "You tell yourself that, but you know as well as I do that you love being popular Gabe, always in the spotlight, who dresses like a twelve-year-old girl and acts like a bitchy queen."

"You're a real asshole," Gabe said. Then he stormed off into the gym.

"Hey!" Kurt shouted, chasing him. "Don't walk away from me."

I followed them inside, realizing what Kurt was trying to do. I had told him to roll with it, after all. Maybe if I just explained that to Gabe, he'd understand.

The gym was black with the exception of the swirling DJ lights mounted over his table, which flashed red and green and blue across the dance floor as they rotated in time to the music. I scanned the perimeter, searching for Gabe and Kurt, but everyone looked the same in the near darkness— grayscale bodies in silhouette, occasionally illuminated by the swirling lights. The movement was disorienting and the thumping bass from the speakers was giving me a headache. One song bled into two, then three as I wove my way around the gym. I was sweaty and tired and ready to strangle the DJ when finally he took a rest to make an announcement welcoming everyone to the dance.

The instant the music fell silent, a voice rose from the back of the gym.

"We're here, bitches!" Esmeralda strutted onto the dance floor, hanging on Thad's arm. "Now the party can start." She'd clearly been waiting for the opportunity to make a grand entrance, and it felt almost as if she'd scripted it with the DJ, who started the music again the instant she reached the dance floor. All eyes were on them. Esmeralda's purple body-con dress barely covered her butt, and when paired with sky-high platform pumps, she looked like she was at least 70 percent legs. Thad's face glistened with a layer of perspiration even though they'd just arrived, and his eyes looked glassy. As they passed, I caught a whiff of stale beer.

Milo followed, flanked by Dakota and Noel, each still claiming half of him. The stepsisters talked from opposite sides, not paying attention to what the other was saying.

"And the salesgirl told me they didn't have it in that col . . . ," Dakota shouted over the music.

Then Noel's turn. "I always get the gluten freh . . ."

"But I made her check anyway because she was such a . . ."

"Because gluten makes me puff . . ."

Milo stared straight ahead, smiling, and began to dance. His dark skin was tinged with pink, and like Thad's, his eyes looked blissfully blank. Since he was dating Dakota and Noel at the same time, I kind of didn't blame him for wanting to get drunk.

Cassilyn and Spencer came last, and I could have sworn the entire dance floor parted to let them through. Even with the rising beat of the music, I could sense that everyone's attention was focused on my friend and his date, as if the royal couple had just arrived. Cassilyn noticed it too. She leaned into Spencer, clutching his arm possessively, and flashed a gleaming smile at her devoted subjects. She wore a gold sequined dress and matching heels, and her hair was perfectly styled, billows of heavy curls shimmering in the DJ's light display. She looked like a living, breathing disco ball.

I would have expected Spencer to look stiff and uncomfortable with all the attention, but he seemed pretty relaxed.

He wore a tuxedo jacket but paired it with black jeans and boots, giving him an *I don't need to try too hard* attitude that instantly made him the coolest person in the room. And as I watched his regal entrance, I realized with a sinking feeling that, in so many ways, Spencer belonged with this group. He was no longer a dorky outcast, sitting in a small booth tucked away into the corner of the cafeteria with his only two friends. He was one of *them* now.

He didn't look at me, and I wasn't sure I wanted him to, but I searched his face as they passed me, looking for signs that he too had been drinking. It was hard to imagine him knocking back a six-pack with Thad and Milo and the jock-tocracy, the same guys who were planning to kick his ass after the dance.

Ugh. That.

Cassilyn tapped Spencer on the arm and stood on her tiptoes to say something directly into his ear. After a few seconds, he nodded, and Cassilyn flitted off to the lobby. She must have been going to the ladies' room.

Spencer wouldn't listen to me. But maybe she would?

FORTY

I RUSHED INTO the lobby in time to spot Cassilyn's sparkling disco ball dress disappear into the girls' restroom. If anyone could prevent him from going to that park after the dance, it was her.

The restroom was empty, except for Cassilyn, who stood in front of the mirror, carefully unscrewing the lid of a travel-size hairspray bottle. She put it to her lips and threw her head back, swallowing the contents.

"Oh my God!" I cried, grabbing her arm. "What are you doing?"

She gulped then giggled. "It's vodka." She held the bottle toward me. "Want some?"

I had to admit, it was a brilliant strategy for sneaking booze into a school dance. Brilliant and kind of sad. "No, thanks."

Cassilyn shrugged, then tilted her head back again and finished off the last drops.

"Can I talk to you for a sec?"

She shrugged by way of an answer, then pulled a compact out of her purse and began touching up her makeup.

"I overheard Milo and Thad talking after school the other day and—"

She sighed dramatically. "And they hate Spencer and want to kick his ass?"

I blinked. "Um. Yeah. How did you know?"

"Not exactly a secret that they both want to tap me." She smoothed some cover-up beneath her lower lip. "And they've pretty much told anyone who'll listen that they're going to teach Spencer a lesson."

She was so cavalier about the whole thing, I was taken aback. "They're planning to jump him tonight after the dance at Bastanchury Park."

"Ah." She clicked her compact shut and dropped it into her purse. "Good to know." She turned to me with a huge smile. "Thanks, Trixie. I appreciate that you're looking out for Spence. You've been a really good friend to him, but I'll be taking over from here. We're going to cut out early anyway and Uber back to his studio, so we should be fine. Thanks!"

I lingered in the restroom, pretending that I needed to readjust my strapless bra. In reality, I didn't want to see Cassilyn and Spencer.

Despite her friendly display, there was a clear message in her words: Spencer was her conquest. And I was pretty sure she was planning to plant her flag on him tonight after the dance.

I mean, not that I cared. Wasn't that really just the ultimate validation of the Formula? I should have been ecstatic that my best friend was dating the most popular girl in school.

Instead I sort of felt like barfing.

One thing was for sure, I was ready to get the hell out of there. Maybe Gabe wanted to bail too? I just needed to find him.

Easier said than done. As I reentered the gym, Gabe was still nowhere in sight.

The first dance of the year was a big deal at Fullerton Hills. Everyone was there: cool kids, dorky kids, new kids, old kids. Most continued to cling together in packs, rimming the fringes of the dance floor or sprawled out across the bleachers like Spencer, Gabe, and I had been all those years ago. Everyone's attention was centered on the writhing mass of dancers who congregated in a large circle around the DJ. He spun an upbeat pop tune that everyone seemed to know the lyrics to, especially the girls, several dozen of whom were screeching along at the top of their lungs with such ferocity I could easily hear them over the amplified sound. I noticed with some satisfaction that Cassilyn was one of the screechers, along with Esmeralda, Dakota, and Noel, but that Spencer hadn't joined in. I caught sight of him standing by the bleachers, arms folded across his chest. But he wasn't bored, checking his phone like the dozens of others standing apart from the action; Spencer's attention was very much focused on the dance floor. On Cassilyn.

Fine, whatever. If that's the kind of girlfriend he wanted, far be it from me to get in his way and tell him that he could do significantly better. I peeled my eyes away and searched the rest of the crowd. It was weird. No Gabe. No Kurt. And, I realized with a start, no Toile and Jesse. Had my little stunt with the Sybille photos banished her from the first dance of the year? I pictured her home alone in pajamas, watching movies and eating ice cream straight from the carton.

And I felt bad for her. Guilty too.

Dammit, why wasn't anything turning out as I'd planned?

I rounded the dance floor. Still no sign of Gabe. Maybe he'd gone out one of the side doors and doubled back to the lobby? It was worth a shot.

The door had just clicked shut behind me, muting the thumping music from inside the gym, when I saw Gabe at the end of the hall near the entrance to the boys' locker room. He had his back to me, head bowed.

"Gabe!" I cried, hurrying toward him. "Are you okay?"

One look at Gabe's face told me he wasn't: his eyes were red and puffy, and when he spoke there was a catch in his voice. "Kurt hates me. Says he never wants to see me again. All because I called him out on that stupid outfit he was wearing."

"Oh, Gabe."

"I thought maybe we could work things out, but then tonight . . . I mean, why would he show up looking like that?"

Uh-oh. "I think he was trying to fit with your new look."

"I don't know why." Gabe sniffled. "I've never even hinted that I wanted him to change. I liked him the way he was."

Guilt overwhelmed me. I'd been trying to help, and now I had totally and completely screwed this up for them. "I think, maybe, Kurt misinterpreted something I said to him."

Gabe caught his breath. "Oh, Bea, you didn't."

"Didn't what?"

He arched an eyebrow, tears gone in an instant. "Get involved in our relationship."

"I didn't get involved. I just, you know, talked to him. Explained why you're doing what you're doing."

"What the hell did you say to him?" His voice was no longer choked up, his sadness replaced by anger.

"I was just trying to help," I said, feeling defensive. "It's not like I told Kurt to show up for the dance like it was White Party weekend in Palm Springs. I merely suggested that perhaps he needed to roll with your school persona if you guys were going to be a couple. And I guess he took that to mean he needed to be more like the new you."

"Goddammit!" The word exploded from Gabe's mouth. "Bea, can't you mind your own fucking business?"

I'd never seen Gabe get angry before, and it caught me off guard. "I—"

"NO!" Gabe held his hands up before him, keeping me at bay. "I don't want to hear it. Just leave me alone." He backed up down the hall.

"Wait!" I called after him. "I'll talk to Kurt and explain."

But it was no use. Gabe rounded a corner and was gone.

"Hey!" I shouted into the empty hallway long after he'd disappeared. "You guys asked for my help."

I should have gone after him, but that felt like begging—for his understanding and his friendship—and I knew it wouldn't do any good. I'd completely screwed up the only two friendships I had, and I wasn't sure Gabe or Spencer would ever forgive me.

I tried to picture what it would be like going through senior year without any friends. But would I really have to? I wasn't Math Girl anymore. I was ASB president. I'd find new friends, more important friends, friends who would appreciate all the awesomeness I brought to the table instead of constantly judging me, arguing with me, and making me feel like a bad person.

It shouldn't be that hard to do. I was relatively sure I could create a formula for finding new friends. Trixie hadn't had much of a problem getting people to like her, so maybe I could transition some of that openness to Bea?

Somehow, that wasn't comforting. I didn't want just any friends. I wanted *my* friends.

Without realizing it, I'd wandered back into the gym. The music had changed; a slow dance was playing. Duos dotted the dance floor, bodies pressed together as they swayed back and forth. This was the domain of the happily coupled, where high school relationships were on display.

My eyes fell on one couple, and I found myself envying the clear intimacy they were experiencing. She had her face nuzzled into his chest, while he rested his cheek against the top of her head, pressing into her voluminous curls. His arms were wrapped around her: one across her shoulders, one lower, near the small of her back. He looked as if he was engulfing her, and though his face was turned away from me, I could picture his blissful smile.

The couple turned in time with a dramatic swell in the song, and I gasped. It was Spencer.

His eyes were open, and before I could look away, he'd caught my gaze. For an instant, I thought perhaps he was going to break away from Cassilyn, come over, and sweep me up in his arms the same way he'd been holding her. But he didn't. Instead, he lowered his face to Cassilyn's and kissed her.

Then everything around me began to spin.

I staggered, my balance shaken, and I was pretty sure that roaring sound in my ears was my chest breaking open as three years of emotions blindsided me, a nauseating wave of joy and pain, sadness and elation.

I was in love with Spencer.

When had that happened? Had I always been in love with him and just not realized it? Was I that incredibly stupid when it came to my heart? I thought of the first day of school, when he'd held me tightly in his arms and my stomach had felt as if it was being twisted up in a knot. And the day after Jesse dumped me, when we'd been wrestling on my bed.

And the day I'd kissed him backstage in the theater.

How could I have been so stupid? How could my brain have ignored the signals from my heart?

Because you were too scared to admit that you were wrong: you'd been in love with Spencer, not Jesse, all along.

The song began to fade out and Cassilyn broke their embrace. She stood on her tiptoes and whispered something in his ear. Spencer nodded. Then she took his hand and led him out of the gym.

He never looked back at me.

I knew where they were going, what they were going to do. The gym suddenly felt oppressive, close and hot and encroaching. I broke into a sweat as the swirling DJ lights left me dizzy and disoriented. I needed to get out of there. I needed fresh air. I turned and ran for the back door.

FORTY-ONE

I WAS RELATIVELY sure I was having a panic attack.

I slumped against the smooth wall and bent forward at the waist, resting my hands against my knees. I gulped for air as if I'd just been running from zombies, and my heart was pounding.

Classic panic attacks included symptoms of: racing heart (check), feeling dizzy or faint (check), sweating (check), sense of hopelessness, difficulty breathing (check). I was experiencing at least 80 percent of these, so even without a medical examination, I felt pretty confident in self-diagnosing.

And, of course, I knew why I was panicking. I finally realized I was in love with my best friend, but it was too late. Any minute now, he and Cassilyn would be back at his studio in some form of undress, about to do something significant and meaningful that would bind them together forever.

Maybe I could stop them? I could go to his studio, pledge my undying love, and beg him to love me back.

My heart ached at the thought, because after watching the two of them kiss on the dance floor, I knew what the answer would be.

He'd be happy with Cassilyn, she'd make sure of it. She wouldn't be constantly at odds with him, challenging him, pushing him, teasing him. Spencer deserved that. He deserved better than me.

My penance would be that I would have to watch their romance blossom and be supportive. If I wanted to keep Spencer as a friend—and the thought of losing him altogether was even more devastating than the thought of him never, ever loving me back—I had to make things right between us, then bury my feelings and never let him know.

But I wasn't ready for that. Not tonight. Tonight I just wanted to go home and cry.

I turned, and was heading for the gym lobby when Michael Torres stepped out of a doorway, his usual MO, blocking my path.

"Hello, *Trixie*." His voice was icy, his dark eyes so narrow I couldn't even see the black of his irises, and a wicked little smile played at the corners of his mouth, taunting me. "I've been looking for you."

Ew. "Can't say the feeling is mutual." I attempted to sidestep him, but he slid to the left, cutting me off.

"I have something here you might find interesting." He pulled his phone out of his pocket, activated the screen, and shoved it in my face.

"Michael Torres, how many times have I told you that

I'm not interested in your manga porn?"

"Just read it."

This was the absolute last thing I needed, and I was tempted just to drop his phone to the tile floor, stomp on it, and march out into the warm fall night. But there was something in his smile that unnerved me, a cockiness that reeked of triumph. So I wrenched the phone from his hand and examined the screen.

It was an article, published on the front page of the *Herald*'s website, and as I read the title, my stomach sank.

FAKING IT: How Three Fullerton Hills Seniors Manipulated Their Way to Popularity

An exposé by Michael Torres

"What the hell is this?" I asked, trying to sound nonchalant and hoping the tremor that was making its way from my hands to my throat didn't show. How had he found out?

"Keep reading."

It was the sudden change that tipped me off. On the second day of senior year, Gabe Muñoz and Spencer Preuss-Katt arrived on campus in character. Gone were their "normal" personalities and styles, replaced by new personae, meticulously calculated to make them popular.

It sounds outlandish, a thing of fiction, but when Beatrice Giovannini—now "Trixie"—joined the charade a few days later, I knew something rotten was going on. Ms.

Giovannini's pet project is applying mathematical formulas to everyday life, and apparently she came up with one to make her and her friends popular. Was this one of her experiments? Was she using Fullerton Hills as a guinea pig for her diabolical machinations?

This reporter needed to know.

After a thorough investigation, I uncovered a series of notes taken by Mr. Muñoz in relation to this undercover endeavor wherein he discusses his new role as a stereotypical homosexual and its calculated effects upon certain social groups at Fullerton Hills. Mr. Muñoz, who is, it must be noted, the coeditor of the *Herald*, kept track of his progress, noting which behavioral characteristics and outlandish antics got the best reactions from his test subjects. He then used this information in an article he submitted to a well-known local newspaper in the hopes of securing a coveted internship.

For her part, Ms. Giovannini used her newfound popularity to get herself elected ASB president, over a much worthier—i.e., less fake—candidate, using a slur campaign. Mr. Preuss-Katt, though not immediately implicated in his friends' flagrant misuse of power, is nonetheless guilty by association.

It is my hope that these allegations will be investigated fully and that during that time, Mr. Muñoz will be suspended from the *Herald* and Ms. Giovannini will be replaced in school government.

I stared at the screen. I had to admit that the writing was surprisingly good—considering Michael Torres only joined the school paper as a way of winning the MIT scholarship—but the content made me so angry my jaw was starting to ache from the force with which I clenched it.

"It went live before the dance," he said. "By Monday, everyone at school will have read it, and I'll be the sole editor of the *Herald*. Your hopes for that scholarship will be dead on arrival, and I'm sure the *Register* will drop Gabe from consideration for the internship."

The internship. Gabe was so excited about it.

"Not that I have anything against Gabe," he continued, "but, you know, collateral damage."

"Why not target me?" I said, fighting the urge to strangle him. "Going after my friends is a dick move."

He tilted his head to the side. "I did."

At first, I didn't know what he was talking about. Then, suddenly, all the pieces came together. His declaration of war, Toile's insistence that she hadn't been responsible for the attack ad. She actually had been telling the truth for once.

"You put up those flyers."

"I can't believe you're just figuring that out."

"You're an asshole."

"And you're not?" he cried. "Look at what you did to poor Toile. She's done nothing but be nice since she got here and what did you do? Ruined her life."

"Her life? What about my life! She stole my boyfriend."

At the mention of Jesse, his face clouded over. "Maybe

if you'd been a better girlfriend, he wouldn't have asked her out. Maybe she'd still be single."

My jaw dropped, realizing his motivation. "You have a crush on her."

"I do not," he snapped.

"Have you told her?"

His sweaty face turned red. "I . . ."

I laughed, more from surprise than actual levity. Michael Torres had ruined my life because he liked a girl and was too afraid to tell her. Unreal.

"This isn't funny!"

He was right. It wasn't. "You know what, Michael Torres? I was wrong. You're not an asshole. You're a giant pussy."

"What?"

"Yeah, a pussy. You want to take me down? Be my guest. I fucking dare you to." I didn't care about the ramifications, I just really, really needed to tell Michael Torres what I thought of him once and for all. "But if all of this is just an excuse to show Toile how you feel about her, then you're just as fake as we are."

His eyes shifted back and forth. "I don't . . . I mean, that's not really . . ."

Awesome. I'd knocked him off balance. "Yeah, that's what I thought. Let me know when you've grown a pair." I held my fist out in front me, parallel to the floor, then opened my palm and pantomimed dropping a mic. I turned and left him in the hallway, still trying to formulate a comeback.

FORTY-TWO

I ROUNDED THE corner, head high, shoulders squared. But the second I was out of sight, I stopped and leaned back against the smooth glass of a trophy case. What the hell was I going to do?

This was a problem like any other. A complicated math problem. If Train A leaves Irvine at 2:30 p.m. traveling north at 25 mph with a steady acceleration of 5 mph until it reaches its max speed of 75 mph, and Train B leaves Fullerton at 2:45 p.m. traveling south at 60 mph with no acceleration, given the distance between the two stations to be 47.6 miles, at what time will Train A pass Train B, and what will be the speeds of the two trains at the time of their passing?

I mean, duh, so easy. I could do it in my head. Train A passes Train B at 3:05 p.m. traveling 65 mph to Train B's 60 mph. Child's play.

So if I can figure out that equation in less time than it

took to read the problem, I should be able to figure out this real-life train collision. I just needed to think.

The lobby was quiet. I strolled past glass display cases full of Fullerton Hills' sports trophy collection, my eyes roaming aimlessly over the fake-gilt placards and posed athlete effigies, trying to lull my brain into a state of functionality. The good news was that Gabe's position on the paper was safe. Mr. Poston had already read Gabe's article on his social experimentation. So that was good. Still, the article would throw Gabe and me back to the bottom of the social pecking order. And what about Spencer? My heart ached at the thought of him, but if he was Cassilyn's new boyfriend, would that protect him from the social repercussions that were about to rain down on Gabe and me? And if so, was there some way I could take the blame for all of this and spare Gabe the fallout? I had no idea. Why couldn't I figure this out? The Formula and its successors had come so easily. And now? Nothing. It was as if math were a foreign language I had yet to study and every variable and operator sounded like gibberish. In my time of need, my mathematical mind had abandoned me, leaving me without—

"Hey, Bea."

I spun around. "Jesse! I didn't know you were here." At the dance, or in the lobby. I certainly hadn't heard him sneak up behind me.

He smiled and edged closer. "I've been looking for you."

"Really?" After Michael Torres, he was the last person I wanted to see.

He nodded. "I've been thinking a lot. About us. I've missed you."

I recognized that smile on his face, small and mischievous. The same one he'd flashed me in the car a week ago when he tried to kiss me. But that was a lifetime ago. I wasn't the same Bea anymore.

"It hasn't *looked* much like you've missed me," I said, folding my arms across my chest. "What did you say at the end of your campaign speech? 'I want to thank my amazing girlfriend Toile. She makes my life better in every way.'"

Jesse hesitated. "Toile wasn't who I thought she was."

"And I am?"

I meant it to sound combative, but Jesse took it as an invitation. He stepped right up to me, backing me against the trophy case until his body was inches from mine. "I know you're smart and cool and fun." He lifted his hand to my chin, tilting it upward. "And now you're ASB president."

So that was it? "You mean, now I'm popular." Toile had been embraced by Cassilyn and her friends from day one, while my friends and I had been threatened by the jock-tocracy. Then as soon as "Trixie" started gaining attention, his focus was back on me. Jesse didn't want a girlfriend who was at the bottom of the food chain, and now that Toile had been humiliated in front of the entire school, our roles were reversed.

"What's wrong with being popular?" Jesse asked, throwing his hands wide. "I mean, you're really cute. I thought so since the first time I saw you in class, and there was no reason you had to be as unpopular as your friends."

I wrinkled my nose in disgust. "You thought you could fix me? Make me less of a loser so I'd look better as your girlfriend?" So that was why he'd wanted us to sit at our own table at lunch and to go to D'Caffeinated instead of hanging out with my friends after school. He'd been trying to separate me from my friends so I wouldn't be tainted by them.

Instead of answering, Jesse stepped closer to me. "Remember how much fun we used to have?" he asked, his thumb grazing my cheek.

A couple of weeks ago, I might have killed to feel Jesse's fingers against my skin one more time, but now it just made me sick to my stomach.

"*Used to* have," I repeated. "Past tense. We're—"

"Jesse!" Toile raced across the lobby toward us. She looked exhausted, as if she hadn't slept in days. Dark circles ringed her usually bright eyes, and I noticed that they were hazel gray, not bright violet. I guess those had been fake too. Her outfit was decidedly not manic pixie as well—yoga pants and a formfitting hoodie with sneakers and a noticeable lack of headwear. She looked like a normal girl home on a Friday night.

So this was Sybille Jeffries.

The instant she saw me behind her boyfriend, she stopped dead in her tracks and I watched as all the color drained out of her face. "What are you doing?" she breathed, her voice hoarse.

Jesse dropped his hand and took a step back. "Just talking."

"You talk with your mouth," Toile and I said in unison. Our eyes met, and she looked about as surprised as I felt.

Meanwhile, Jesse swayed back and forth, shifting his weight forward and backward, almost as if he was trying to decide between the two of us. I intensified my glare, hoping it gave a crystal-clear *Back off* vibe. It worked. Jesse turned to Toile and took her hand.

"Bea was just reminding me of old times. It was nothing, I promise."

Oh, that was it. I shoved him. Hard. "Are you kidding me?"

"Don't push him," Toile said, getting between us.

I threw up my hands. "Don't defend him. And definitely don't listen to him. He's as full of shit as you are."

She tensed. "I am not full of shit, *Trixie*."

But I wasn't going to let this be about the two of us. Right now, our anger needed to be focused on Jesse. "Do you know what Jesse did the week of the election? He drove me home after school and tried to kiss me."

Toile's eyes shifted to Jesse's face. "I . . . I don't believe it." But she kind of sounded like she did.

"Believe it," I said. "And just now he was about to do the same, but I stopped him." I pointed my finger in Jesse's face. "I don't want you anymore. And I certainly don't have to put up with your shit. I deserve to be treated better, and so does Toile."

"I do?" Toile said.

"Yeah," I said. "You don't have to settle for a boyfriend

who only likes you when you're getting attention from the popular people. He should like you all the time. No matter who you are."

Toile blinked. "You're right." She turned to Jesse. "I do deserve better."

I backed Jesse toward the exit. "Got anything to say to that? Any excuses to make?"

"I . . . I just . . ." He swallowed. "I like you both. I was confused."

"Was?" Toile asked.

"Yes. I mean, no. I mean . . ." He stumbled over his Converse. "I gotta go."

Then he sprinted out the door.

FORTY-THREE

TOILE AND I stood shoulder to shoulder as we watched Jesse flee down the hallway and out of our sight. Hopefully, out of our lives.

It felt so ridiculous now that I'd ever fought over him.

"I'm sorry," I blurted out.

"It's not your fault he's an asshole," Toile said, in a very un-Toile-like manner. Hmm, maybe I was going to like Sybille better.

I turned to face her. "Not that. The photos I posted. I know now that you didn't put up those flyers."

She sighed. "I tried to tell you, but—"

"I know, I wouldn't listen. But Michael Torres just admitted to it."

She shook her head. "Michael Torres? Why?"

I smirked. "Why do you think?"

Her cheeks flushed. "Oh."

I was mostly there. Might as well just cop to it all. "I told

311

myself everything I did was about winning Jesse back, but it wasn't. It was about beating you."

She half smiled. "Well, I kind of figured with the whole Trixie thing."

"I was angry," I said, feeling defensive. "I mean, you did steal my boyfriend."

"I know," she said. "But I swear, when he asked me out he said you two had broken up weeks ago. He told me . . ." She dropped her eyes to the ground. "It doesn't matter what he told me. I understand why you hate me."

"I don't hate you."

Toile arched an eyebrow. "You sure about that?"

"I was hurt when Jesse picked you over me," I conceded. "And when Spencer explained the whole manic-pixie-dream-girl thing, I thought maybe I could reinvent myself and win Jesse back. Then that day in Principal Ramos's office when I realized you were playing a role too—"

"How did you know?" she asked. "I mean, know for sure."

I grinned. "You quoted a line from *Garden State*. Which I'd just watched."

She sighed. "I love that movie."

Ew.

"You're right," she continued. "I was playing a role. Those photos you found . . . My dad's a navy doctor. A specialist. It's kind of hard to fit in when you're in a new school every year."

"Every year?"

She nodded. "Since fourth grade. Even by military family standards, it's been ridiculous. But he retired last spring, and we settled in Fullerton. I wanted to make some real friends here before college, so I came up with the manic-pixie thing."

"Which I just ruined."

Toile shrugged but didn't say a word.

I felt horrible.

We wandered down the hall in silence and popped out the front door of campus into the warm fall night. It was eerily quiet, especially considering that the dance was going on inside. We were in that dead zone: everyone had already arrived and no one had left yet. "Can I ask you something?" Toile said. She was watching me acutely.

"Sure."

"Did you love Jesse?"

"Yeah." The answer was automatic, and even as the half-assed admission came out of my mouth I realized how hollow it sounded.

"Really?" she pushed.

"No."

"Look, it's none of my business . . ."

"No," I repeated. "It's not." I felt my voice crack, that dreaded tightness forming in the pit of my stomach as I desperately fought to remain in control of my emotions.

"But I kind of thought you and Spencer—"

"Please don't . . . ," I managed, my voice a whisper.

"Oh." She paused. "Cassilyn."

Between Michael Torres and Jesse, I'd managed to forget Cassilyn and Spencer for a few minutes. But now the thought of the two of them together in his studio hit me with its full weight.

I didn't even realize I was crying until my wet cheeks tingled in the evening breeze. I felt Toile's arm around my shoulders. She didn't say anything, just held me until the sobs slowed and finally ceased.

"Are you going to be okay?" she asked.

"No," I said, for perhaps the first time in my life.

She guided me toward the stairs. "Come on. I'll take you home."

The lights were on in the kitchen and dining room when I stepped into the foyer of my dad's house, but no one called out my name or asked me how the dance had gone. Small mercies. Maybe Sheri was still sick and everyone had gone to bed early? That would be perfect. I wasn't ready to explain to anyone what had happened.

I dropped my clutch on the dining room table and dragged myself into the kitchen. I needed chocolate ice cream. All the chocolate ice cream. I was going to take it to my room and bury myself in my misery.

But the moment I rounded the island into the kitchen, I froze. My dad stood in front of the counter with his back to me, head bent as he embraced a woman. I could see her slender arms, brown skin, and hot-pink fingernails. Though her body was hidden behind my dad's heavy frame, I knew one thing for sure: it wasn't Sheri.

I only stood there staring for half a second, 1.5, tops, but it felt like an eternity. After all he'd put us through—his first wife, my mom, Sheri, and even me—and after I'd caught him in the act with Tonya, here he was up to his old bullshit. And this time in our house.

"What the hell are you doing?" I said.

Instead of releasing his new girlfriend and spinning around, his face a reddened mask of shame and embarrassment, my dad hardly moved. His arms remained wrapped around the woman I still couldn't see, and he didn't even look up. "Hey, BeaBea," he said casually. "How was the dance?"

"How was the dance? Are you kidding me?"

But I never got an answer to my questions. As I spoke, my dad turned, and the skanky home wrecker came into view.

"Mom?"

"Hello, Beatrice." Her head rested against my dad's chest, one hand draped around his neck while the other was wrapped around his thick waist. She was barefoot, her heels discarded on the kitchen floor, and the look on her face was one of absolute contented happiness. She didn't even correct me for calling her "mom."

Something was horribly wrong.

"No," I said.

My mom's head popped up. "What?"

"You guys are *not* getting back together." It was a statement of fact, one that I would fight for with every fiber of my being.

My dad laughed. "What are you talking about?"

"No way," I repeated. "You were miserable with each other. Don't you remember that? You fought all the time. And I know you've both been completely crazy since you divorced, but you've also been happier than I ever saw you together. So no. I might be the only teenager in Orange County who doesn't want her divorced parents to get back together, but this is not happening."

My parents stared at me for a moment, then my mom glanced up at my dad and both of them burst out laughing.

"Get back together?" my mom said between heaves.

"Bea," my dad added, "your mom and I are definitely not getting back together."

Okay. Well, that was good. "Then what the hell is this?"

My mom broke free of my father and held her left hand toward me, fingers downturned, exposing a flashy solitaire diamond. "Benjamin proposed."

I blinked. "What?"

She nodded, smiling from ear to ear, and for the first time in years, she looked like the carefree mom I remembered from my childhood.

"And your mom came over to tell me because he's a colleague and she didn't want me to hear from someone else." He squeezed her shoulder. "Which was very thoughtful."

I was still having difficulty wrapping my brain around this turn of events. "But you've only been dating for like two weeks. How could you possibly know him well enough to marry him?"

She snorted. "I knew your dad for a year before we got engaged, and look how that turned out."

"I listened to what you said, Bea." My dad's eyes softened. "About how I needed to grow up. Tonya has been reassigned. I have a new secretary. I think you'll like him."

Him. Finally.

"I want to apologize to your mom. And to you. I've been an ass."

"True," my mom said with a nod of her head. "But I'm sorry too. I wasn't exactly the easiest person to live with."

My dad lifted my mom's hand to his lips and kissed it. "You're going to make Benjamin very happy."

"And you and Sheri," she said, "are going to make a wonderful parents to that baby."

I caught my breath. "Baby?"

My dad beamed. "Sheri and I had an appointment today. Apparently, she didn't have the flu after all."

I stood there, stunned. Everything in my life had gone tits up. My friends hated me. My parents didn't hate each other. And I was going to be a big sister.

None of this was in the Formula.

"What's wrong, Bea?" my dad asked. "We thought you'd be happy. This is what you were hoping for, right?"

My parents, who, for most of my life, had behaved like spoiled children, had finally taken some initiative toward actual adult behavior. And I, who had always aimed to be practical and rational and completely adult in my decision making, had regressed to a little girl who threw a tantrum when she didn't get her way, and who ended up hurting those she cared about in the process.

Maybe, for once, it was time to take inspiration from my parents?

My mom had gone home. My dad and Sheri had gone to bed. My ego had gone on vacation.

It was my own fault that I'd lost my friends. Worse, I'd lost myself. I'd tried to hang on to Jesse because I didn't want to face some scarier emotions lurking within, while my parents, and my friends—for good or for bad—had embraced theirs. Gabe and Kurt. Spencer and . . .

"Spencer and Cassilyn," I forced myself to say out loud. The words hurt more, piercing my heart in the same way they pierced the silence of my room.

I pushed away my despair. I didn't deserve it, not after what I'd done. There was a good chance that Spencer and Gabe were better off without me screwing up their lives. It would have been simple just to slip into anonymity and hide from the social interactions at school until I graduated and could run away to college. That would have been the easy way out, but I'd hurt too many people and I needed to take responsibility for my actions. Michael Torres's article attacked the people I loved. I had to find a way to fix it.

I walked over to my patchwork tote and removed my trusty notebook and pen. There was only one way to figure this out. I needed one last formula.

But as I sat at my desk, pen poised over an empty notebook

page, I couldn't bring myself to write down any numbers or symbols. I'd found so much comfort in my precise, flawless formulas, and yet life wasn't precise or flawless. Life was a mess. A beautiful, unpredictable mess, and trying to impose some kind of mathematical order on it had only resulted in disaster.

Maybe this time, I needed to trust my feelings.

FORTY-FOUR

MY PLAN FOR Monday's assembly was actually the least of my worries. I was pretty sure Principal Ramos wasn't going to expel me for what I was about to do (I mean, she didn't like me, but I wasn't going to break any laws, so I felt relatively safe in that regard) and as far as my social standing at Fullerton Hills went, I'd already resigned myself to eight and a half more months of pariah status. (It was part of my penance. Catholic much?) I could live with that. What was stressing me out was making things right for my friends.

I didn't know if my scheme could save Kurt and Gabe's relationship, or Toile's reputation, or make Spencer hate me less, but my calculations suggested that two out of three were certainly within my control.

Live by the Formula, die by the Formula.

I'd managed to avoid my friends all morning, made easier by the fact that Spencer wasn't in first period again, but I hadn't been able to escape the whispers.

They were everywhere, following me down the hallways, rippling through my first- and second-period classrooms in undulating waves. Michael Torres had been right: everyone in school had read his article.

No one spoke to me. There were no *Hi, Trixie*s in the halls. I ran into Giselle and Annabelle on the way to class and they studiously avoided eye contact. It wasn't outright hostility, though—more like I was a plague victim and no one wanted to catch my disease. I cringed at the idea that Gabe and Spencer—if he was even at school—were enduring the same kind of treatment, and only took solace in the fact that by lunchtime, their suffering would be over.

I ducked out of second period early to meet Principal Ramos in the theater as requested. The stage was set with a microphone front and center, and I could see the shifting stage lights moving from blues to oranges to a pleasant mix of the two as the tech cycled through lighting cues from the booth to find a good mix.

"So," Principal Ramos said. She was pacing the edge of the stage as I walked down the carpeted aisle, her heels clicking against the scuffed wood floor. "Is your speech ready?" No mention of Michael Torres's article. She either hadn't read it or didn't care.

Knowing Principal Ramos, it was the latter.

"Well?" she prompted impatiently.

I cleared my throat. "Yes." *And, oh, what a speech it's going to be.*

"Good. I'll introduce you," Principal Ramos said. "Then

you'll have five minutes." She pointed at me with her forefinger. "Do not go over. We've got presentations by the drama department and the cheer squad, and I don't want to go into the lunch period. Got it?"

"Got it."

"Good." Then she strode purposefully up the aisle to discuss the details of the assembly with the theater tech.

I wandered backstage and found a quiet chair in a corner near the lines that raised and lowered the flies. The area was dimly lit by orange work lights, a good place to stay out of sight until I was needed. I felt like a death row inmate waiting for my last meal. I remembered the day of the election speeches, when I'd kissed Spencer right here in an effort to make Jesse jealous. I would never forget the way I'd felt when his tongued grazed my lips. Now, as then, a shiver went down my spine. If only I'd actually spent some time analyzing what that feeling meant at the time, none of this would have happened.

The bell rang, signaling the end of second period, and things began to move quickly. Cheerleaders and members of the drama class arrived backstage, warming up and chatting about their upcoming performances, totally ignorant of my presence. In the theater, I could hear the dull murmur as students filed in, slowly filling up the seats. The murmur became a roar as the house edged closer to full capacity, then I heard Principal Ramos's voice through the speaker system, asking everyone to take their seats and quiet down.

I stood up then and slowly walked to the curtain legs

near the edge of the stage. I couldn't understand what she was saying, my brain unable to process a single word until I heard her speak my name.

There was a decided lack of applause as I stepped out onto the stage, with the exception of Principal Ramos, who seemed determined to make up for it with her own raucous clapping as she backed away from the microphone.

This was it. I'd memorized my speech, practiced it all weekend, tweaked it, and now was the moment of truth. Somewhere in the faceless darkness of the theater sat people I loved and who I'd hurt. I couldn't take back what I'd done, but I could certainly try and set things right.

"Any day, Miss Giovannini," Principal Ramos growled in my ear.

Five minutes. Right. Not a second over.

"My name is Beatrice Maria Estrella Giovannini, but until recently most of you didn't even know my name. 'Math Girl.' That's what everyone called me. No name, just a title.

"It hurt, to be honest. The fact that after three years at this school no one even knew who I was. But it shouldn't have. I had great friends, who accepted me and supported me and probably knew me better than I knew myself. Unfortunately, I kind of screwed things up."

"What are you doing?" Principal Ramos whispered.

I grabbed the microphone, holding it firm. She wasn't going to stop me, not until I'd said what I'd come to say.

"So while I've got the mic, I just want to set the record straight. Gabe Muñoz and Spencer Preuss-Katt are totally innocent of the charges leveled against them by Friday's online article in the *Herald*. The Formula was my idea. I wanted to win a scholarship to MIT, and my friends were just trying to help me. I mean, yes, we'd been picked on since we were freshmen, and I thought if we changed who we were, all of our problems would go away. Only it didn't work that way, and instead, we just discovered a whole new set of problems."

I swallowed, my mouth cottony dry, and spoke quickly.

"But we're not fakes and phonies. Not really. Gabe and Spencer and I are the same nameless nerds you didn't really know two weeks ago. We may dress differently, or act a little more outgoing, but we haven't changed deep down inside. I still prefer math to meeting new people, Gabe is still going to pursue interesting and important articles for the *Herald* no matter who he pisses off in the process, and Spencer would still rather spend time with paint and canvas than a football or basketball. You like us better now because you actually got to know us, not because Gabe came up with a catchphrase and I wore mismatched shoes. My friends are awesome people, and you shouldn't punish them for my sins. I'm the only one at fault here."

Principal Ramos grabbed my hand. "Give me that," she said, trying to wrench the microphone away, but I managed to slip it from the stand and rushed to the edge of the stage. I was almost done.

"Lastly, Toile Jeffries, I apologize for posting those old photos of you. I don't care if you were playing a role or not, you made a lot of people at this school feel good about themselves. To everyone here, you are very real. So, Principal Ramos and the esteemed student body of Fullerton Hills High School, I hereby resign as ASB president and hand the position over to someone who deserves it a lot more than I do: Toile Jeffries, who rightly should have won in the first place."

FORTY-FIVE

I'M NOT SURE what I was expecting when I dropped that bomb. Mass hysteria? A pelting with rotting vegetables? An angry pitchfork mob? I certainly wasn't expecting applause.

It was slow at first, like an ironic golf clap, but grew exponentially faster and louder with each passing second until the entire student body was applauding, whistling, and cheering. I certainly hadn't anticipated a positive reaction to my speech—there had been a less than 5 percent chance of it. I mean, I'd basically just told the entire school that I'd manipulated them for my own personal gain, and yet everyone seemed to approve. Everyone but Principal Ramos.

"For the love of all that's . . . ," she grumbled as she walked across the stage and snatched the microphone from my outstretched hand. "Well," she said cheerfully after the applause died down, her demeanor instantly sunshine and rainbows, "in light of these unexpected events and keeping in mind that we will not under any circumstances be holding another election at Fullerton Hills, I hereby declare Toile Jeffries your new ASB president. Toile, can you join me onstage?"

I stepped back and watched the shadowy bodies in the theater. After a few seconds, a silhouette moved down a row and into an aisle, then slowly made her way to the stage. Toile wore a look of complete astonishment as she climbed the steps. She paused before me, her eyes searching my face for an explanation.

"Why?" she asked.

"Because you deserve it." I smiled. "And you'll do a better job than I would."

She glanced at Principal Ramos at the microphone, then back to me. "That's the nicest thing anyone has ever done for me."

And then, I don't know why (maybe, for once, I had nothing to say, or maybe it was just a physical manifestation of my blurter nature), but I hugged her. Just a quick embrace, a gesture of thanks and apology and understanding all wrapped up together. Then I let her go and hurried offstage.

Gabe was waiting in the wings, Kurt at his side.

"Oh, Bea," he said.

Kurt corrected him. "Trixie."

I shook my head. "No more Trixie. I'm just Bea. Or Math Girl. Whichever you prefer."

Gabe took my hands in his. "You didn't have to do that."

"Yes, I did."

"Yes," Kurt said. "She did."

My eyes darted back and forth between them. "So, you two . . ."

"We talked last night," Gabe said. "And decided to try again."

"Bea," Kurt said, "what you did today. It reminded me of why Gabe is friends with you. And why I'd like to be friends with you too."

"Of course," I said with a smile. "If you think you can put up with me."

"If I can put up with Gabe," he said, "I can put up with anyone."

I squeezed Gabe's hand. "Have you seen—"

"He's not here," Gabe replied quickly, not even waiting for me to finish my sentence.

"I don't mean Jesse," I said.

"I know. Spencer didn't come to school today."

"Oh."

"And so, while I appreciate the opportunity," Toile was saying, mic in hand, "I'm going to have to say no. I wouldn't be your best candidate for ASB president."

"What?" Principal Ramos cried. "Neither of you want it?"

Toile looked to the wings and smiled. "Nope." Then she curtsied and skipped offstage, waving at me as she passed. "I think there's someone who deserves the job even more than we do."

"Huh?" She didn't stop to answer, exiting into the hallway.

"Un-freaking-believable. Mrs. McKee," Principal Ramos said. "Who came in third behind these two in the original election?"

Mrs. McKee didn't even need to look up the information. "Gabriel Muñoz."

Gabe gasped. "Me?"

"Wonderful. Would Gabriel Muñoz please come to the stage?"

I hadn't expected Toile to turn down the job, and I had no idea that Gabe had been the runner-up in the election, but it was as if the stars aligned, the angels sang in heaven, and suddenly all was right with the world.

Kurt gave him a shove toward the stage. "Get out there before Ramos changes her mind."

"Gabriel Muñoz?" Principal Ramos asked. Gabe nodded. "Do you want the job?" He nodded again. Then she sighed. "Thank God. Can you please just give an acceptance speech?"

Gabe took the microphone from Principal Ramos's hand. There was a moment of hesitation, and then Gabe realized he was in the spotlight he'd always wanted and took control of the situation. "I don't have a speech prepared," he began, "because I definitely didn't see this coming." The audience laughed. He had them.

I patted Kurt on the arm and headed to the stage door. It was as if the fatigue and stress of the last three days hit me all at once, sapping my energy and leaving me with a sick, empty feeling in the pit of my stomach. Maybe I'd go home early? Plead illness or girlie cramps or whatever. Surely, after what had just gone down, no one would mind if I skipped the rest of the day.

As Gabe continued to address the student body, I stepped into the hallway. Where I ran right into Toile, who was holding hands with Michael Torres.

"Are you?" I asked. "Is he?"

Michael Torres beamed from ear to ear. "Toile just agreed to go out with me."

Well, it certainly wasn't a pairing I'd seen coming—by my calculations, there'd been barely a 17 percent chance of Toile actually agreeing to go on a date with Michael Torres. But apparently my percentages were completely off base anyway, so what the hell did I know?

"I'm glad," I said, smiling at Michael Torres for the first real time in my life. "I mean it. She deserves someone who'll treat her well."

"Th-thank you," he stuttered, as unsure how to take a compliment from me as I was to give it.

We stared at each other a moment—archenemies calling a silent truce—and when I turned to leave, he stopped me.

"Bea, thank you."

"Me?"

He nodded. "I wouldn't have asked her out if you hadn't called me a pussy at the dance. So yeah, thank you."

Well, at least something I did this week worked out. "You're welcome."

FORTY-SiX

GABE, KURT, TOILE, and I all ate lunch together at the table Cassilyn had allocated to us, right in the middle of the cafeteria. Because, dammit, why not? We weren't going to lurk in the shadows anymore. This was our time.

Cassilyn congratulated Gabe warmly (I think she even meant it), but Esmeralda and the stepsisters sat with their backs to us, steadfastly refusing to acknowledge our presence. It hardly mattered. They weren't the most interesting people in the cafeteria anymore. Gabe had a steady stream of classmates stopping by to congratulate him, and he introduced Kurt to all of them as his boyfriend. Toile, now a sort of toned-down version of the manic pixie who had infiltrated our school a couple of weeks ago, proved to be significantly less annoying. In fact, I kind of liked her. She was smart and funny, and took no shit. And she was way more like me than I'd ever have cared to admit.

We never saw Jesse. I'm sure he was at school, but he

stayed the hell away from us. Which proved he had at least two brain cells to rub together.

So yeah, things were good. And I was even able to put Spencer and Cassilyn out of my mind.

Mostly.

After school, I took the bus to Dad's instead of Mom's. He and Sheri wanted to have dinner with me to celebrate the soon-to-be Giovannini baby.

It was comfortable in the house again. Sheri was over the moon to be an expecting mom, and it was wonderful to see my dad doting on her—pulling out her chair before she sat, fetching items from the kitchen, and asking repeatedly for her to "take it easy."

Sheri glowed, and judging by her apparent happiness, I guessed that my dad hadn't confessed his affair—or whatever it had been. And to be honest, I was okay with that.

At least until he screwed up again. Then I'd kill him.

"So, how is Jesse?" my dad asked after I'd picked at my food and left most of my meal on my plate. "I haven't heard you mention him in days."

"He's fine," I said, not even sure if that was true.

"He's a nice one, Bea," Sheri said. She kept her left hand on her belly as she ate, as if she was protecting the precious cargo within. "And really cute. Is he still doing that painting thing?"

I stiffened. She was talking about Spencer. She thought Spencer was my boyfriend.

I felt the lump rising in the back of my throat, but instead of fighting it off like I'd been doing all day, I let the bubble of sadness wash over me. Tears welled up, and I dropped my head just as they cascaded down my cheeks.

I heard a loud clank—my dad's knife and fork hitting the ceramic dinner plate. "Are you okay?"

"No."

Sheri rested her hand on my arm. "What happened?"

I couldn't have explained it all even if I'd wanted to. I didn't understand half of it myself, how I'd been dating Jesse and in love with Spencer, all without even knowing my own feelings. I'd hurt my friends, and though Gabe had forgiven me, I was afraid that Spencer never would.

Did it matter? I mean, even if he could get past what a selfish moron I'd been, could I really just swing back into a friendship with him? No, I don't think I could. I remembered all of our time together: hanging out in his studio, art shows, concerts, watching TV on the sofa, our bodies so close together you'd think we were a couple. How could I watch silently while he dated Cassilyn? Feeling my heart break afresh every single time he looked into her eyes, held her hand, kissed her?

The tears flowed. I took a deep breath, attempting to steady myself. I'd been so stupid. So ridiculously, blindly idiotic.

"Bea?" Sheri repeated, her calmness oddly soothing. "Is there anything we can do to help?"

Another breath, and I trusted my voice. "No. Nothing." I swallowed. It was probably easier just to give them the quick and dirty version than to explain the mess I'd caused. "Jesse and I broke up."

"Oh, Bea." Sheri squeezed my arm. "I'm so sorry."

Strangely, saying it out loud stopped the tears. Jesse was no longer my sore spot.

Dad cleared his throat, as if he was about to impart some timeless parental wisdom. "Well," he said slowly, "I guess the song applies now."

I glanced up at him, confused.

"Andrew . . ." Sheri's voice imparted a warning.

He smiled at me, oblivious. "You know, 'I wish that I was Jessie's girl.'"

"I don't think you're being appropriately sensitive to Bea's feelings," Sheri said while she stroked my arm. "A girl's first breakup is a traumatic event."

He picked up his fork. "Not as traumatic as her first divorce."

She ignored him. "Besides, that's not even the right lyric. It's 'I wish that I *had* Jessie's girl.'"

"No, it's not."

"Of course it is." Then she sang a line. "'Where can I find a woman like that?' It's by Rick Springfield. Do you think he was singing about wanting gender reassignment surgery?"

Their ridiculous argument faded in the background as my mind raced. The tune and the lyric were familiar. I closed my eyes, desperate to recall the moment. Gabe had sung a line from a song—once in Spencer's studio, once at school—and when I asked what it was, he'd just winked and said something. What was it?

"'Where can I find a woman like that?'" I repeated.

"Exactly," Sheri said.

Spencer's face. When Gabe made that joke, one I didn't understand, Spencer's face had gone ashen. My heart began to race. Had I read that reaction wrong? Had Spencer been upset because he was in love with me?

I bolted from my chair, yanking my phone from my pocket. I had Gabe's number dialed before my dad and Sheri could react.

"Bea!" Gabe said, answering before the first ring was finished. "What's up? Kurt says hi and wants you to know he's—"

"Did Spencer have a crush on me?" I blurted out.

Silence.

"Is that a yes?" I prompted.

"He swore me to secrecy," Gabe said. "Said he'd tell you in his own way. He . . . he made you a video."

A video? Fibonacci's balls. The thumb drive. He'd given it to me the day after my breakup. He'd asked several times if I'd opened it, which I thought was super annoying of him at the time. I was too hung up on all my Trixie BS to even think why he was so upset that I never saw what was on the drive.

"I have to go." I ended the call before Gabe asked any questions. My brain was focused on that thumb drive.

What had I done with it? Tossed it on my desk in my other bedroom. Then what?

The other day in my room, I'd been about to plug it into my laptop. I'd been interrupted by Jesse's campaign email and dropped the flash drive back into my tote bag.

"Can I be excused?" I asked.

"Of course," my dad said. "Is everything okay?"

"You know what, Dad?" I said, turning toward my room. "It just might be."

My breath caught in my chest as a video of Spencer popped onto my screen. He was sitting on the sofa in his studio, wearing his usual work outfit of paint-smeared jeans and a ratty old T-shirt. His hair was mussed up, the long bits sticking up in front as if he'd been running his fingers through it repeatedly, and his face was flushed.

"Hey, Bea," he said, a tremor in his voice. "I've been wanting to tell you something for a long time. I was going to do it when I got back from Europe, and then when I found out you were dating Jesse, I just couldn't." He kept his eyes cast down toward the coffee table, occasionally glancing up at the camera as if he was afraid of what he might find there. "Gabe called me twenty minutes ago with the news, and, well, I figured I'd better do this before I lost my nerve." He smiled. "Here goes."

The video stopped and cut to a photo montage while music played in the background. The song might not have been familiar, but the images were. Spencer and me. A montage of our friendship. In each photo, we were smiling, laughing, making faces, teasing each other. And pissing each other off. Lunch at the café in the Getty, pretending we were fancy LA art patrons while we sipped our coffee on the veranda. Huddling under a torn plastic bag when a freak rainstorm erupted during an outdoor concert. Our trip to Magic Mountain, where Gabe and I took a picture of Spencer puking his guts out after a ride on one of the crazy roller coasters. In each photo there was lightness and joy, and anger and frustration.

A lyric caught my attention, familiar because Sheri and my dad had just been fighting over it ten minutes ago, and I realized that I was listening to "Jessie's Girl." Spencer had put together a love letter.

My heart leaped in my chest before a cold realization dawned on me. That was two weeks ago. Before Trixie. Before Cassilyn. Before our friendship had been blown to smithereens. Could I really believe for a second that his feelings were still the same?

There was only one way to find out.

FORTY-SEVEN

THE LIGHT WAS on in Spencer's studio when I walked up the driveway. He was working. He always worked when something was bothering him. Was that something me?

Probably. Though maybe not in the way I hoped.

Still, I had to find out. I gripped the thumb drive in the palm of my hand and marched up to the side door. It was unlocked.

Spencer stood at his easel, still tucked away in the corner of the garage. He was wearing almost the same outfit he'd had on the day he filmed his video—the same outfit he wore most days when he was fixated on his work—and as his brush raced furiously over the canvas, he seemed oblivious to my presence.

In other words, situation normal.

Except it didn't feel normal. The exact opposite of normal, in fact, which technically is "abnormal," although that word wasn't appropriate somehow. More like the absence of normal. And though I was relatively sure, based on the bulging lines of his tightly clenched jaw, that he felt the awkward semi-abnormalness too, I tried to act like we were the old Spencer and Beatrice with our easy, fun friendship, and not the new Spencer and Beatrice, who interacted beneath a cloud of unspoken words and unrequited feels. It was the only thing I could do.

"Hey," I said, hands shoved in the pockets of my jeans.

Spencer's eyes never left the canvas. "Hey."

"I don't know if you heard what happened at school today."

"I heard."

He clearly wasn't impressed with my efforts to fix what I'd broken. Not that I blamed him.

Part of me wanted to leave right then, just walk away from our friendship and save myself from the arrow that was aimed straight at my heart. But I couldn't. I had to finish this, even if it meant hearing from his own lips how I'd ruined everything.

"I, um, looked at that thumb drive. The one you gave me a couple of weeks ago."

He set his jaw. "A bit late."

Late. As in, I was too late. He was in love with Cassilyn.

I felt a sob heave up from my stomach, and I pinned my lips together in an effort to suppress it. What good would tears be now? They wouldn't change Spencer's feelings.

"Anything else you want to say?" His voice had an edge, and his brushstrokes became harsher.

"I . . . I'm so sorry," I sputtered out.

He still refused to look at me. "Sorry for what?"

"That I didn't know."

The strokes from his paintbrush slowed. "You didn't know I was in love with you?"

I shook my head as heavy tears rolled down my cheeks. I may not have wanted to admit it, to myself or anyone else, but somehow I'd always known his feelings. What I didn't know were mine.

I took a deep breath, steadying my voice and forcing back the tears. "No, I knew that," I said quietly. I watched him closely, desperately hoping for any sign that he wouldn't hate me forever. I could live with losing him, but I couldn't handle the idea that for the rest of our lives, he'd always think of me with bitterness. "What I didn't know was that I was in love with you too."

"Was?" he asked, sounding perfectly calm.

I wasn't expecting that. "Huh?"

"Past tense. You *were* in love with me?"

"Was. Am." My voice trembled and I felt dizzy, disoriented. "I'm in love with you, Spencer. I always have been."

"You have a shitty way of showing it."

"I know."

"I had to stand by and watch you make an idiot of yourself over Jesse."

"I know."

"Making yourself into something you thought he wanted." He glanced up at me briefly. "The right guy would never want you to change. He'd like you, flaws and all."

I opened my mouth to respond, but the words stuck in my throat. He was right. Spencer had always liked me the way I was: when I was dorky and unpopular and spitting out percentages and equations like a camel. He would never have wanted me to change.

He returned to his easel. "And then Cassilyn came along."

My eyes drifted to the back of the canvas. Cassilyn's portrait. "She'll . . ." I swallowed, trying to stay the tremor in my voice. "She'll make you happy."

He paused then, finally. Dropped the paintbrush into the jug of water and slid his palette onto the table. "Cassilyn *is* super into me."

I bit the inside of my cheek, hard, hoping the pain in my mouth would drown out the pain in my heart.

He grabbed the easel and angled it so I could see the portrait clearly. It was Cassilyn, no doubt about it. Golden blond hair, slender features, and soft curves. But it was the style of the painting, not her beauty, that momentarily took my breath away. The brushstrokes were strong, haphazard, and yet deliberately placed. The background and foreground were delineated by drastically different color palettes—dark purples and teals in the back and a mix of oranges and yellows in the front—and Cassilyn's stylized features practically leaped off the canvas. It was the first real piece of his art that I'd ever seen, and it was truly spectacular.

"Spence," I breathed. "It's beautiful."

"She was all over me Friday night after the dance." He grabbed a rag and wiped his hands. "But nothing happened."

"What?" My eyes were glued to the painting.

"I told her I couldn't see her anymore."

"Why?"

He dropped the rag on the table and stood before me, his deep blue eyes fixed on mine. "Because I'm still in love with you."

I thought I might faint. Or cry. Or laugh. Or pee my pants. Maybe all of them at once. I'd never felt like that before: like I was standing with my toes on the edge of a precipice about to jump.

"You're still in love with me," I repeated, just to make sure I hadn't imagined it.

He stepped closer, his body inches from mine. So close I could feel his heart hammering in his chest. And though we'd been that close a gazillion times during our friendship, it was the first time I'd done so with my eyes open. Literally and figuratively.

"What was the probability of that?" he asked, smiling.

"Less than ten percent."

Spencer shook his head. "Maybe it's time to lay off the numbers?"

Maybe he was right. "But I've made you so miserable."

"You've made me better."

"I have?"

"That manic-pixie-dream-girl thing isn't total crap, you know. You can inspire someone without sacrificing yourself in the process. You were right about my art—I needed to be more confident. And if Cassilyn was good for anything, it was that."

"I don't deserve you," I said.

"Bullshit." He took my hands in his, squeezing them gently. "I've been a total dick to you. Angry. Bitter. You were right the other day—I've been a bad friend."

"No worse than I've been."

Spencer placed his hand on my cheek. "Beatrice Maria Estrella Giovannini, I love you. You *and* Trixie, if that's who you want to be. But you don't have to. Not with me."

And then he kissed me. It wasn't the first time our lips had touched, wasn't the first time I'd felt that unnerving thrill deep in the pit of my stomach, but it was the first time I'd allowed myself to enjoy either of them. I closed my eyes and leaned into him. Spencer wrapped his hands around my waist, pulling me close as he kissed me more deeply. I could have stayed like that forever, his lips against mine, our hearts pounding together. I felt vulnerable and alive and scared and excited all at the same time, and I never wanted that feeling to end.

"Spence," I said, breaking away. "Do you know what this means?"

He nuzzled my cheek. "I'm going to have to find an art school in Boston?"

I snorted. "Yes, but that's not what I'm talking about."

"Okay." He cupped my face with his hands. "What does this mean?"

I smiled, feeling wicked. "It means the Formula worked."

■

ACKNOWLEDGMENTS

To the smart and insightful Ginger Clark, who saw the pitch for this quirky, "off-brand" book and said, "You need to write this. NOW." She knows me so well.

To the supportive, inspiring Kristin Daly Rens, who always believed I could write a book without murder, even when I wasn't so sure.

To the Wolfpack, hands-down the sexiest critique partners around: Jennifer Bosworth, B. T. Gottfred, Nadine Nettmann, and James Raney.

To the team at Curtis Brown: Holly Frederick, Jonathan Lyons, Sarah Perillo, Tess Callero, and Nicholas J. L. Beudert. You make what I do possible in every way.

To the amazing folks at Balzer + Bray: Alessandra Balzer, Donna Bray, Kelsey Murphy, Elizabeth Ward in marketing, Caroline Sun in publicity, Kathryn Silsand, my long-suffering copy editor, and Sarah Kaufman for the drop-dead gorgeous cover.

To Dr. Robert Boostanfar, Katie, Maribel, Leticia, Claudia, Ivy, Dr. Alison Peck, and everyone at HRC. You didn't know you were a part of *this* process, did you?

To Simone Baud, Jkena Davidson, Keanna Eady, Jo Finlay, Lisa Middleton, and Talia Weingart Wilson, the strongest women I know.

To John Griffin, without whom none of this means anything.

And special thanks to Nathan Rabin, who—for better or for worse—coined the phrase "manic pixie dream girl."